SHE HAD TO DIE

SHE HAD TO DIE

HUGO AUGUST DETECTIVE SERIES, BOOK TWO

REBECCA BARRETT

WITCH CREEK

PUBLISHING

She Had to Die
Hugo August Detective Series, Book Two

Copyright ©2025 by Rebecca Barrett

Published by Witch Creek Publishing

All rights reserved.

Library of Congress Control Number: 2025915409

ISBN: 979-8-9883075-2-5 (Paperback)
ISBN: 979-8-9883075-3-2 (eBook)

Cover Design and Interior Formatting by Becky's Graphic Design®, LLC
www.BeckysGraphicDesign.com

Printed in the United States of America

For my dear, dear friends without whom this novel wouldn't be.
Susan Tanner, Carolyn Ladner, and Ginger Davis McSween

*Do not expect to just take and hold
Give friendship back, it is pure gold.*

—Gillian Jones

One

THE NEON PHOENIX stood out starkly against the night as it rose above the horizon with wings spread wide. Hugo ran his palm down his face and felt the stubble of a five o'clock shadow. He angled his watch toward the dim light of the instrument panel on the dashboard of the Thunderbird. A quarter past four in the morning.

"Christ," he muttered.

The two-way radio on the seat next to him crackled with the dispatcher's voice. "Time to scene?"

He picked it up and adjusted the volume knob with his thumb. "Arriving now."

"Forensics is headed your way."

"Ten-four."

The flashing lights atop a patrol car formed a landmark in the mist rising off the water that edged both sides of the seven-mile-long narrow strip of land that bridged Mobile Bay and linked the city of Mobile with the Eastern Shore. Hugo pulled onto the oyster shell parking lot and surveyed the scene as he put the Thunderbird into park and killed the engine.

Chief Goode was easily identifiable, the beginning of a

paunch at his midsection well defined by the back lighting of the motel entrance. He stood with a taller man in casual clothing. Behind and just to the right of them, under the peaked portico over the glass double doors leading into the building, two people stood in intimate conversation. Smoke from the cigarette in the woman's hand drifted upward.

Hugo folded a stick of Juicy Fruit gum into his mouth and got out of the car.

The Chief let his gaze travel over Hugo's tall frame. "You look like shit."

"It's four in the morning."

"You sober?"

"As a judge."

The Chief studied Hugo then nodded toward the man with him. "This is Chief Stanton. Spanish Fort Police."

Hugo shook Stanton's hand, waiting for an explanation as to why the Mobile Police Chief and, more particularly *he,* was standing outside a motel in the wee hours of the morning in what was clearly not their jurisdiction.

The Chief cleared his throat. "We have a murder in one of the rooms. The victim is Buzz's niece. Ruby."

Hugo looked from Goode to Stanton. "How?"

Stanton turned his profile to the two Mobile police officers and stared across the highway into the mist dancing in the swamp grass along the far shore. "Single gunshot to the heart."

"What was she doing here?"

Neither Goode nor Stanton replied.

The movement of the female smoker caught Hugo's eye as she ground out her cigarette with the toe of her shoe.

One corner of her mouth lifted in a knowing half smile as she touched her companion on the arm and the two of them went through the double doors into the motel lobby.

"Okay," Hugo said. "The forensics team's on the way. Anything I need to know before they get here? Like why we're here and not the state police? Or the county?"

"Ruby was engaged to Sam Hollingsworth. He's highway patrol for Baldwin County. She broke it off about a year ago." Stanton rubbed the back of his neck and exhaled a weary sigh. "And I don't want the new sheriff all up in my business, if you want to know the truth of it."

Chief Goode gave Stanton a slap of consolation to his upper arm. "Buzz and I go way back, don't we?"

Stanton nodded, studied the ground at his feet, and blinked rapidly. "God Almighty," he said in a soft voice. "How am I going to tell Beth?"

Goode cleared his throat. "Look, Buzz, you pull your guy and high tail it out of here before anyone shows up. We'll do what we can to keep everything as low key as possible. Won't mention the family connection but you know it'll get out. Be sure her mama's prepared. And Nora, too."

Hugo and the Chief watched as Stanton walked toward the motel entrance. He was almost as tall as Hugo with broad shoulders and an Uncle Sam recruitment poster physique. His hair was cut high and tight. He could have easily passed for a drill sergeant. Just before he reached the door, he swayed a couple of steps, a small drunken dance of grief. Or perhaps it was simply a trick of the flashing light of the neon sign. The weight of the door almost defeated him as he went inside to collect the patrolman guarding the room. As soon as it closed behind him, Goode turned to Hugo, his voice a fierce, low growl.

"Keep a lid on this, August. Not one word to the press about it. Not one, you hear me? Make sure everyone else gets the message." He opened the door of his car and as he slid onto the seat he looked up at Hugo. "I want a detailed report of the initial findings and progress reports on every little detail. I won't be blindsided. You hear me? This is going to be one hell of a mess."

The Chief sped away as Stanton and a uniformed patrolman came out the entrance of the motel. Both of them looked shell shocked. Neither of them spoke to Hugo as they got into the patrol car. As they pulled away, the driver killed the flashing lights and turned east toward Spanish Fort.

The smoker was behind the registration counter when Hugo entered the motel. She was already lighting another cigarette. With a flick of her head, she sent blond curls cascading behind her shoulder. She appraised him from head to toe as he crossed the small lobby.

"What's your name?" Hugo asked.

"Dixie."

"You the night manager?"

She nodded.

"Who found the body?"

"Me."

"What time?"

"Two forty-five or there about."

"You randomly check the rooms at two forty-five every morning?"

That garnered him a hint of a smile.

"Not usually. She wanted a wake-up call for two. No one answered so after a couple more calls, I decided she had left already and I went to check the room."

"Was anyone else in the room?"

"Not when I got there."

"Anyone come and go before you checked the room at two forty-five?"

"Not that I saw."

"How'd you get in?"

"Pass key."

"Anyone else have a key?"

"There are two keys for each room. The guest gets one. Sometimes two if the circumstances call for it."

"And what might those circumstances be?"

"Oh, shuga, you know what circumstances. This ain't the Ritz."

"By that you mean The Thunderbird Inn is a rendezvous establishment?"

"That's a fancy mouthful."

"Were you here when she checked in?"

Dixie nodded.

"When was that?"

"About ten, I think. Something like that."

"Was anyone with her?"

"No."

"Anyone show up looking for her?"

"Not that I know of."

"Did you hear the gunshot?"

Dixie shook her head.

"Did you hear anything?"

"No."

Hugo watched her in silence for a couple of beats. "Two in the morning or thereabouts on a quiet weeknight and you didn't hear the gunshot?"

Dixie shifted her weight from one hip to stand upright. "That's what I said."

Hugo looked past her into the open office where a pegboard mounted to the wall held keys under their allotted numbers. "Which room is it?"

"Lucky number seven."

"You think it's lucky?"

"She did."

"Yeah?"

"Always the same room. Lucky number seven."

"She asked for it specifically? On a number of occasions?"

"You *are* a bright boy."

Hugo let his gaze travel around what passed for a lobby. There wasn't much to it. Two easy chairs angled toward each other in a corner of the small space. Off to his right a glass door led into a darkened room that appeared to be the restaurant. To his left a long hallway was the conduit to the rooms. There were only two dimly lit fixtures spaced far apart along the whole length. At the far end he could barely make out a door to the outside.

"Is the door at the end of the hallway locked at night?"

"It's supposed to be."

"Was it tonight?"

"I haven't checked."

"Did the police officer who was here earlier check it?"

"I don't know."

Hugo walked around the counter and into the office. Hanging under number seven was a single key. "Is this the key you used?"

"No." Dixie opened a drawer of the registration counter and pulled out a ring of keys. "People are always walking off with the keys so we keep a back-up on the master ring." She handed them to Hugo then leaned against the doorframe of the office, the smoke from her cigarette spiraling upward. "They're all marked with the room numbers."

"Is the desk always manned?"

"Mostly."

Hugo looked around the office at the recliner in the corner with a blanket over the arm rest, the empty coffee cup with Dixie's hot pink lipstick smudging the rim, and a plate with the remains of a sandwich on it.

"Did you use the master key to let the police into the room?"

"Yes."

He nodded at the single key still on the pegboard. "Has anyone touched this one?"

She shrugged. "Not since it was placed there after the last occupant, I guess."

Hugo opened drawers on the office desk until he found a stack of envelopes. He took a tissue from a box of Kleenex and used it to remove the key from the pegboard and drop it into the envelope. Dixie watched without comment.

"Did anyone go into the room after you found the body?"

He saw the flicker of indecision before she could control her reaction.

"Who?"

"I didn't know what to do. So, I called Harry."

"The guy you were standing with outside?"

She nodded.

"He works here?"

She nodded again.

"Did he go in alone?"

"No, I was with him."

"Did either of you touch anything?"

She thought a second and shook her head. "No. Except the light switch. When I opened the door, I flipped the switch. That's when I saw her."

"How did you know she was dead?"

"The bullet hole in her chest. And the blood."

"You didn't touch her? Check for a pulse?"

Dixie shook her head and looked away from his steady regard.

Hugo jangled the master keys in his hand then walked the length of the hallway to the emergency escape door. There was a deadbolt lock mounted above the doorknob which had a thumb lock. When Hugo turned the doorknob, the door opened onto the pre-dawn light and the smell of damp and decay.

He retraced his steps to room number seven. It was locked. He used the master key and stepped inside, closing the door behind him. The room lay in darkness, broken only by pulsing flashes of neon light slanting intermittently through the partially open venetian blinds and illuminating the body.

Ruby lay on her back on the floor at the foot of the bed.

Her face was turned slightly toward the window, her lips parted as if on a sigh, her eyes open as if watching the strobing light of the motel sign. One hand lay on the floor, palm up, in the tangle of long red curls that framed her face, the other lay across her abdomen. Her legs were pulled up slightly as one does in sleep. A short, sheer robe was tied at the waist. A single dark ribbon of red trailed from a small entry wound on the inside rise of her left breast. Her face and limbs were the white of a delicately sculpted marble statue. She was beautiful, and she was dead.

Two

THE DOOR OPENED behind Hugo. At the sound of the wall switch being flipped, the room sprang into harsh relief with light from the overhead fixture. The illusion of life evaporated from the body like mist in the reality of the cheap motel furnishings, taking with it the siren's spell that had held Hugo motionless.

"Christ," Junior said and then whistled softly, that low sissing sound he made with a trick of his tongue against his front teeth. "Drop dead gorgeous."

Hugo grunted.

"Know who she is?"

"Ruby."

"And why are we here?"

"A favor to the Spanish Fort police chief."

"I see."

"His niece."

"Oh."

They stood a moment staring down at the redhead.

"Damn shame," Junior said.

Hugo tore his gaze from lips that no longer beckoned,

from eyes that had ceased to glitter with invitation in the neon light. "Where's the team?"

"Just pulling in."

Hugo crouched beside the body. "She's a regular according to the night manager."

"A working girl?"

"I don't think so. I'm guessing she met the same guy every time."

"Don't tell me. Mr. Jones."

"Mr. Smith, actually."

"Well, that narrows it down. The night manager give you a description?"

"Not yet. But she didn't see him tonight she says."

"A no show."

"Someone showed up. Obviously. We just don't know who. The exit at the end of the hallway is unlocked. Poor lighting. Anyone could have come and gone without being seen."

"My money's on Mr. Smith."

"Maybe. She used to be engaged to a highway patrolman. This is his turf."

"Who called it in?"

"The night manager."

"She didn't see the shooter?"

"She says not."

"You believe her?"

"Early days, yet."

"So, what's the plan?"

"There's a handy man or cook hanging about. Find out what he knows. We need a list of any other guests. There are four cars and a Harley in the parking lot. Get the tag numbers." Hugo took in the rumpled state of the bed. He stepped over Ruby's body and, with his elbow, pushed open the door to the bathroom. A small cloth draw-string bag was open on the top of the toilet tank. A woman's cosmetics lay in a jumble within it and across the porcelain top. Neither of the two towels had been used but a wet washcloth lay in the sink. He pulled back the shower curtain. There was no indication that it had been used. The faint smell of mold overpowered a whisper of feminine scent.

He stepped back into the motel room and went to the window. He stared through the venetian blinds. The throb of the neon lights revealed a shroud of fog slowly rolling across the parking lot. His car was barely visible through the mist.

Evie entered the room with her large scene-of-crime bag. She pushed her dark rimmed glasses up the bridge of her nose with a gloved forefinger as she eyed the body. Her assistant appeared in the doorway behind her.

"Do we have a name?" she asked.

"Ruby."

When he said nothing more she looked up at him. "Just Ruby?"

"For now."

The assistant peered over Evie's shoulder. "She a hooker, then?"

Hugo realized the assistant had taken out his notepad. He didn't recognize the guy. "She's the victim. Only facts as to the state of the scene and body for the record. No one's to know what we're working on. Don't talk to the press. Or your girlfriend or your mother." He saw the speculation in the assistant's eyes. "That's straight from the chief and I'll throw anyone who leaks to the wolves without a second thought. Got it?" He stared at the assistant until he looked up from the body.

The guy hesitated as he watched Hugo a long moment then slipped the notebook back into his pocket.

Hugo circled the body and stopped in the open doorway as he surveyed the room and Ruby. "Looks like a small caliber gun was used. We'll need to do a preliminary check of the night manager, the handy man, and any guests for gunshot residue."

Evie looked up from the body then turned to her assistant. "I've got clear tape in the case. You know what to do?"

"I'm guessing I need to dab the tape over their hands to see what it might pick up."

"Think you can handle it?"

"It can't be that hard. But wouldn't they have washed their hands?" There was a speculative look in the assistant's eye.

"Humor me," Hugo said.

"The motel guests too?"

"For the sake of elimination, yes," Hugo said. "Collect their prints then check them against any found in this room and on the exit door at the end of the hallway. Once they leave here, they're in the wind. Keep everyone in their rooms until we can interview them. I want a thorough search for the gun."

Evie was already extracting the camera from her

bag. Hugo summoned Junior from the room with a jerk of his head.

"The night manager is Dixie. Get a look at the registry for anyone staying here within the last twenty-four hours. We need to start the process for phone records. Calls in, calls out. The exterior will be a nightmare for the search team."

Junior nodded and looked back at Evie snapping photos with a high-powered flash. "My guess would be it's lost forever somewhere in the marsh grasses of the delta."

"Probably but we have to look."

"Why didn't Spanish Fort call in the sheriff?"

"The Chief's tight with Goode."

Junior reached into his inner coat pocket for a pack of cigarettes, a worried look on his face. He glanced at the assistant then lowered his voice. "Does Stanton think the smokey's involved?"

"Sam Hollingsworth. Nothing was said but she broke off the engagement about a year ago. He's in the frame."

"Crap."

"Who's the kid with Evie?"

"Old Doc Allen's grandson." Junior grinned. "Taking a break from med school, I hear."

Hugo gave a humorless grunt. "Lucky us."

⁂

HUGO SLIPPED ON a pair of gloves and started at the end of the hallway. He worked his way back, checking each room. It was evident that most of the rooms had seen little use. There was a staleness to the air and a forlorn drabness to the furnishings. The towels in the bathrooms were threadbare and coarse. He skipped over the two rooms that were occupied by guests and the room where Evie and her assistant were finishing up with the body. The front desk was unmanned when Hugo reached the lobby. He found Dixie standing out front under the peaked portico of the building smoking a cigarette as the sky began to glow in the east with predawn light.

"When did the fog start?" he asked.

Dixie flicked her cigarette butt into the deepening mist. "Not sure. Before midnight. I stepped out to stretch my legs."

"What do you remember?"

Her brows arched briefly then she shook her head. "The fog was wispy. It hadn't settled in."

"How many cars in the lot?"

"Three, I think." She was silent a moment. "Yeah, three. And mine. The Beetle. So that makes four."

"The same three that are here now?"

"I suppose."

"These belong to the guests?" A white Caddy riding low was flanked on either side by a red Mustang and a powder blue Chevrolet Woodie.

Dixie nodded.

"And the Harley?"

"Harry."

"The handy man? Cook?"

She nodded. "Cook."

"Which car's hers?"

"The Mustang."

Hugo had guessed as much. "The reporters will be all over this."

"I figured as much."

"You know who she is?"

"I've lived here all my life."

"Gossip will complicate things. For everyone."

"Is that a warning, officer?"

"Let's call it a suggestion. For the Stanton's sake."

"Do I look like someone who's disloyal?"

"You feel loyalty to the Chief?"

She remained silent.

"You know who he is, don't you? Mr. Smith."

"Just another motel guest." She watched Hugo with a bland look of innocence.

"We'll find out soon enough."

"I'm sure you will."

"Was he the only one?"

Dixie hesitated. "For the past year or so."

"Before that?"

"She was engaged, I hear."

"But?"

Dixie arched her eyebrows again. "Who knows."

Hugo stood beside her feeling the cool of the damp fog on his face and watched the gray mist glow with bright colors as the sign flashed on and off repeatedly.

"When she didn't answer the phone, why didn't you check the lot for her car?"

"Didn't think of it."

"Umm." He turned back toward the motel. The aroma

of brewing coffee greeted him when he opened the door of the lobby.

The ambulance attendants were wheeling the gurney bearing Ruby's body down the hallway. A man in an undershirt and plaid Bermuda shorts stood near the door to the restaurant with a steaming cup of coffee in his hand.

"What the hell's going on?" he asked.

Hugo saw the black smudging of print powder on the man's hands. He turned and watched the gurney. A long tendril of a red curl escaped the sheet and bounced with each turn of the wheels. It looked so alive.

He blinked the image away and gave the man in the plaid shorts a quick up and down.

"An unexpected death," he said. "Are you a guest?"

The man followed the progress of the gurney with his gaze until the door closed behind it. He glanced at his blackened fingertips. Then he, in return, gave Hugo a quick up and down. "You a cop?"

Hugo nodded.

"How'd she die?"

"Unknown at this time."

"Right." The guy sipped his coffee then grunted. "Hell of a thing. To die in a two-bit motel on the road to nowhere."

"Did you see her at any time last night?"

"Why?"

"Trying to establish time of death."

"Ask the cook."

"Yeah?"

"Saw him coming out of her room about midnight."

"How'd you know it was her room?"

"The red hair. Caught a glimpse as the door closed."

"Which room is yours?"

"Number twelve."

Hugo looked down the hallway. "Near the exit?"

"Two doors away."

"See anyone using the exit?"

"Other than the cook?" He shook his head.

"You hear anything unusual?"

"Like what?"

"Like anything that you wouldn't normally hear in the dead of night on an isolated strip of road to nowhere."

The man eyed Hugo a moment then shook his head.

"What's your name?"

"W. A. Roth. Everyone calls me Dubya."

"Where're you from, Mr. Roth?"

"Atlanta."

"New to the area?"

"Come down to Gulf Shores a few times a year to do a little deep sea fishing."

"You're a ways from the Gulf."

"Plan to meet up with a fella about a boat."

"Where?"

"Fairhope. At the yacht club."

"Before you go fishing?"

"Nine a.m."

"You planning to buy the boat?"

"Don't know, do I? 'Til I see it."

Hugo let the silence lengthen but Dubya had nothing to add. He took down his address and phone number before going in search of the cook.

᠁

AN OLDER COUPLE was sitting at a table in the dining area when Hugo passed through on his way to the kitchen. They followed his progress with their eyes and leaned in toward each other to murmur with their heads together. The word was out. News would spread quickly. Hugo felt his stomach muscles tighten with a sense of urgency.

He pushed through the swinging doors as the cook threw a ration of bacon onto the hot grill and covered it with a heavy cast iron weight.

The cook was probably mid-to-late twenties. His dark hair curled over the neckband of his white tee shirt and he had a foo Manchu mustache. He cast Hugo a glance from eyes as dark as his hair and proceeded to crack eggs into a bowl.

"Harry?"

"Yeah," the cook said as he whipped the eggs, flipped the bacon, and dropped bread into an industrial sized toaster.

"Got a last name, Harry?"

"I already told the other cop."

"Well, how about you tell me."

"Chapman."

"How well did you know Ruby Stanton?"

He shrugged and kept his attention on the sizzling bacon as he poured the eggs onto the grill. "I see her come and go."

"Would you say you're on speaking terms?"

"Sure."

"You speak to her last night?"

Again, the shrug. "Could be." He glanced at Hugo. "Probably."

"A good-looking woman like that and you don't remember if you spoke to her last night?"

He was silent a couple of beats. "Yeah. I saw her. But I don't know nothin' about her getting shot."

"How'd you know she was shot?"

"Dixie called me. Hadn't hardly fallen asleep good. Wanted someone here while she waited for the cops."

"What time was this?"

"When I got back?"

"When Dixie called."

Again, the shrug. "Two o'clock, maybe?"

"How long did it take you to get back to the motel?"

"Five minutes? Ten minutes? Something like that."

"You live close, then."

"Temporary situation. Camping out over a boat house up on Confederate Drive. Keeping an eye on the place for the owners."

Hugo watched as Harry plated the two breakfast platters with quick, practiced movements.

"They've got a phone in the boat house, have they? The owners?"

The cook scraped the grill with a metal spatula then banged it against the surface to dislodge food scraps. "I was sleeping in the house. I do that sometimes."

"Enough times for Dixie to have the phone number?"

"So?"

Hugo shrugged. "You went straight home after work?"

"No. I went to the Paradise for a beer."

"What time was this?"

"About nine, I guess. The restaurant closes at eight. No room service. So," he did a little side to side movement with his head, "out of the kitchen by eight-thirty, eight-forty."

"What time did you leave the Paradise?"

He didn't reply immediately. Finally, he shoved the spatula into a slot on the side of the griddle. "Can't say. I was off the clock. I had a couple of beers. Walked down the trail to the bay for a while."

Hugo watched him move on to the coffee pot. He gestured with it and Hugo nodded.

The coffee was strong but good. As he went out into the foyer, he saw a uniformed policeman turning away a couple of men at the front door.

"Breakfast regulars," Dixie said as she came from the office to join Hugo. "We generally do a decent business on the weekdays."

"No waitress?"

"Dick Tracy talked to her and sent her back home."

Hugo drank his coffee.

Dixie adjusted her purse strap on her shoulder. "So, can I go now?"

Hugo glanced at his watch. It was five-thirty. "This your usual time to knock off?"

"More or less."

"Which is it? More or less?"

"The waitress gets here about quarter to five. The dining room doesn't officially start serving until five-thirty. I grab breakfast and head out by about five-forty or so. Dickie is generally here by then."

"Dickie?"

"The manager. He usually gets here just before six. I thought, under the circumstances, I'd head on out. They've put yellow tape across the entrance. Your guy woke all the guests and has them in the dining room with orders they can't go back to get their things until their rooms have been searched. I was told to touch nothing. So," she shrugged.

"How'd you get in touch with Harry?"

She hesitated. "I called him at the Brennan's house."

"And what time was that?"

"I told you already."

"Tell me again."

"About two-forty, something like that."

Hugo drained the last of the coffee from the cup. "Sure. Head on home. We'll call you if we have any more questions."

At that moment a raised voice beyond the glass door of the entrance drew Hugo's attention. A man in a lime green polo shirt and pink, green, and yellow plaid trousers was shouting at the patrolman guarding the door. Hugo had no doubt that this was Dickie.

Three

JUNIOR WATCHED DUBYA as he left the dining room and walked straight down the hallway toward his room. He was the last of the potential witnesses to be interviewed. Something about him didn't sit well. Maybe it was the greasy look of his bottle black hair or the Mediterranean hook of his nose. Or the calculating way he studied Junior, as if weighing each question, trying to extract any knowledge from the asking.

He sighed and closed his notebook. He was feeling that familiar letdown when the early euphoria of the chase came up against a blank wall. Finally, he rose from his chair and made a circuit through the kitchen to refill his coffee cup, disregarding the acid burn at the back of his throat. He needed the caffeine.

He decided it was time to see what might be of value in the motel office. It had been searched already for the weapon, but you never knew what dirty little secrets were squirreled away in the most obvious places.

The file cabinet held nothing but old folders that looked as though they hadn't been touched in years with the exception of half a dozen in the front of the top drawer. Mainly they had to do with insurance, maintenance, and regular bills for the motel.

Junior's brows shot up when he opened the third drawer. "Well, well. What have we here?" Neatly folded in the bottom of the drawer were three pairs of a sexy lace panties, one black, the other two red. He also discovered slippers with feathery pom-poms in black, and a packet of condoms.

"Dixie, you are a naughty girl," he murmured.

From the file cabinet he moved on to the desk. There wasn't much of interest among the usual office supplies until he got to the bottom right drawer. It was locked. A brief search of the center drawer of the desk and behind the file cabinet failed to locate a key so he took the letter opener and jimmied the lock.

Inside was a treasure trove of feminine products. Lipstick, brush, make-up, nail polish, sanitary napkins. Junior felt the blush warm his face. She also had half a dozen packs of Marlboros neatly stacked. He started to close the drawer but realized there was a notebook in the very bottom. He pulled it out and sat back in the desk chair, thumbing through the pages.

There were notations of dates and initials marching down each page. Occasionally there would be a question mark beside a date. Sometimes Dixie had jotted down a question. *Ask D.* Toward the end of the book a notation read *Sully.*

Now we're getting somewhere, Junior thought. He read back through the dates trying to find a pattern and he did. The dates were two weeks apart with the notation

Due every twenty-eight days. Junior frowned. He sat back and stared at the ceiling for a couple of minutes. Then realization struck. He blushed more deeply and returned the notebook to the bottom of the drawer.

⁂

JUNIOR TOOK A deep pull on the Marlboro and held the smoke a couple of seconds before exhaling. He extinguished the cigarette against the sole of his shoe. The early morning sun did little to penetrate the mist. An egret alighted gracefully a few feet from where he stood at the edge of the marshy shore of the Blakeley River.

He had followed a little trail that managed to survive the rampant growth of a variety of wild plants. It meandered around muddy depressions north from the exit door near Ruby's room.

A small, raised earthen promontory jutted out into the water. A good spot for viewing the expanse of the delta that was the culmination of the five rivers which meandered down the state and emptied into the bay and eventually the Gulf of Mexico.

A cane pole stuck upright in the water about three feet out from the little earthen dock. At some point in the past, it had been corded with a rope-like string to mark the various depths of the water.

A mullet jumped about ten feet from shore, barely visible in the mist. The egret stalked closer to water's edge with slow, deliberate steps. A good fishing spot, Junior decided. It was evident from the imprints in the dark soil of the earthen pier that it was well used. By the motel staff? Or did the guests know about it? Anyone taking a stroll could happen upon the path, especially if they slipped out the emergency exit for a smoke or a view of the large expanse of waterways. If the gun didn't show up, someone would need to take a dive into the murky depths. This was a logical place to dispose of a weapon, especially if the killer was familiar with the hotel grounds.

He retraced his steps along the path. As he neared the exit door at the west end of the building, he took a left and made his way along the rear of the motel. All the windows of the rooms on this side had their blinds closed.

At one time an effort had been made to keep the encroaching vegetation at bay and crepe myrtles formed a ragged line of defense. They were being rapidly overtaken. An inadequate attempt to shape them had long since been abandoned.

A raised wooden deck at the rear of the building near the restaurant gave a view of Blakeley River shrouded in a heavy layer of fog. A flatbed fishing boat faded in and out of visibility as it eased across the calm surface. The sound of its trolling motor reached Junior. He made a mental note to ask Dixie if she had heard a boat motor in the night.

Two doors opened into the restaurant from the deck. The one on the left lead directly into the kitchen and the other into the dining room. It would be easy to move between the kitchen and the west emergency exit of the building without being seen by reception.

From the deck, Junior watched as two policemen from Mobile worked the tall grass to the east of the motel, looking for anything that might be linked to the crime. He let his gaze travel from right to left along the expanse of wild growth, water, and wetlands and knew it was a hopeless task. It would take a miracle to find anything useful, especially something as small as a handgun. So far, the search of the motel had turned up nothing.

The kitchen door opened and Harry, the cook, stepped out onto the deck with only the barest hesitation when he saw Junior. With a nod in Junior's direction, he lit a cigarette and turned his gaze northeast.

Junior followed his line of sight. "Nice place to live," he said as he looked along the eastern shoreline of the delta. He could see the rooftops of boat lifts, their access hidden from view by the marsh grasses and swirling fog. It would be easy enough, he decided, to slip into the unlocked door of the motel, shoot Ruby, and slip away to any of the houses along the embankment. Someone Ruby would open the door to his quiet knock. Mr. Smith, no doubt.

"Who lives up there?" Junior asked the cook.

"Don't know."

"You don't know any of the residents along Confederate Drive?"

The cook flipped his cigarette over the edge of the deck. "A few of them, I guess."

"Seeing as how you live in one of the boat houses."

The cook cut his eyes at Junior then nodded toward the first house peeking through the trees. "The O'Sullivans."

"Like the funeral home O'Sullivans?"

"The same." He nodded again. "Next is the Brennans. That's where I'm housesitting."

"Where are the Brennans?"

"The mountains somewhere. North Carolina, I think."

"Do they know you're housesitting?"

Harry clenched his jaw then gave a *meh* movement of his head and shoulders.

Junior remained silent for a long moment, staring out across the water. "Look, it's not my patch and I really don't care what the arrangements are. As long as you scratch my back."

"How's that?"

"You live on the bluff overlooking the motel. You work at the motel with a front row view of the action on this strip of water. I don't imagine you miss much."

"Nothing much to see."

"Boats. Who's in them. Where they're going."

"How would I know? Fishing? Up the delta? They could be going anywhere."

Junior considered this. Finally, he said, "Squatting in a rich man's house. Most likely with the wife's approval." He clicked his tongue against the roof of his mouth. "I think I'd pay attention. Just in case."

"O'Sullivan," the cook said. "He comes by boat to the motel."

"Where does he dock? There's no way to get from the boat to land without wading in water."

"Next door. The marine repair shop. About a hundred yards west."

The length of a football field. Convenient. "Married?"

"Very."

"Know the wife?"

"Everyone knows the wife."

"Think he was visiting Ruby?"

"Couldn't say."

"And here we are, all chummy and the like."

The cook sighed. "I'd guess not."

"Dixie?"

"You'd have to ask her."

That's a yes, Junior thought. "Regular?"

"Yeah."

"Last night?"

"Couldn't say."

"And the house after the Brennans?"

"That belongs Bama and Lord. Don't know the fourth house. He drives a woody wagon. Crane, I think. Got some kids."

"Ever see any of them here at the motel?"

Harry looked at him. "At the motel?"

"Yeah, eating lunch maybe. Or whatever."

"No."

"Other than O'Sullivan."

Harry cut his eyes toward Junior. "Other than O'Sullivan."

✺

THE MORNING WAS ticking away. Hugo needed to speak with Ruby's parents before her murder became common knowledge. But first there was Dickie to contend with.

Hugo watched Dickie hitch his pants as his gaze

traveled around the foyer with a belligerent, I'm-in-charge expression on his face.

Dickie's full name was Richard "H" Leeton. The H short for Harris of the Mobile Harrises. As if anyone was asking.

Hugo assured him he would bear that in mind, but he still needed to ask him some questions.

"But I wasn't here!" Dickie protested.

"What time did you leave the motel yesterday?"

"About six. Quarter to, actually."

"Do you know the victim?"

"Ruby? Sure. Her family's lived in Spanish Fort since way back."

"When was the last time you saw her?"

Hugo had maneuvered them into the office and closed the door.

Dickie tugged at the waistband of his polyester plaid trousers and swelled his chest, filling the small space with his importance.

Hugo stood his ground and waited.

Dickie stopped blustering and sat heavily in the desk chair. He cleared his throat. "It's been a while." He leaned back in the chair. "Matter of fact, the last time I saw her was at Mary Mahoney's."

"Biloxi?"

The corner of Dickie's mouth lifted in a sneering smile.

"What was she doing over there?"

"My guess would be having a late lunch."

"How late?"

Dickie shrugged. "After two. Couldn't say exactly."

"Alone?"

"She was when I saw her."

"Did you get the impression she had a lunch companion?"

"Have you ever seen Ruby?"

Hugo gave a small grunt. Ruby wasn't the kind of woman who dined alone. "Did you see her companion?"

"No."

"Did you see anyone you knew other than Ruby?"

Dickie lowered his gaze to the desktop. "Can't say I did."

Can't, Hugo wondered. Or won't?

⁂

HUGO LEFT DICKIE with instructions that all the rooms and common areas were off limits until the forensic team had finished. He took the ring of master keys and made his way down the long hallway. From the list of registrants, he knew that only three rooms had been occupied the previous evening. Apart from number seven where Ruby had lost her life, numbers twelve and four were occupied.

W. A. Roth and the couple from St. Louis in number four had been sequestered in the dining room where Junior interviewed them. Once a search of the motel was completed, they were escorted back to their rooms to collect their belongings. Dickie wasn't happy about the fact that the motel would be shut down until the police finished processing the scene. He had blustered and fumed until the implications behind Hugo's questioning about his activities of the last twenty-four hours silenced his tongue.

On his first inspection of the vacant rooms, Hugo had

discovered all the odd numbered rooms were made up in readiness for occupation. The air, as Hugo entered each one, had exuded a staleness and faint hint of mildew.

Nothing in the two occupied rooms seemed out of the ordinary. The beds had been slept in, wet towels lay on the floor, and damp lingered in the bathrooms.

It was room number two that piqued Hugo's interest.

The room was made up and tidy and yet there was something. Hugo stood still in the center of the room, his eyes closed, the only sound the hum of the window air conditioner, and let his thoughts drift.

It was the lingering scent in the back of his throat, the smell of rot, decay, and damp that lived in the leeways and marshes here on the edge of the delta. The memory stirred in the back of his mind. The earthy, moldy scent of the jungles of Vietnam, the humming air conditioner mimicking the patter of the incessant rains of July drenching his platoon, drowning out all other sounds. Something was there, just beyond his vision, beyond his reach, drifting like the mist outside the motel. The unknown danger. Yet, somehow, he knew. He wanted to shout. *Stop! Stop!* But they hadn't stopped.

Hugo eyes opened with a start. His chest heaved with his breathing. He swallowed the bile in the back of his throat and wiped cold beads of sweat from his forehead, banishing the image to that dark corner of his mind then began a thorough search of the room. It was clean. Too clean. And unlike all the other unoccupied rooms of the motel, it was cool. He stared at the rumbling air conditioner. Someone had occupied the room last night.

Four

THE SPANISH FORT police station was quiet with a somberness that bordered on unease. Hugo was directed to the only office by a middle-aged woman with a deep crease on her forehead, her lips compressed tightly as if it required a monumental effort to contain her thoughts. The office door had a glass upper panel with Chief William "Buzz" Stanton lettered in gold.

Stanton sat at his desk, the phone receiver at his ear. The change in him was profound. Hugo tapped on the glass of the door.

Stanton looked up, said something into the mouthpiece of the phone, and hung up. He motioned for Hugo to enter.

A window air conditioning unit had the office cold enough to hang meat but still the Chief's forehead was beaded with sweat.

"Sorry to have to do this right now, Chief," Hugo said as he took the chair opposite.

"I know the drill." Stanton fixed him with a look that would curdle milk. "I want this bastard. In my jail."

"If Goode—"

"No ifs. My jurisdiction. My terms."

He understood Stanton's rage, the need to punish. "Let's start with the fiancé."

"Ex-fiancé."

"Who broke it off?"

Stanton sat back in his chair. "Ruby."

"How did he take it?"

"Not well."

"I'll need more than that."

"He wouldn't let it go." Stanton paused and looked away from Hugo. "I had to step in."

"Did it become physical?"

"No. But I let him know I had no problem taking it there."

Hugo could easily imagine the exchange between Stanton and the ex-fiancé. "What about with her? Did he ever cross that line with her?"

"He's still alive, ain't he?"

"Would she have told you?"

Stanton fell silent for a couple of beats. "I don't know," he said. "She could be secretive. Didn't like anyone up in her business."

"Anyone being?"

"Her ma. Me. The family in general."

"I take it there was someone new in her life. Do you know who?"

Stanton lowered his gaze to his desktop and picked up a pen. "I couldn't say for sure."

"I'm good with an educated guess."

"I wouldn't want to send the investigation off in the wrong direction."

"Let me be the judge of that."

By way of an answer, Stanton studied Hugo. "How old are you?"

"I'm good at my job."

Stanton grunted. "The Haywood case."

"Actually, it was the Camden case."

"But she was a Haywood."

"She was a victim."

"Right." Stanton tapped the pen against his desk blotter. "Right," he said again. "I'll give it some thought and get back to you."

✺

JUNIOR STARTED WITH the last house on Confederate Drive that was visible from the motel. There was no answer. He walked around the side of the house to find a two-vehicle carport. It was empty.

At the next house, he checked his notes then rang the bell.

He was about to ring it again when the door opened. A petite brunette stood in the foyer fixing an earring to her left earlobe as she looked up at the stranger on her porch.

"Yes?" Her greeting held a note of distraction as her gaze flitted beyond Junior to the unmarked car in the driveway.

The cook hadn't provided Junior with a last name, so he took his shield from his coat pocket.

"I'd like a word if you don't mind."

She glanced at the shield and called out, "Lord!" The earring secured in place, she gestured for Junior to come inside. "He's on the deck. He'll have to give you the details."

She was moving down a hallway as she spoke, impatience underscoring her words. "I'm late already and I don't know anything about the boat. It isn't as if it's missing."

Clearly, the lady of the house had misinterpreted Junior's appearance on her doorstep, but he made no comment.

The hallway opened into a large living room with two couches facing each other in front of a massive fireplace, the brick chimney exposed all the way to the high-pitched ceiling. The walls on either side of the fireplace were mainly glass with French doors onto a deck that overlooked the delta and the barely visible skyline of the city of Mobile beyond a very distant miniature and ghostly presence in the diminishing fog.

The French doors to the left of the fireplace stood open and Junior saw a man of medium height with a thatch of sun-bleached curly hair standing on the deck, a pair of binoculars trained on the water.

"Lord!" the woman said, "the cops are here." She turned away from the doorway in the direction of the left wing of the house. "I'm sorry," she said to Junior in passing, "but I've got to run." With that, she disappeared beyond an archway.

Lord stood on the other side of the French doors and gestured toward Junior. "Out here," he said.

Junior stepped onto the deck and held up his shield for Lord's inspection. Like his wife, he barely gave it a glance.

"It's not moored where I left it. And there're footprints everywhere."

"I'm not sure I understand the problem."

Lord flung his hand holding the binoculars in the direction of the dock below. "It's those damn kids! I told Stanton the last time that he'd better do something about it or I would."

"About what?"

Lord stared at him in disbelief. "The boat! They've taken it out again. Last night."

"Are you sure? Did you see or hear anything?"

"Am I sure?" Lord's face reddened with his rising anger. "Of course, I'm sure. Since all this started, I make a point to double check every afternoon." He stared out across the water. "Little shits!"

"When did all this start?"

Lord stared at him, disbelief on his face. The expression changed to puzzlement. "Who are you?"

"Junior Knight. Mobile Police."

"Mobile? What the hell does the Mobile police have to do with anything?"

"I'm here to ask about what you may have seen or heard out on the water last night."

"Why is Mobile investigating this?"

"There was an incident on the causeway near here. We're helping the Spanish Fort Police with additional manpower." Junior hoped that version would keep Lord from asking too many questions before he could get some answers.

"Must be something serious."

"There was a death."

"Anyone I know?"

"I couldn't say."

"How did it happen?"

"Undetermined at this point in the investigation."

"An accident? Where?"

"There's not a lot we know right now. Anything unusual that you saw or heard would be helpful."

"Drowned, I guess. You think it was one of the Crane kids?"

"No positive ID yet. Were you and your wife home last night?"

Lord nodded. "I took the boat out in the late afternoon. Checked the crab traps." He nodded toward a white buoy with red stripes about a hundred or so feet out in the delta. "Got four good sized crabs. Bama made West Indies salad to go with dinner."

"Just the two of you home last night?"

"Yes. There's only the two of us."

"No guests for dinner, anything like that?"

Lord's eyebrows rose briefly. "Just the two of us." He gestured with a nod of his head toward an outdoor table and chairs. "Out here. Watched the sunset. Back inside around eightish."

"You say someone moved your boat?"

"This is the fifth time since Easter. It's those Crane kids. I'm sure of it."

"Did you see them?"

Lord expelled a loud breath of exasperation. "If I had seen them, you can believe I would have stopped them."

"How?"

"How?"

"How would you have stopped them?

"I have a pistol. I warned Stanton I'd take care of the situation if I caught them."

"You planned to shoot them?"

Lord's scowl deepened. "Of course not! But I planned to make them piss themselves."

"What kind of pistol?"

"Smith and Wesson. Why?"

"Can I see it?"

"Oh, for God's sake, I'm not really going to shoot anyone."

"Still, I'd like to see it."

Lord's expression turned speculative. "It wasn't an accident, was it? Someone was shot."

Junior knew it was pointless to deny the fact. He also knew he wasn't leaving without seeing Lord's gun.

"If you could get it for me, please."

Lord nodded. "Sure." He looked out across the water toward the causeway. His gaze lingered on the Thunderbird Inn. "Sure," he said again and disappeared into the house.

Junior watched from the doorway as Lord disappeared through the archway on the opposite side of the house from the one Bama had taken. While questioning Lord, he had heard the faint sound of a garage door opening. Bama was, he assumed, on her way to her appointment.

He picked up the binoculars Lord had left on the deck railing. Slowly he panned along the view before him.

The First National Bank building rose from the lingering mist of the Mobile skyline in the far distance. Patches of the roadbed of the Causeway were visible. The top of the bridge over the Apalachee River faded in and out of view through the drifting fog as did the nearer Blakely River bridge.

He saw a patrolman walk out of the restaurant door at the Thunderbird Inn and light up a cigarette. The two patrolmen he had seen earlier doing a grid search had worked their way east of the motel almost to the marine repair shop. Lord and Bama, Junior realized, had a bird's eye view of the happenings at the motel.

Lord returned with a Crown Royal bag that contained the pistol. Junior removed it by carefully gripping the end of the barrel. He gave it a sniff.

The gun was clean, no evidence that it had been fired recently.

"I'm going to need to take this in."

"Aww, come on!"

"You'll get it back." Junior slipped it back into the sack and placed it into his pocket. "This the only gun you got?"

"I have a one-ten and a twelve gauge. I suppose you want them, too."

"No, I don't think that'll be necessary. Unless you still have the urge to scare the piss out of the little shits?"

Lord shook his head.

"And you say you didn't hear anything last night?"

"No. But we had a couple of bottles of wine with dinner."

Junior gave a small grunt. "You know Ruby Stanton?"

"Well, well. Someone finally got shot over Ruby."

"No. Someone finally shot Ruby."

Five

RUBY'S MOTHER WAS a redhead like her daughter, that shade of red that wasn't carroty but held a hint of gold in its depths. She was naturally pale but, Hugo suspected, the news of Ruby's death had intensified the lack of color. To Hugo, it felt as if the pin pricks of his questions would shatter her.

"Mrs. Stanton, I know this is very difficult, but I have to ask."

Her eyes had a glazed look when she turned toward him. "Where's Buzz?"

"I'm Hugo August. The Chief thought it might be a good idea to have an objective party in the early stages of the investigation."

Frown lines appeared on her forehead. "Investigation?"

Hugo sat across from her at the kitchen table. He took her hand in his. "Can I get you anything?"

A cold cup of tea sat in front of her. She glanced at it then quickly away as she shook her head.

Hugo gave her hand a gentle squeeze.

She looked up at him, fear in her expression. Fear at

the questions she knew he would ask, he wondered? Or something else.

"I'm so very sorry," he said.

She took a breath and nodded.

"When did you last see Ruby?"

"Last night. About seven."

"Where?"

"Here." She glanced around the room as if she didn't recognize it. "The kitchen." She gave Hugo's hand a squeeze. "She was hungry."

"Did she eat?"

Mrs. Stanton nodded. "There was cold lasagna." A fleeting quiver of her lips might have been an attempt at a smile. "She liked it cold."

"What did she do after that?"

"Went back to her apartment."

"Where's her apartment?"

"Over the garage."

"Did you see her go out last night?"

She shook her head. "No. But I heard the car. Her little Mustang."

"What time was this?"

"It was still light out. Maybe eight?" Her face took on a stricken look. "I should have looked at the clock." Her mouth drew down at the corners and gaped open on a silent cry of despair.

The other woman in the room, who Hugo suspected was Nora, Chief Stanton's wife, moved quickly to Elizabeth's side. She wrapped her in her arms and made shushing noises.

Elizabeth buried her face against the other woman's apron. "If I had known!" her wail of anguish muffled.

"There, there, Beth. There, there."

Hugo rose from the table. There was nothing to be gained by further questioning.

"I'd like to see her apartment."

The woman continued to run her hand over Elizabeth Stanton's hair. She jerked her head toward the back door. "Go on, then."

STAIRS RAN UP the far side of the Stanton's garage. You couldn't see them from the back porch of the main house which guaranteed Ruby a certain degree of privacy in her comings and goings.

From a tiny landing at the top of the stairs, Hugo had a view of the neighbor's back yard and kitchen window. A woman stood at the sink of the house, a glass in her hand. She was watching Hugo.

So much for privacy, he thought.

The door to the apartment was unlocked. Hugo could see the signs of a careful and neat search. That would be Stanton, he decided, rather than one of his men.

The space was small. A room with a single bed, vanity table, and an armchair invitingly overstuffed and covered in print material of fading flowers in multiple hues.

It was a woman's room. The two windows were draped with a lacy fabric that was tied back to one side. The standing lamp beside the armchair was fringed at the bottom of the shade. An array of feminine potions cluttered the mirrored vanity table.

It took only a few minutes to repeat the search of the apartment. He noted the absence of a phone book or diary. There was a calendar on the back of the bathroom door. It featured a pin-up from the forties.

Ruby had noted appointments going back to January and a couple in the upcoming three weeks. Hugo took the calendar. He found Ruby's diaphragm in the drawer of her bedside table. Interesting, considering where her body was found and the implications of that location. The fact that Stanton had resisted the urge to remove it from prying eyes surprised Hugo.

On the bottom shelf of the bedside table was a stack of books. The top one was *Br'er Rabbit and The Tar Baby*. He looked through the stack. All of them were children's books.

He lifted the receiver of the phone and checked for a dial tone then he made note of the number. They would need to subpoena her call record.

When he closed the door of the apartment as he was leaving, he saw the neighbor at the kitchen window. She looked away as he stared down at her.

⁂

THE NEIGHBOR AND her little mutt of a dog eyed Hugo suspiciously as he dug his shield out of his pocket. She examined it thoroughly before stepping back so he could enter her house.

"Mobile Police." She looked him up and down. "What're you doing in Spanish Fort?"

"I expect you know already, Mrs...?"

"Gorton. Adele Gorton." She sighed. "It's about Ruby, then."

"Did you see her leave home last night?"

"Maybe."

"You have a clear view of her apartment." Hugo said with a hint of a smile. "I don't imagine much gets past you."

They had moved into the living room just to the right of the entry.

"I'm not nosey, if that's what you're implying."

She motioned for Hugo to take a seat on an old-fashioned, high-backed sofa covered in needle point. It was as uncomfortable as it looked.

"Have you been neighbors with the Stantons for a long time?"

"Over twenty years. They moved in back in 1948. Beth was pregnant with Ruby."

"Then you know them well."

"Ruby and Nelson played together as kids."

"Your son?"

Adele nodded.

"You know what happened last night?"

She nodded and looked away. "Bad business, that. And Henry dead not two years."

"Who's Henry?"

"Elizabeth's husband. Henry Stanton."

"That would be Chief Stanton's brother?"

"First cousin."

"Tell me what you saw last night."

"Why are the Mobile Police investigating this?"

"Stanton can't be involved because of the family ties. He and Goode are longstanding friends."

"I'm surprised Buzz would let anyone other than himself handle it."

"It's protocol."

"He's never been one to be bothered by such."

"Yet here I am."

Adele studied him. "She came home in the afternoon. About three. Which was unusual, even for her."

"Home from where?"

"Mobile. Work."

"Where does she work?"

"You don't know?"

Hugo shook his head.

"That lawyer. Talbot. Davis Talbot. Has an office in downtown Mobile in the old LeClede Hotel building."

"She doesn't normally come home early?"

"Sometimes she doesn't come home at all."

"How long has she lived over the family garage?"

"Just over two years, I guess. Since the summer after her year at Alabama."

"Why only one year?"

"The usual. Too much partying, too little studying."

"She's worked for the lawyer since then?"

Adele shook her head. "Took that first summer off as the kids say. Went to work for Buzz for a while after that but it didn't last."

"Why?"

"Too much partying, not enough working, I would guess. But there was talk about one of his men."

"What kind of talk?"

"Have you seen Ruby?"

"Yes."

"Well, there you are."

"Which officer?"

"Don't know. They kept it hush-hush."

"But?"

"People gossip."

A wail, long and drawn out, came from the rear of the house. It was a cry of utter despair.

Adele rose wearily from her chair. "That's Nelson. The news about Ruby has upset him. I need to go to him."

Hugo stood. "Of course." He glanced down the hallway that centered the house as he made for the front door. Three doors opened off the hall. All of them were closed. The sound seemed to come from the last room on the left near the rear of the house.

Nelson's wailing turned to low moans as Hugo stepped onto the front porch and the door closed behind him.

⁂

JUNIOR DECIDED IT might be a good idea to check the Brennan's where the cook was house sitting. He started around the back down by the dock.

The apartment over the boathouse was barely that. The peaked roof left enough space for a room about eight by twelve. It was accessed by a rail ladder. Inside was a blow-up mattress, a folding table with a couple of chairs, and a low chest of drawers overflowing with what Junior assumed was the cook's clothing. A Coleman lantern appeared to be the only source of light although the dock below was marked at intervals with lights mounted on the tops of pilings and there was another one over the boat lift.

On the pier, a metal pipe had been run to a fish cleaning station with a splinter off to a pole that created an outdoor shower. A bamboo mat provided scant privacy for anyone using it.

Junior retraced his steps along the pier to a long staircase leading up the face of the bluff to a stone paved patio and the house. When he tried the French door, he discovered that it wasn't locked. He did a walk through and found the room the cook was using. The only thing of interest was a dime bag of weed. He didn't think the Brennan's would be best pleased with the state of the kitchen, but that wasn't any concern of his.

What did concern him was a fine glass fronted cabinet that housed a collection of guns. He tried to open it but realized it was locked. On a shelf of handguns, an empty space caught his eye. Had a pistol been there? If so, where was it now?

The casualness with which the cook squatted in the house amazed Junior. He had no doubt that Mr. Brennan was unaware of the fact his home was being used with such reckless disregard for the white sofa in the great room. A dirty plate and fork sat on the pristine middle cushion.

Two things were certain. Harry Chapman had a brass

pair, and the residents on this strip of Confederate Drive had a clear view of the Thunderbird Inn.

Junior checked his watch. It was getting to be mid-morning and he hadn't had anything except coffee all day. His pre-dawn dash to get to the scene also meant his grandmother hadn't had time to pack him a lunch. Maybe the cook could rustle up a late breakfast. If he was still at the motel.

As if in answer to Junior's thoughts, a motorcycle came roaring up the driveway as he was getting into the police sedan.

So much for breakfast, Junior decided, as he watched Chapman kick down the stand and kill the motor.

Chapman stared at Junior as he dug a pack of cigarettes from his tee shirt pocket. "You looking for me?" he asked in a sullen voice.

"Not particularly," Junior replied. "Checking out the view from the houses along the bluff." He studied the Harley. "Nice bike."

"Belongs to a friend."

"Yeah?"

"Yeah."

Junior didn't push it. "You ever see a bunch of kids taking Lord's boat out on the bay?"

Chapman grinned. "The Crane kids?" He shrugged. "Can't say that I have."

"Not last night?"

"Not any night."

"You know Lord's boat?"

"Sure. See him and his wife out on it most days. Late afternoon usually."

"How about the other neighbors?"

"What about them?"

"They out on the water much?"

"Can't say I paid much attention."

"But you notice Lord."

"I notice Bama."

Junior conceded that Bama was worth noticing.

"Is there much activity on this stretch of water?"

"Some. They follow the Blakeley into the delta."

"Fishing? Skiing?"

"Not really suited for skiing. Too much trash and logs beneath the surface to run at any speed except in the heart of the five rivers. Plus, there's the gators and sand bars."

"So, just pleasure boating, fishing?"

"That would be my guess."

"Are you a fisherman?"

Chapman shook his head.

"When do you expect the Brennans to return from the mountains?"

"Football season."

<h1 style="text-align:center">Six</h1>

HUGO DROVE DOWN the hill on Highway 98 from Spanish Fort, the view of Mobile Bay opening before him softened by lingering mist over the water. The Thunderbird Inn parking lot was empty except for Dickie's car and a Spanish Fort police cruiser. He saw Dickie in his office looking morose.

"All the guests gone?" he asked the patrolman sitting on a folding chair in the foyer near the front door.

"The couple were the last to go. Kind of creepy the way they kept hanging around."

"It's just you and the manager?"

He nodded. "Your search team packed it in. Don't know if they'll be back after lunch or not. They didn't look too happy. A guy showed up about twenty minutes ago, banging on the door. I ignored him."

"You didn't get a name?"

"I know his name. Pete Donahue with the Press Register."

"Christ."

Hugo crossed the foyer to the office. Dickie looked up from a racing form from the dog track.

"What happens now?"

"You got any reservations on the books for the next few days?"

Dickie made a show of looking through the logbook and shook his head.

"That works then. The motel is a crime scene 'til further notice. I'll take your keys. We'll set up in the dining room."

"You can't do that! What about my business? I'll go broke if we have to shut down for more than a couple of days."

"You're not making any money on accommodations if the room rate and occupancy records are accurate." Hugo indicated the registration book with a lift of his chin. "Unless there's something else you're selling that I should be checking into."

Dickie stood and blustered around the small space. "It's the dinner crowd that generates most of our cash flow. Guys on the road like to stop in for a few beers."

"And?"

"And nothing!" He hitched his plaid slacks. "Just drinks and telling fishing tales. Guys that don't want to hurry home is all."

"Guys like Ruby's friend?"

Dickie cut his eyes away from Hugo's steady gaze. "Don't know who you're talking about."

"Davis Talbot."

Dickie tapped his finger on the edge of the desk. "Don't think I know him."

"Sure you do. Lawyer. Office in the LeClede building."

"Oh." Dickie feigned enlightenment. "I thought you were looking at someone on this side of the bay."

"Is he one of your guys who likes to drink beer and tell fishing tales?"

Dickie shrugged. "You'd have to ask Dixie."

"How long has Dixie worked for you?"

"Three, four years now, I guess."

"So she knows the comings and goings around here pretty well."

"Sure."

"Knows the regulars."

Dickie decided to study his fingernails a long moment. "Don't know what you mean by regulars. Other than the breakfast crowd."

"She always works the night shift?"

"Mostly. Once a week, or on a slow night, Skip fills in."

"Skip have a last name?"

"Harris."

"Related?"

"Nephew."

"Does Skip know Ruby?"

"How would I know?"

"Where's Skip now?"

"At the bay house I'd imagine."

"Down the bay or over the bay?"

"Over the bay."

"Got a number?"

Dickie rattled off a number with a 978 prefix.

Hugo made note of it then returned his notebook to his pocket. "I'll have the keys. You can head out."

Dickie made a show of producing his key ring from his pocket and extracting a key. He slammed it onto the desk. "I'll be talking to Buzz about this."

"You do that." Hugo picked up the key and bounced it in his hand. "But If I were you, I'd give it a day or two. Your dentist would probably give you the same advice."

Dickie glared at Hugo and pushed past him on his way out the door.

HUGO TOOK HIS time going room to room throughout the motel once again. There was something off about the whole set-up that kept nagging at the back of his mind. He saved room number two until last. Aside from the murder scene, it was the anomaly.

He opened the curtains and tilted the blinds. From the window, he could see two houses on the high bluff overlooking the bay. He recognized them as number one and two of those visible from this section of the causeway.

He saw someone standing on the patio of the second of the houses, looking out over the water. Hugo squinted. The cook, judging from the dark hair, stance, and the white tee shirt. After a few seconds, he turned his gaze directly at Hugo. Or so it seemed. What had drawn his eye? The motel or this window specifically? From this distance it was impossible to tell but Hugo had that sense of being watched even though he knew he couldn't be seen from that distance.

He turned his attention to the room. The musty odor

of damp and decay that lingered faintly in the other rooms of the motel was absent. Why was that, he wondered?

Nothing about the Thunderbird Inn gave the impression of a prosperous establishment. And yet it managed to keep the doors open.

He glanced at his watch. The lawyer would surely be at his office about now. Unless he had a court case that was ongoing this morning. Either way, Hugo needed to question him before the news about Ruby reached him. If it hadn't already. Next on the list would be the wife. He was certain there was a wife.

It would be best to tackle them separately and before they had the opportunity to talk to each other. Hugo wondered where Junior was.

As if he had conjured him up, the dark blue city issue sedan Junior drove pulled onto the oyster shell parking bay.

Hugo turned to the Spanish Fort patrolman. "I imagine there's a phone jack in the dining room. See if you can locate it. Check the bar area. And I saw a chalk board for menu specials. We'll need that. A Mobile police officer should be here shortly to set up an incident room."

The patrolman frowned. "I need to ask the Chief."

"Stanton can't be involved. That's why he called MPD. We need a neutral command post."

"I don't know."

"Well, I do. The whole Spanish Fort force will be under scrutiny because of the situation with Ruby."

Hugo saw that he had surprised the patrolman with this inside knowledge. "How long have you been with the department?"

"Just over a year."

"Before that?"

"Vietnam."

"You from the area?"

He nodded.

"Then you knew Ruby?"

"From school."

"Knew her well, did you?"

"Just school and stuff."

"You ever date?"

"Geez! That was our sophomore year. I took her to the spring dance. Her daddy drove us!"

"Since then?"

"Since then! Nothing. Ruby dated lots of guys."

"How about after you joined the force?"

"She left. Quit. I hadn't been on the job two months."

"Why did she quit?"

"I thought you knew."

"I'd like to hear your version."

"Boo and Ruby got into it. He had a thing for her. Always has."

"Boudreau Vansant. The sergeant with the Chief last night?"

The patrolman nodded.

"How'd you know he was with the Chief last night?"

"Everyone knows. He's still green to the gills this morning."

"So, this thing he had for Ruby, care to elaborate?"

"They got into a fight. At the station."

"They were dating?"

"No. I don't think they ever dated. Boo was just crazy for her. He couldn't stand being around her all the time and her not even giving him the time of day." He shook his head. "It was sad really, the way she treated him."

"How did she treat him?"

"Ignored him. Looked right through him. The worst part was she flirted with everyone else. And I mean everyone."

"Why was she so cruel, do you think?"

He shook his head and shrugged. He wouldn't look at Hugo.

"You must have some idea."

"She's the Chief's niece."

"That's why I'm the one asking the questions."

"You don't understand." He gave Hugo a pleading look. "The Chief and Ruby, you just don't go there, man. He thought she could do no wrong. Even when she got caught out, she could convince him black was white."

"So why Boo?"

"Because she could."

"Could what?" Junior asked as he walked through the door.

The patrolman looked away. Hugo studied him and realized how very young he was. He turned to Junior. "Dickie pretty much confirmed that Mr. Smith is one Davis Talbot."

"Lawyer," Junior replied.

"You know him?"

"Know of him. Office across from the courthouse. Lives in Springhill."

"You take the wife. I'll pay a visit to our boy scout."

"There's a wife?"

"I'm betting there is. Otherwise, they wouldn't be meeting in this fleabag."

JUNIOR PULLED INTO a parking space in front of the old stucco structure on Royal Street that housed the Mobile Police Department and the city jail. The detective bullpen was at the top of the stairs on the second floor.

He lifted the massive 1968 edition of the City Directory onto his desk and flipped through the heavy volume. Davis and Melissa Talbot lived on Yester Place. That was about as near the heart of Springhill as you could get.

No kids listed.

Melissa was a housewife.

Junior took down the address and phone number and made his way down the stairs to his police issue sedan.

At Broad Street he turned onto Old Shell Road. The drive through Midtown to Springhill took less than fifteen minutes. It was important that he question her while Hugo had her husband occupied.

A maid in a white uniform answered the door.

"Yes?"

"Mrs. Talbot home?"

She hesitated. "Who you?"

Junior took out his shield. The maid's eyes widened slightly.

"Wait here," she said.

Melissa Talbot was tall. The short tennis skirt she wore accentuated her long legs. She was still wearing a sun visor.

"Yes?"

Junior showed his shield and introduced himself.

"What do you want?"

"I'd like to ask you some questions."

"About what?"

"May I come in?"

The diagonal line on her forehead deepened as her lips thinned briefly in annoyance. She turned from the doorway, leaving Junior to follow after her.

The room was sunny with tall windows and formal Queen Anne furniture. She gestured with a sweep of her hand for him to take a seat before sitting on the sofa across from him.

"Are you Melissa Talbot?"

"Yes."

"Married to Davis Talbot?"

The line on her forehead deepened again.

"Yes."

"Where were you last night?"

"What?"

"Can you tell me your activities last night? Where you were, who you were with?"

"I'm not telling you anything until you tell me what this is about."

"There's been an accident. A death, actually."

"Davis? He was here at breakfast."

An interesting response, Junior thought. "What time was that?"

"Eight-thirty. I had a match at the Club at nine. We

left at the same time. About ten of." She frowned. "It isn't Davis, is it? Dead, I mean."

"No."

"Then what do you want with me?"

"If we could go over the past twenty-four hours, Mrs. Talbot."

"Lissa. Everyone calls me Lissa." She watched Junior take his notebook out. "Gardening. George came early to beat the worst part of the heat. We're putting in a new patio, so he had to dig up the azaleas along the south wall of the house. After that, I went to a committee meeting at the church."

"What church is that?"

"Dauphin Street Methodist. We discussed funding issues and the new rose garden though I don't imagine that's relevant to whatever you're here about."

"After that?"

"I stopped in at the A&P for a few things, came home, and had a late lunch. George finished the yard work about two, I think. I was home until a little after four. Went to the Club for cocktails, then dinner."

"Were you alone?"

"No. I had drinks with friends. Davis joined me about seven."

"What time did you and your husband get home?"

"I came home about eight-thirty, quarter to nine. Davis stayed to play poker."

"When did he get home?"

"I don't know."

"You didn't wake when he came in?"

"No."

"But he was here when you got up this morning?"

"Yes."

"Do you know Ruby Stanton?"

Melissa Talbot leaned forward and opened the lid of a lacquered box on the coffee table. She took her time selecting a cigarette. "So, this is about Ruby."

"Do you know her?"

"I know who she is. She's my husband's secretary. And his current mistress." She took the lighter out of the box, flicked it to life, and lit her cigarette. "What happened?"

"She was shot."

"Who shot her?"

"That's what I'm trying to determine."

She leaned back into the cushions of the sofa and studied Junior through the drift of cigarette smoke.

"You think it was Davis. Or me."

"Why do you say that?"

"Scorned wife. Jealous lover."

"Did you kill her?"

"Why would I?"

"As you say, scorned wife."

Melissa Talbot laughed. Not a hesitant, nervous laugh but a heartfelt laugh of true amusement.

"Do you think I care what Davis does? Ruby is just the latest in a long line of women."

"And that doesn't bother you?"

"Not really. I understand him. He entertains himself with a new mistress every couple of years. As long as he's discreet, I turn a blind eye."

"Why do you put up with it?"

She smiled at Junior. "Because I don't care. I like my life. The house, the garden, the Club. He strays then gets bored and things return to normal."

"You're not jealous?"

"No."

"You're not afraid he'll want a divorce?"

"Not really."

"Why?"

"This house, this lifestyle. He can't afford to divorce me. But he doesn't really want to no matter what he tells them."

"Do you love your husband?"

"I love being married to him."

Seven

THERE WAS NO one at the front desk when Hugo entered Davis Talbot's outer office.

He was about to knock on a heavy door which bore the attorney's name in brass letters when a young woman came hurrying from an alcove.

"Don't!" she said as she rushed toward him. "You can't go in there."

"Is Davis Talbot in there?"

"Yes, but—"

Hugo opened the door and saw the lawyer sitting with his feet on the desk and staring out the window that overlooked Government Street.

Davis turned toward him as the young woman rushed in behind Hugo.

"I'm sorry, Mr. Talbot. I—"

Talbot lifted a hand in a gesture for silence. "Where's Ruby?"

"Still not here, Sir."

Talbot shooed her out the door with a wave. As it closed behind her, he said, "Well, well. If it isn't our world famous lawman. What can I do for you, Detective Hugo August?"

Hugo took the chair across from Talbot. "You can start by telling me where you were last night."

Talbot brought his feet to the floor and sat forward at his desk. He studied Hugo a moment. "What happened?"

"You first, if you don't mind."

"Dinner at the Club. Our card game afterwards ran rather late. Then home."

"How late?"

"One o'clock or so. Whiskey was involved so don't quote me on the time."

"Who won?"

"Cortland."

"Who else was in the game?"

"The usual suspects. Young, Heinrich, Waverly."

"Do you own a gun?"

Talbot was silent. He ran a hand down the length of his tie. "Yes. I own several."

"Hand guns?"

"Two. A Smith & Wesson, and my father's old Colt."

"Tell me about Ruby."

Talbot settled back in his chair. "She's late."

"She's your secretary?"

"Yes."

"And?"

Talbot rose from the chair and went to stand by the window. He watched the traffic below as he asked, "What happened?"

"She was shot."

He closed his eyes and turned his head so Hugo couldn't see his expression.

"Where?"

"In the heart."

Talbot swung around to face Hugo. "Where was she?"

"You don't know?"

"How would I?"

"You weren't supposed to meet her," Hugo paused a heartbeat, "in lucky number seven?"

Talbot visibly paled. He swallowed, returned to his chair and sat heavily, his head against the high back. "Who did it?"

"That's my question."

"Me? You think I would shoot Ruby?"

"Would you?"

"Never!"

"Then who?"

Talbot looked away. "I don't know."

"Your wife?"

"Lissa? No."

"Did she know?"

Talbot shook his head. "I don't think so."

"But it's possible."

He glanced at Hugo then away. He shook his head again. "Not Lissa. She's not the jealous type."

"You weren't planning to divorce?"

"No."

"Was your wife at home when you returned from the poker game?"

"Yes."

"Did she wake up when you came in?"

He hesitated. "I don't know."

"She either did or she didn't."

"I didn't actually see her. We sleep separately sometimes. When I've been out late."

"Then how do you know she was home?"

Talbot had no answer.

"How long have you been having an affair?"

"Since she came to work for me."

"When was that?"

"About nine months ago."

Nine months. The wife knew, Hugo thought. "You always meet at the Thunderbird?"

Davis shook his head. "We go to the Fountainhead sometimes. Stop at Mary Mahoney's for lunch. You know."

"I'm afraid I don't know."

Davis lifted his hand from where it rested on the arm of his chair and let it drop back, a helpless expression on his face. "We needed someplace we could be ourselves. Away from prying eyes."

"So, when you weren't meeting at the Thunderbird you ran over to Mississippi for a little alone time."

Davis turned his profile to Hugo.

"This happen often?"

"Not so much lately."

"Why's that?"

He didn't answer. Instead, he sat forward in his chair and pulled a file folder from the corner of his desk. "I have a client due any minute and I need to review the file." He flipped the dust jacket open and picked up a typewritten sheet of paper. It trembled ever so slightly. "If you have any more questions, call and make an appointment with Betty."

Hugo accepted his dismissal. For now. Until he knew what the wife had to say, he would give the lawyer a little rope.

The moment the door closed behind him Betty popped out of her little cubby. She caught Hugo's sleeve.

"He had nothing to do with it."

Hugo looked down into her brown eyes slightly magnified by glasses. "To do with what?"

"Whatever happened to Ruby."

"And what do you think happened to Ruby?"

"She's dead."

"Have you been listening at keyholes, Betty?"

"No!" She stepped back from Hugo. "Lonnie called. Said she was dead."

"Who's Lonnie?"

She glanced away. "A friend."

"How does Lonnie know she's dead?"

Betty shrugged. "Don't know."

"What exactly did Lonnie say?"

"That Ruby's dead."

"Did Lonnie say how she died?"

"No."

"So why the need to tell me Talbot had nothing to do with it?"

His question momentarily flustered Betty. She shook her head and threw out her hands in frustration. "Because he didn't!"

"You know they were having an affair, don't you?" He realized Betty was older than he had initially thought. The fine lines around her eyes, a tiny sagging along the jawline.

She looked away from Hugo's scrutiny. "It wasn't serious. Just a flirtation."

"Nine months? Seems pretty serious to me."

The color rose from Betty's throat until her face was a blotchy red. She started sorting a stack of files on the secretary's desk.

"She's not the first. He gets bored and these things happen. He was over her."

"How do you know?"

She pushed her glasses more firmly into place with her forefinger. "I've seen them come and go. I know the signs."

"How long have you worked for Talbot?"

"Almost seven years. Since he first went into practice on his own."

"And what do you do?"

Her hands stilled from the busy work with the files and she looked up at Hugo. "Everything. The books, the scheduling, the filing."

"So what did Ruby do?"

"Not much."

⁂

HUGO STEPPED OUT of the relative cool of the LeClede building into the enveloping heat and humidity of a Mobile summer day. A quick glance at his watch told him that it wasn't quite eleven o'clock. He glanced around and let his gaze come to rest on the courthouse across the street. He jaywalked to the other side. In the office of the Probate Court he asked to speak with Judy Fohl.

Judy swept through the inner door behind the counter. At the sight of Hugo, she smiled a one-sided smile. "Hello, handsome. Long time, no see."

"It hasn't been that long."

She arched an eyebrow black as a crow's wing.

Hugo gave a sheepish grin. "You quit coming to the Royal Flush."

"And you've been busy. Is that it?"

"I didn't think you'd miss me."

She gave him that smile again, the deep red of her lipstick striking against her alabaster skin and raven hair. "What you need, Honey?"

"Lunch?"

"It's a little early and I'm trying to watch my figure." She studied him a moment. "But I wouldn't object to a drink."

"Doobie's?"

"Ten minutes," she replied."

Doobie's was three short blocks from the courthouse. Hugo walked. There was no one else in the place at this late morning hour. He glanced at his watch again. The lunch crowd would start soon.

He was halfway through his first beer of the day when Judy arrived. He watched her cross the room in her pencil slim skirt and very high heels. She wasn't beautiful. He supposed she was what you would call striking. Men always looked when she entered a room. But she was so much more than that in her own way. There was a confidence about her that didn't come from her appearance, a calmness, and perhaps a sense of authority. A rarity among women, he realized.

Since the age of eighteen Judy had worked in the office of the clerk of the Probate Court. Now in her mid-thirties, she ran the place. At her fingertips was the who, when, and how of everything that happened in Mobile County. She made it a point to know and understand it all. She also made it a point to lend an ear to all the facts, gossip, and innuendo that wasn't couched in the legalese of the dry pages of the ledger books. Hugo felt fortunate that she had, for some reason, decided to befriend him when he first became a detective with the police department. But it wasn't just her knowledge he valued. It was her friendship.

She slid into the booth across from Hugo and took out a pack of Marlboros.

He watched the small blue square of the tax stamp flutter to the tabletop as she opened the pack. It had been a long three years since his last smoke. At moments like this he thought he missed them. Maybe he did.

Judy studied him as she lit a cigarette and blew smoke toward the ceiling.

"You look like crap."

"Thanks. You're the second person to notice."

"An all-nighter?"

"Something like that."

"You want to tell me about it?"

"Ruby Stanton. Know her?"

"First the Barbie dolls and now the Rita Hayworth. No wonder you look like something the cat dragged up."

"She's dead."

Judy's eyebrows arched briefly. She watched smoke

drift across the table toward him. "I take it she didn't die of natural causes."

He shook his head and took a long drink of beer.

"Did you do it?"

He gave her a half smile and shook his head again.

"I'd go with the jilted lover."

"How do you know there's a jilted lover?"

"There's always a jilted lover. And I know Ruby."

"Do you know her well?"

"No. She works for Davis Talbot."

"Tell me about him."

She shrugged. "Worked for Trehearn and Young when he first got his degree. Set up on his own a few years back."

"Why?"

"Don't know but rumor has it that the senior partner developed an intense dislike for him."

"What prompted this change of attitude?"

"The usual reasons, I would imagine."

"I don't suppose the senior partner had an attractive wife?"

"Daughter."

Hugo gave this some thought. "When did he marry his wife?"

"Lissa? Can't remember exactly but I think it was while he was still in law school."

"Is she local?"

Judy nodded and took a sip of the martini the waitress placed before her. "She went to high school at Shaw then to the University."

"Did they know each other before college?"

"Couldn't say. But if I had to guess, I'd say she majored in the time-honored tradition."

"Oh? What's that?"

"Husband one-oh-one."

"Ah. Looks like she did all right."

"She did better than all right."

"How's that?"

"Let's just say you won't find her photo among the Camellia Ball debutants."

"How do you know?"

"Shaw?"

Hugo turned his beer glass around and around in the same wet ring. "Right," he finally said.

"You think it was him?"

"Early days. You think he's capable of killing someone?"

Judy tilted her head slightly. "You know what they say. Everyone's capable of murder given the right circumstances."

"Is that a yes?"

"Talbot considers himself a ladies' man. He's had a string of affairs over the years."

"Are his affairs well known?"

"Around the courthouse, yes. Whenever he gets a new secretary, the handicapping begins."

"Yeah? What's the bet?"

"How long she'll last."

"Does he end the affair before or after they quit?"

"Or get fired."

"For what?"

"Poor job performance would be my guess."

"Ouch." Hugo considered this. "So he and Ruby were still involved."

"Why do you think that?"

"The dog's body. Said Ruby didn't show up for work this morning."

"Could be covering for him."

Hugo grunted and took another long pull on his beer. "You think that's the way the wind blows?"

"Don't you?"

He sighed.

Eight

THE LAWYER WAS a serial adulterer. How many jilted women were in his past? Would any of them feel strongly enough to take it out on Ruby?

The office help certainly was smitten. Was she to be believed? Had Talbot really broken it off? Ruby had died at their rendezvous spot. What did that mean? Was she meeting someone new? Rubbing salt in the wound by choosing their place for a dalliance?

Or, had Talbot decided she was the one? The one that would end his marriage to the social climbing wife? The one worth the price of social outrage, ostracism, lost clients?

Hugo had a long list of questions and potential suspects but very few answers. Best to start with the known possibilities. The ex-fiancé and the lover. According to Dubya, the bartender had been in her room just before she was shot. And a Spanish Fort policeman was smitten with her. He needed to see what Junior thought about the wife. He could hear him now. *It's always the wife.* But in this case, Hugo wasn't so sure.

HUGO STEPPED OUT of the dim, smoky atmosphere of Doobie's into the bright noon light of St. Emanuel Street and squinted up at the sky. When he lowered his gaze, he saw Bebe Prescott walking toward him as she dug around in her purse.

She wore a bright orange sleeveless dress that fell from her shoulders in an A-line. It was covered in bold flowers of yellow, white, and green. They looked like a child's painting and she looked like a dream.

As she drew a pack of cigarettes from her purse, she looked up and saw him. She stopped in her tracks.

"Hugo."

The sun glowed in her pale blonde hair.

Hugo couldn't speak.

"What are you doing here?"

He took a couple of steps and closed the gap between them.

"I work here."

Bebe glanced away with a humorless little laugh. When she turned back to face him, her eyes were rimmed with the threat of tears which she quickly blinked away. She dispelled any illusion of tenderness when she replied, "At Doobies? Maybe I should get a city job."

Hugo touched the knot of his tie. "It's a life." He glanced at the cigarette pack in her hand. "Can I light that for you?"

Bebe looked at the pack then shoved them back into her purse. "I changed my mind."

"How've you been?"

"Good." Her gaze traveled over his features. "Okay."

He nodded. What else was there to say.

"Hugo—" Bebe raised her hand as if she would adjust his tie or place her palm against his chest as she used to do oh so long ago to feel the beat of his heart. But she did neither of those things. Instead, she took a step back. "Take care of yourself, okay?"

"Sure. You too."

Then she sidestepped him and continued down the sidewalk. At Conti, she took a left.

Hugo continued to stare down the sidewalk long after she disappeared from sight.

⁂

HUGO WAS COLLECTING legal pads, file folders, and an assortment of office supplies from paper clips to a staple gun into a box when Junior topped the stairs at the Mobile police station.

"What's the plan?" Junior asked.

"We're going to set up at the motel. At least for now. That'll hopefully keep Stanton at arm's length."

"Good luck with that."

"We have to make the effort and it's neutral ground between Mobile and Spanish Fort. Our killer could be from either side of the bay. Besides, he probably has his stooge over there already."

"So, what about our other cases?"

"That's the Chief's call. The only thing I've got going is

the floater they found in Shit Creek. Waiting for the coroner's report." Hugo lifted the box and balanced it against his hip. "How about you?"

Junior shook his head. "Nickel and dime stuff. Nothing patrol can't handle."

"Speaking of which, the search team's been pulled from the motel. They didn't find anything. As of now we've been allotted one patrolman to man the phone and keep us organized."

"I prefer to keep my own notes."

Hugo gave a grunt of agreement. "He's the Chief's eyes and ears so let's hope he's hard of hearing." He patted his coat pockets checking that he had his notebook. "Tell me about the wife."

"She didn't seem too concerned when I told her we were investigating a death. Even when she thought it might be the husband."

"Alibi?"

"Home alone. She wasn't concerned that he might be about to divorce her. Or so she said. Knew he had a wandering eye. She acted like it was a bad habit rather than a real concern."

"Think she could have done it?"

"She could have. I get the impression she wouldn't skip a beat if the bullet had been in the husband's chest."

"Maybe that was the plan. And he skipped the rendezvous."

Junior gave a small shrug. "I could see him as the target. The question is, who's the shooter and why would they shoot Ruby?"

"It's been suggested that we look at the jilted lover."

"Oh, yeah? By whom?"

"Judy Fohl."

"It's as good a guess as any. She have a name?"

"Other than the lawyer?" Hugo shook his head. "But it did start me thinking."

"About?"

"Ruby was at the motel in Lucky Number Seven. Her usual room. Davis was at the Club playing poker. Which one is the jilted lover? Or is it the Smokie? He fits right into the role."

"It's been a year since she broke off the engagement. Why would the Smokie wait this long to exact his revenge, or whatever this is? As for Ruby and the lawyer, you think she was the one who ended it?"

"I don't even know if it was over. Maybe she was bored, ticked off about something, or got off on jerking his chain."

"Or vice-versa."

"Either way, we need to find out who else was in the running. Something happened between her and one of Stanton's men. See if you can get to the bottom of that. And there's a nosy neighbor. Clear view of anyone who comes and goes at Ruby's apartment. I don't imagine the mother missed much either. She's in a bad way right now but at some point, we're going to have to push her."

Hugo punched Junior in the upper arm. "I'll take the mother and the neighbor. Go butter up the dispatcher. She looked like she was about to pop when I was there earlier. Find out what's in her malicious little heart."

"Malicious?"

"Anyone that eager to gossip has something nasty to say. Find out what."

It was the nature of the job. Junior knew that murder was the ultimate expression of malice. He also knew there were those with repressed anger, hatred, envy. Sometimes all they needed was an excuse to release their pent-up rage.

"What about the ex-fiancé?"

"I'm meeting him at the Thunderbird," Hugo checked his watch, "in about ten minutes."

"Okay. I'm going to run home and pick up a fresh shirt."

"Don't tell your grandmother."

Junior turned slightly, his profile to Hugo. "I'm not a rookie."

"Not saying you are. But she'll ask. You know she will."

She would ask. Junior knew that. He shouldn't resent the warning, but he did. She was a worrier. About him, especially. And about Hugo, too, since the year Father Gregory showed up at their door one December night with Hugo, bloody knuckled and wild with rage, in tow. He couldn't stay at the orphanage anymore. There had been an incident, Father had said. The situation was untenable, he had said. Junior had looked the word up in the big dictionary in the library at St. Andrews's Catholic School the next day.

Even though Hugo was his best friend, to this day, he still didn't know what he had done to cause the Archbishop to cast him out of St. Thomas More's Home for Boys.

Junior sighed. "I'll skip the fresh shirt." He dug into his pants pocket and produced a pack of chewing gum. "You better have this."

Hugo looked at the Wrigley's spearmint gum in Junior's outstretched hand, then took it. "Touché," he said.

⁂

SAM HOLLINGSWORTH KEPT Hugo waiting for nearly twenty minutes. An intentional snub, Hugo realized, as he watched the sandy headed patrolman with the buzz cut saunter into the dining room of The Thunderbird Inn, his sunglasses hooked into the neckline of a black tee shirt that sported the image of Jack Dempsey suited up for a fight.

"I hear you're looking for me," he said, as he stood over the dining table Hugo was using as a desk.

Hugo motioned toward the chair on the opposite side of the table.

Instead of sitting, Hollingsworth asked, "Who the hell are you, anyway?"

Hugo let the silence draw out for a couple of seconds. "You know who I am and why I'm here." He closed the file in front of him. "But, hey, we can do this all afternoon if you want."

Hollingsworth snatched the chair out and sat. "I gave Stanton my statement already. This is just a waste of your time."

He didn't add *and mine,* but Hugo had no doubt that was what he wanted to say.

"You and Ruby were engaged."

"That's old news."

"But not to me. So walk me through it beginning with when you first started dating."

Hollingsworth crossed his arms over his chest, reared back in his chair, and stared at the ceiling before lowering his gaze to glare at Hugo.

"We both know I'm the prime suspect. I'm the jilted fiancé, after all. So why don't you just ask me what you want to know."

Hugo sat forward, his forearms resting on the table. He gave a little bob of his head. "I hear Ruby was a friendly girl."

Hollingworth clenched his jaw then relaxed it. "That's supposed to light my fuse? Cause me to blurt out a confession?"

"It's supposed to confirm or deny what I've heard so far." He leaned back from the table and opened the file jacket. "So far, other than Stanton and Ruby's mama, no one has any kind words for her. You thought enough of her to propose, to take the break-up hard. So, tell me about the real Ruby."

Hollingsworth turned toward the window of the restaurant and stared out across the parking lot and roadway. He seemed to diminish as he sat there, as if something essential had escaped somehow.

He sat in silence.

Hugo waited.

Finally, he spoke.

"We met in Tuscaloosa. That was my area back then. The first thing to catch my eye was her hair." A faint smile of remembrance touched his lips then faded. "The sun made it glow like it was on fire. Like a low burning blaze."

He cleared his throat and looked at Hugo, once again in control of himself. "I stopped her for speeding in that

Mustang of hers in late September. She flirted her way out of a ticket. Told me she would be at the Beef & Bitters that night. That I should come by.

"We started dating that night. We would talk for hours. She had a bright mind, interested in everything, wanted to learn to fly a plane." Hollingsworth paused, a look of remembrance softening his features. "There was something fragile about her, a hint of uncertainty. I couldn't understand why. She had everything going for her. Beauty, brains, personality." He shook his head.

"She could be emotional at the drop of a hat and in many ways she was naïve. When she came back to campus after Christmas, she seemed different but gradually she was herself again. She didn't want to go home for spring break. Her mood was all over the place. I tried to convince her to stay in Tuscaloosa, but she said she had to go home, that there would be hell to pay if she didn't. After the break she hadn't been back at school but a few days when her dad died."

He cleared his throat and sat straighter in the chair. "She was hysterical when she got the news. Said it was her fault. Of course she went home. I went to the funeral. She was like a zombie. It hit her hard." He cleared his throat again. "She didn't come back to campus. Wouldn't take my calls. I thought she'd get over it. The worst of it, I mean. That she needed to grieve.

"I had it bad. In the beginning I'd call her, and she seemed to be better. We'd have long talks, but then it got harder and harder to catch her at home. She seemed to have lost interest in everything. I came down a couple of times and it was like it was when we were in Tuscaloosa together but different. She seemed guarded. Secretive. One night in early August she said she wasn't coming back to school. No explanation, just not coming back. I thought she didn't want to leave her mama, you know? That it was too soon after his death. And maybe it was. But I didn't want to let her go.

"It took about eight months. I finally managed a transfer down here. Everything was wonderful for a while. We got engaged pretty soon afterwards. There were periods of moodiness after that. I thought it had to do with being back in Spanish Fort. It's hard to explain. I wouldn't be able to connect with her for days at a time. She was always vague about why. She suddenly quit her job with the police department. Then one day she gave me my ring back and said she didn't want to marry me."

"Was there another guy?"

Hollingsworth shook his head and shrugged. "At first, I thought that had to be it but after a while I realized she just didn't want to marry me. Or have anything to do with me. It was as if she wiped me, our history, from her mind. As if we never happened."

"Did you know about Talbot?"

"Yeah. She went to work for him about four or five months after we split. Gossip travels fast in small towns."

"That didn't make you angry?"

"Of course, it made me angry. And it hurt for a while, but I had already accepted that we were over."

"That's not what Stanton says."

"I was pissed, okay? In the beginning. I couldn't

understand what had happened. Mainly, I couldn't understand how she could just look right through me with no sign of what we had been to each other. It was like I was a stranger." He frowned and looked up at Hugo. "But it was also like she was someone else. Not Ruby at all. Not my Ruby. So I let it go. I moved on."

"Where were you last night?"

"Working."

"Between the hours of ten and two."

Hollingsworth pulled a notebook from the pocket of his slacks and flipped through the pages. "At 10:12 I got a call about a traffic accident on 31 south of Atmore. I was just north of Bay Minette at the time. It took me almost twenty minutes to get there. A kid hit a deer. The windshield cut the kid up pretty bad. A couple of cars had stopped to help by the time I got there. I didn't think we could wait for the ambulance, so I loaded him up in my car with one of the locals. We got him to Atmore around 11:00. By the time I left the hospital, it was after midnight. I went home, showered, changed uniforms, and was back on patrol by 1:30."

"Where's home?"

"Daphne. Tanglewood Apartments."

"We're going to need your gun."

"Stanton already has it."

❧

PEGGY SUE WAS exactly as Hugo described. She couldn't hide the spite that simmered just beneath the surface.

Junior caught her in the parking lot as she was leaving

Spanish Fort police headquarters for lunch. She clearly wanted to vent but she didn't want to be seen doing it.

"I don't know anything," she said as she fished in her purse for her car keys. "I didn't know her well enough to be able to tell you anything helpful."

"Sometimes it's the thing you don't know you know that's useful."

"Look, I've only got thirty minutes for lunch. Everything's crazy around here."

"I hear ya. The chief's niece," he sighed sympathetically. "She was something else, I hear."

Peggy Sue shifted her purse onto her shoulder and glanced side to side. "You don't know the half of it."

Junior gave a tut-tut shake of his head. "Caused a lot of trouble on the job, did she?"

She glanced at her watch. "Look, I'm having lunch at the Blue Gill. It's quick at this time of day and close by. If you want to know the real Ruby, meet me there."

With that she crossed the parking lot to a blue Ford Pinto and drove off in the direction of the Causeway.

Junior went inside the station and asked the officer manning the front counter for a map of the town.

The officer stared at him. "Does this look like a filling station? Go across the street to the Texaco."

"Right." Junior looked around the open squad room. There were two desks side by side in a small bullpen. On the other side of the room was the Chief's office and beyond that, a door that led to the rear of the building. Behind the officer manning the reception counter was the switchboard. He was the only person in the place. Junior turned and left.

Peggy Sue had taken a table outside on the wide, dilapidated deck that sat on pilings above the swamp grasses and water of the delta.

The smell of fried fish had Junior's mouth watering. His stomach rumbled. He ordered sweet tea and fried flounder from the waitress who had trailed after him through the restaurant. As she disappeared through the screen door, he turned his full attention to Peggy Sue.

"So, tell me about Ruby."

He could see that she was having second thoughts as she took her time taking a long sip of tea.

"I already know about her and Boo. That they had a thing going on."

It was the prompt she needed.

"There wasn't a 'thing' between them. He was crazy about her. She liked making sport of him. Like a cat toying with an injured bird."

"She sounds like a nasty piece of work."

"She used her beauty like a carrot. Until she wanted to use it like a hammer."

"Who did she hammer besides Boo?"

"That highway patrolman. The one she was engaged to. And just about every woman in Spanish Fort. Including her Aunt Nora."

"The Chief's wife?"

"You didn't hear it from me."

"How do you know this?"

"Nora and I have been friends since she first came to town to take a teaching job at the elementary school."

"What did Ruby do to Mrs. Stanton?"

"The Chief. She kept him wound up. Every time things settled down Ruby would stir them up again. Kept Buzz in a mood. They couldn't plan anything. Two weeks ago was their anniversary. They were supposed to go with friends for Memorial Day weekend to a cabin at Lake Martin. Nora planned it especially because Buzz loves to fish."

"So, what happened?"

"Ruby. That's what always happens. Since she left grammar school she's led him around by his nose."

"What happened two weeks ago?" Junior prompted.

"Someone was following her she claimed."

"And they canceled their trip because of it? Was someone following her?"

"Of course not. She just wanted to ruin Nora's trip. To prove she could."

"Why?"

Peggy Sue sat back in her chair and pushed her plate aside. "Control. Whatever. She loved her little games."

"And Stanton let her get away with it?"

"Always has. It's like she has some kind of power over him."

Nine

THE PARADISE SAT just beyond the intersection in Daphne where the Hwy 98 truck route diverged from old Hwy 98. The scenic route followed the shoreline, more or less, of the eastern shore of Mobile Bay down to Mullet Point.

At one-forty in the afternoon Hugo pulled up in front of the night club. Nothing stirred in the harsh sunlight. At the far edge of the pea gravel parking lot a long white Caddy was practically hidden in the shade of a Formosa tree.

Hugo tried the door of the cinder block building. It was locked. He banged against it and waited a couple of minutes. He glanced at the car in the shade then banged again. Finally, he heard the turn of the lock and the door opened a few inches.

"We closed," a woman with her head bound up in a mustard yellow cloth said through the narrow opening.

Hugo held up his shield.

She studied it a moment, then studied him. "Manon!" she called over her shoulder as she opened the door, "Po-lice."

Hugo stepped into the dim light of the bar. As his eyes adjusted, a large black man with a circlet of white hair came through a doorway on the far side of the building. He looked Hugo up and down but said nothing.

"You the owner?" Hugo asked.

"Manager."

"What's your name?"

"Manon."

"Manon what?"

"George Manon."

Hugo took his notebook from his inside coat pocket. "Do you know Harry Chapman?"

"Can't say I do."

"White guy, black hair, mustache and goatee. About five-ten. I hear this is his favorite joint."

"Lots of folks come to the Paradise. They like the music."

"You get a lot of white people in here, do ya?"

"More than we used to."

Hugo looked around the bar, sizing up the space, then he sized up George Manon. "You know Chief Stanton over in Spanish Fort?"

Manon nodded.

"Know his niece?"

Manon glanced at the woman then returned his attention to Hugo. He said nothing.

"She's dead."

Manon crossed his arms over his chest.

"Murdered."

Hugo waited.

Manon remained silent.

"The Chief was very fond of his niece. So you can imagine how he's feeling right now. That's why I'm here." Hugo gave a little side to side movement of his head. "Sort of a go-between. Considering the Chief's temper and all." Hugo had no idea if Stanton had a temper but odds were he did. And he doubted whether or not Manon knew either. He glanced at the woman then shrugged. "But maybe it would be better to let the Chief check out Chapman's alibi. I hear he can be pretty persuasive."

"He comes in here sometimes."

"Regular?"

"Regular enough."

"When did you last see him?"

Manon glanced at the woman again. She moved behind the bar. "Last night."

"What time?"

He looked off over Hugo's head then shrugged. "Can't say for sure. Nine maybe."

"When did he leave?"

Manon shook his head. "Couldn't say."

"You have a big crowd last night?"

Manon shrugged.

Hugo closed his notebook and returned it to his coat pocket. "I'm sure someone will remember. Maybe some of your regular patrons. I suspect the Chief knows a lot of them."

The woman spoke up. "'Bout eleven. He left 'bout eleven."

Hugo kept his gaze squarely on Manon. "Did he come back later?"

"Naw," the woman replied.

HUGO FOLLOWED A track that led from the back of The Paradise about a hundred yards or so down the bluff to a strip of sandy shore and Mobile Bay. At some point in time a fallen tree had washed partly onto the beach, anchored by its weight and the sand, the trunk and remaining stubs of limbs bleached almost white by the sun and surf. It was obviously a gathering spot for patrons of the club. Beer bottles and cigarette butts littered the sand and bobbed in the lazy wash at the water's edge.

His mouth tasted stale and of beer, his eyes itched from lack of sleep, and he felt a weariness deep in his bones. He climbed onto the dry end of the tree trunk and sat, staring out into the bay, listening to the shushing of the wake against the beach. The sun was hot, but he didn't have the energy to remove his sports coat. Seeing Bebe suddenly, out of the blue like that, had almost buckled his knees. It had been nearly six months since he last saw her. He knew he had crossed the Rubicon with his accusations about her aunt's death. Knew it even as he had done it, slamming her with his words, with his hurt and anger. But she had betrayed him first, hadn't she? Five months ago, five years ago. It didn't really matter. The cut was bone deep. And still, she had this power over him.

He wanted a beer. He wanted to sleep, to forget. But he could do none of those things. Ruby Stanton was dead. Someone hated her enough to shoot her through the heart. Or loved her enough. He would find out who. That was his job. That's what he was good at. That's what kept the memories at bay.

Hugo took one last look at the calm waters of the bay and climbed down from the log. He removed his jacket and started up the bluff. The seat of his car was blistering hot when he slid onto it, throwing his sports coat onto the passenger side, the steering wheel equally hot. He glanced toward the shade of the Formosa tree on the edge of the parking lot. The white car was gone.

He turned the key in the ignition. His limbs felt heavy with the heat and fatigue. A hot shower was what he needed. A good steamy shower to clear his head and make him clean again.

⁂

AFTER HIS LATE lunch, Junior drove the short distance between the Blue Gill and the Thunderbird Inn. He entered the dining room to discover he had the place all to himself. He and Hugo had been promised someone from MPD to man the phone and be a conduit to Chief Goode. Even the Spanish Fort patrolman had abandoned the scene. That suited Junior just fine. The thought of someone looking over his shoulder all the time always made him doubt himself.

He sat at the table they had set up as a desk and took out his notebook. The blank chalkboard stood directly in front of him. Where to start?

Access. That was key. He picked up the chalk and wrote CAR and BOAT under this heading. Could someone have walked down the hill from Spanish Fort? Doable but a pretty good hike and the possibility of being seen was a risk. But maybe not with the fog. Easy enough to slip into the brush on the side of the road if a car came along. If you weren't afraid of gators.

Who? Good question, Junior thought, as he added this heading to the board. It was a long list that covered both sides of the bay.

Motive. He grinned and wrote JILTED LOVER. Below this he listed Fiancé, Lawyer, Wife, Boo. O'Sullivan?

He felt pretty sure they could eliminate O'Sullivan. That's where he'd start. He drew a line under O'Sullivan. First, he called information and got the number of O'Sullivan's Funeral Home. He identified himself and asked to speak with Mr. O'Sullivan.

"Which one? Junior or Senior?"

He did a quick mental calculation. "Junior."

"Could I tell him what it's about?"

"No."

"One moment."

Junior held much longer than a moment. Finally, the receptionist came back on the line. "I'm afraid Mr. O'Sullivan isn't available right now."

"I see."

"Would you like to leave a message?"

"No, no. That won't be necessary. I'll call Mrs. O'Sullivan with my questions. I'm sure she can tell me about her husband's activities last night."

There was a brief silence at the other end of the line. "Just a second," the receptionist said. "I think Mr. O'Sullivan might be finishing up with his client."

Good decision, Junior thought.

Ten

O'SULLIVAN KEPT JUNIOR waiting just long enough to establish how important he was. His, "Yes, what is it?" was brusque when he finally came on the line.

An interview over the telephone wasn't ideal. Junior liked to watch for the tell-tale signs a suspect was prone to exhibit under the stress of being in the hot seat. But time wasn't on their side and by now he was pretty sure everyone on both sides of the bay knew that Ruby Stanton had been murdered at the Thunderbird Inn. The afternoon edition of the paper would be hitting doorsteps within a couple of hours. He needed to get O'Sullivan's story before the particulars were all over the news. He decided to lead with his best gambit.

"Just a few questions, Mr. O'Sullivan, about what you saw last night at the Thunderbird Inn."

There was the briefest hesitation.

"I don't know what you're talking about."

"The walk from the marine repair shop. That's what? About a hundred yards, give or take? And the fog hadn't settled in yet. Or maybe at the motel? Late hour like that, hardly any guests. It would be hard to miss someone coming or going." Junior paused, letting that sink in. "Other than yourself, of course."

O'Sullivan didn't speak for a long minute. "I don't think I can help you...what was your name?"

"Knight. Junior Knight. The Chief can tell you how to spell it."

"Look. You've got some cockamamie idea that I know something about Ruby's death, but I don't. You should be checking out that long haired cook. Or her fiancé. Ruby was no angel. But I never had anything to do with her." O'Sullivan was working himself up to righteous indignation. "Go do your job and stop spreading gossip."

"The funny thing about gossip, Mr. O'Sullivan, is that it usually has a kernel of truth in it. And Ruby isn't just dead. She was murdered. So pardon me while I get on with my *job*. Which we can always do downtown if you prefer." He paused a couple of heart beats. "Now, tell me who or what you saw."

"No one."

"Other than Dixie."

Junior could almost feel the rage traveling over the phone line.

"Other than Dixie," O'Sullivan said in a low growl.

"What time?"

"Midnight. I left the house at midnight. Docked at the repair shop. About twelve fifteen."

"And you left the Thunderbird at what time?"

The lie purred over the line. Junior heard the subtle shift and knew he was about to get the sales pitch.

"Around one."

He had no doubt the murder occurred sometime after one in the morning. O'Sullivan was covering his tracks.

"You're sure about that? It wasn't closer to two o'clock?"

"I'm sure."

"Did you hear the gunshot?"

"I told you, I left at one."

"But you don't know when Ruby was shot, do you, Mr. O'Sullivan? It's entirely possible that it happened while you were there. Between midnight and one in the morning. In which case you would have heard the shot. And we both know how sound travels over water. Maybe you heard something after you got back home."

O'Sullivan was silent. Finally, he said, "I have a client. If you have any more questions you'll need to speak with my attorney."

But Junior already had what he needed. O'Sullivan knew without being told that he was calling about Ruby's murder. He'd cornered him into admitting he was there when it happened. Dixie had obviously warned him. O'Sullivan was putting himself well out of the time frame of the shooting. What else were they lying about?

⁂

THE STEAMING HOT water ran over Hugo and down his back as he stood under the mineral corroded showerhead of the bath of his shotgun house. He could feel his pores opening in the steamy confines of the tiny room. Something was niggling at the edge of memory. Something important. It eluded him as the water began to run to the temperature of tap water. He reached for the spigot just as the first boom sounded. Reflexively he ducked and his feet went out from under him in the ancient tub. He felt the pain in his side through a shower of starbursts and reverberations.

Incoming. Incoming! Rockets explode all around him, sending showers of earth into the air, blinding him. He hunkers down as he feels for his M-16. It isn't there. Lost. Lost in the dirt and damp and darkness. It hurts to breathe. It hurts to move but he has to do both. Charlie is coming.

The chill is deep in the bone. The dense canopy of the jungle has turned the endless rain into an ice bath. A sense of urgency stirs in the back of his mind. He needs to move. He can't see beyond the white curtain of rain. A deep breath sends a flash of pain through his chest and he opens his eyes.

Hugo stared up at the thin spray of water falling from the corroded showerhead. He lay curled in the tub, shivering, entangled in the white plastic shower curtain. As he pushed himself to a sitting position a stab of pain shot through his left side. It took a minute to muster the will to stand. He ground his teeth against the pain and examined his side. There was a red welp slanted across his ribs. He turned off the water, grabbed the towel bar, and climbed out of the tangle of the curtain. With a towel he wiped the mirror over the sink and examined his forehead. There was a red mark on the left side above his brow.

A deep throated revving of an engine followed by a loud pop caused him to flinch. Pain shot down his left side once again. He looked out the small bathroom window to see a two-toned white-over-blue 1954 Ford F100 parked on the empty lot between his shotgun house and that of his neighbor. Maurice was admiring the truck as a young kid who didn't look old enough to drive gunned the engine once more.

Hugo felt the bile rise in his throat. He hawked and spat into the sink then rinsed his mouth before lathering his face. He took his time shaving. His hand was steady. Not a single nick. Better, he decided, as he wiped away the excess lather with a hot steamy washcloth. Better.

⚜

IT WAS ALMOST four o'clock when Hugo drove into the parking lot of the Thunderbird. Junior's city issue sedan was the only vehicle there.

He looked up when Hugo entered the room. "What happened to you?"

"Slipped in the shower." Hugo raised his hand in a swear-to-God gesture and gave Junior a one-sided grin.

"You okay?"

"I'll be sore a day or two but no real damage. It only hurts when I breathe." He read through the notations on the chalk board. "What's new?"

"O'Sullivan. And Dixie."

"He's her gentleman caller?"

"Yep. Says he arrived at about midnight. Left at one. Didn't hear a thing. Didn't see anyone."

"You believe he was coming to see Dixie rather than Ruby?"

"Yeah. But they're both lying. There's no way they didn't hear the shot."

"Unless the shooter used a silencer."

"What local yokel is going to have a silencer for their gun?" Junior sat back in his chair, his hands clasped behind his head.

"Nobody."

"It's a crime of passion. Heat of the moment."

"Maybe."

"What else could it be?"

"I don't know." Hugo studied the board again. "The thing that bothers me is that she was shot here. Her rendezvous place. What if it was intended to point us in that direction? The lover. The ex-fiancé?"

"A misdirection. And premeditated."

"It was always premeditated. Someone came with a gun to shoot the occupant of Lucky Number Seven."

"You still think the lover could have been the target?"

"Chapman was in the room with her at midnight according to Dubya. O'Sullivan, if he's to be believed, arrived at midnight."

"Said he left his house on the bluff at midnight. Fifteen minutes, give or take to ease the boat from his dock without disturbing the wife, cross the short distance of water to the repair shop, tie up, then walk a hundred yards to the motel."

"So, Chapman leaves, O'Sullivan arrives. What's his story?"

"Said he didn't see or hear anyone. Dubya's wandering the halls of the motel. That Hog the cook rides isn't exactly quiet. And at that hour of the night, someone should have heard it. Both when he left and when he came back after Dixie called him."

"Not to mention the gunshot," Hugo said.

"Yeah. There's that." Junior let his gaze run down the list of names. "So who's lying?"

Hugo was silent for a minute as he stared at the board. "Everyone. The question is, why?"

Eleven

THE PHONE RANG and Hugo and Junior stared at it then looked at each other. Hugo lifted the receiver.

"August," he said.

He angled the earpiece so Junior could hear. It was Chief Goode.

"What have you got?"

"The usual suspects. The lover, the lover's wife, the ex-fiancé. Something with one of the Spanish Fort patrolmen."

The Chief cleared his throat. "I wouldn't worry too much about the cop. They're a tight bunch over there. No one would cross Stanton."

Hugo looked at Junior. "You mean the highway patrol cop or the local cop?"

"You know damn well what I mean. Call me when you find something that resembles a lead. Or are the two of you just sitting on your asses? The autopsy is at nine in the morning. Be there." With that the Chief hung up.

"What was that all about?" Junior asked. "And where's the help he promised?"

Hugo studied the board. Finally, he turned to Junior. "There's no help. We've been hung out to dry. He knows something and he's distancing himself and the department from the train wreck. He only called to see if we had anything damning."

"You don't think he'd withhold evidence?"

"Goode has managed to hang on to his job for over twelve years. He might not withhold evidence, but he can make it hard for us to find it if it involves his betters."

"Same difference."

Hugo lifted his chin slightly in acknowledgment. "Let's see what the autopsy shows tomorrow. I'll attend. For now, I'm going to interview Elizabeth Stanton. She may be the grieving mother, but we've got to get ahead of whatever's going on beneath the surface."

"I'll take the cop since the Chief is so sure that's a blind alley."

"Good. Then head home. Get a hot shower and a decent meal. See what the six o'clock news has to say." Hugo returned his notebook to his coat pocket. "And see what Mrs. K has heard. She'll know what everyone's saying."

Junior grinned. "I'm sure she can't wait for five o'clock Mass. Myrtle Crum and her friends will have the scoop."

"Speaking of scoop, be on the look-out for Pete Donahue. He's snooping around."

"I'd bet the Press Register already has a juicy write up waiting on everyone's doorstep. Nothing like a sex scandal to get the public's attention."

"Not to mention the murder of a police chief's niece."

"Yeah, that."

⁂

THE FRONT DOOR was opened by Nora Stanton. She stepped back to let Hugo enter the house.

"Beth's asleep. I gave her another valium."

"I really need to talk to her."

"Maybe tomorrow. She's a mess."

Hugo studied the woman standing before him. She was slim but in an athletic way, toned, well tanned, with a bit gray streaking her brunette hair. "This must be hard on you, too."

She turned her profile to him and gestured toward the living room. "Would you like a cup of coffee? Or tea?"

"No, thanks." He followed her into the tidy room that gave a view of the street through a bay window. He could hear the faint ticking of a clock. "Did you always live in Spanish Fort?"

She took an armchair and Hugo sat on the sofa.

"I moved here from Tallahassee to take a teaching job right out of college." She looked out the window, gathering the memories. "I was so green. And naïve. I boarded with the principal's sister. Rosemary." A sad smile touched her lips fleetingly. "Spanish Fort is very inbred. Everyone's connected to everyone either by blood or long association. I had just left behind the easygoing life of a campus practically on the beach. Rosemary took me under her wing and just before Christmas, she introduced me to Buzz. Six months later we were married."

"Have you always been close to Elizabeth?"

"Not at first. Buzz and I got married just before Ruby was born. The first time I even knew anything about Beth was when he insisted we visit her in the hospital after the birth."

"So you've known Ruby her whole life."

Nora Stanton's gaze was upon the past. Hugo let her drift among her memories.

"She was a beautiful baby. She had Beth's red hair, that creamy white complexion. There was nothing of Henry about her." With a sigh she turned back to him. "Buzz fell under her spell that day. And he's been under it ever since."

"Were the families always close? Your kids play together?"

"I have no children."

"Perhaps that's why he cares so deeply about Ruby."

Nora stared out the window again. After a brief silence, she said, "Perhaps."

∙ı�∕

BOO VANSANT WASN'T at Spanish Fort police headquarters. By the time Junior finally found him sitting in a folding lawn chair behind a travel trailer set up on Blakeley River Road, the day was fading. Vansant was nursing a Pabst as he watched the sun lowering over the river and the large and small land masses through which the five rivers traversed on their way to Mobile Bay. The sun glinted on the ripples of the water causing Junior to squint against the brightness. Mosquitoes sang around his ears as he made his way through calf high grass to stand beside Boo.

"Peaceful setting," Junior said.

Boo glanced at him then took a pull on his beer.

"We need to talk about your fight with Ruby."

"Nothing to talk about."

"That's not what I heard."

"You shouldn't listen to gossip. Peggy Sue isn't the most reliable source of information."

"Who said it was Peggy Sue?"

Boo squinted up at him. "An educated guess."

"Why would Peggy Sue lie about it?"

Boo didn't respond.

"So, what *did* happen?"

His sigh was soft and shallow. "She heard that I applied for a job with Mobile."

"Police department?"

He nodded.

"Why would that make her mad?"

Boo shrugged. "That was Ruby. No rhyme or reason, just rage."

"I thought she didn't care about you."

"Who knows what Ruby cared about. I sure didn't. Not since we were kids. But when Alma told her I was going to move to Mobile if I got the job, she blew a gasket. Had a meltdown at the station in front of everyone."

"Huh." Junior studied Boo as he sat there watching the late afternoon sky. "What happened?"

"The Chief took her in hand. Marched her out of the office. When he came in the next morning, he said to forget about her outburst. She was emotional. It was that time of the month. Told me to forget about Mobile, too. That he didn't want to lose a good, seasoned officer. Ruby never came back to work."

"You withdrew your application?"

He shook his head. "I never heard back from MPD."

They were silent a long moment then Junior asked, "Who's Alma?"

"My girlfriend. I guess."

Twelve

HUGO STOOD ON the front porch of Elizabeth Stanton's home. The lawn was manicured to a fault. Not a blade of grass out of place. The flower beds were neat, compact, and weed free. Even the hedges marched along in military precision.

He walked around the house to the garage and up the stairs to Ruby's apartment. The door was closed but the latch hadn't fully engaged. Hugo pushed his coat back from the revolver holstered at his side and eased the door open with the toe of his shoe.

There was sudden movement and a whimper from Ruby's bed. Against the headboard a slight young man lay balled up with a book clutched to his chest as he stared at Hugo in fright.

"Hello, Nelson," Hugo said quietly. He stood still in the doorway, his arms loose at his side. "What have you got there?"

Nelson squeezed himself more tightly into a ball and said nothing.

"I'll bet it's Br'er Rabbit."

"And the Tar Baby," Nelson said in a soft voice.

"That's my favorite, too."

Hugo moved slowly to the armchair across from the bed and sat down. "I like Mary Poppins, as well."

"She's nice."

"Like Ruby."

Nelson nodded.

"She read to you, didn't she?"

Tears rose in Nelson's eyes. "She's dead."

"I know."

"Someone shot her with a gun."

"Yes."

"Why?"

"I don't know but I'm going to find out."

"Are you her friend?"

Hugo shook his head. "I never met her. I'm a policeman."

Nelson shrank tightly against the headboard. "I don't like policemen."

"Why don't you like policemen, Nelson?"

He turned his head and watched Hugo from the corner of his eye. "Ruby said never be a policeman. Never, never, never."

"Why did she say that?"

Nelson didn't answer. Instead, he opened the story book. "Br'er Fox, *please* don't throw me in that briar patch."

For a while Hugo watched Nelson turn the pages and pretend to read a disjointed version of the story. There was a spoon full of sugar in the narration as well as Mr. McGregor. Finally, he rose from the chair. "I have to go now, Nelson. But first, could you tell me something?"

Nelson looked up from the book.

"Did Ruby's friends visit her here? In her apartment?"

Nelson thought about this a moment. "I'm Ruby's only friend. She told me so."

* * *

WHEN HUGO ENTERED the Spanish Fort police station there was no one around. He could see Stanton through the glass of his door, leaning back in his chair, staring into space. Hugo tapped on the glass and the police chief turned toward the sound but not quite registering, not yet there in the present.

He pulled himself from some faraway place, sat up straight, and motioned for Hugo to enter.

"Chief. Anything new?"

"That's my question."

"Talked with her boss."

Stanton's eyelids narrowed slightly. The image of a crocodile came to Hugo's mind. He made no comment.

"He's known for his affairs. The wife could be in the picture. Early days yet. The ex-fiancé has to be considered. We'll see how his alibi holds up against the time of death. Autopsy is scheduled for tomorrow morning. We haven't found the gun. No one in the area seems to have heard the shot."

"In the dead of night and on the water."

"My thought, too."

"The hotel guests?"

"Nothing. But the couple take something to help them

sleep when they travel. Don't like being in an unfamiliar bed, apparently."

"Huh."

"As I said, early days still." Hugo hesitated, "Tell me about Dixie."

Stanton's brows shot up briefly. "Nothing to tell. She's lived here all her life. Married when she was a kid hardly out of high school then divorced. Went to work at the motel soon after, if I recall."

"Know her well?"

"Well enough. Stop in at the motel occasionally on my rounds. Have breakfast there once in a while. They do a good business at meal time. There's been an unruly guest to deal with here and there over the years."

Hugo turned to go but hesitated with his hand on the doorknob. "Tell me about Nelson Gorton."

"The neighbbor's kid?" He shrugged. "What's to tell. Waterhead baby. The IQ of a first grader, if that. Real attached to Ruby. Harmless. Why?"

"Nothing. Just saw him this afternoon. Ruby's death really upset him."

"She was kind to him, them being the same age and him living right next door. Treated him like a kid brother. Don't waste your time there. He can't tell you anything. Doesn't have the wherewithal."

"Right," Hugo said and left the office.

✦

THE SETTING SUN was blinding when Junior popped out of the west entrance to the Bankhead Tunnel into the heart of downtown Mobile. He dropped the sun visor and stopped at the traffic light. In front of his car, he recognized Evie as she started across the street in the crosswalk. He gave the horn a light tap and she looked up at the sound.

She came to the window on his side of the car. "What's up?"

"Nothing exciting. Just a lot of leg work." The traffic light turned green, but Junior ignored it. Downtown was dead at this hour of the day. "Why are you still here? Thought you'd be long gone home by now."

"Walked over to St. Andrew's for Mass. Left my purse at the office."

"Want a ride?"

A car came out of the tunnel behind Junior and blew his horn. Junior flashed the car's blue light without even glancing at his rearview mirror and waited for Evie's response.

Evie looked at the angry driver and laughed. She walked around to the passenger side of the sedan and got into the car. Just as the traffic light turned red, Junior did a U turn in the intersection and took her the short block to police headquarters and the crime lab in the building's basement.

When she got back into the car after retrieving her purse, Junior noticed that she had applied fresh lipstick and brushed the tangle of curls back into soft waves that framed her face. The thought pleased him.

"Hungry?" he asked.

"I wouldn't mind getting a bite somewhere. Not too expensive, though."

"How about Korbet's? My treat."

"Oh, no, Junior. I couldn't let you do that."

"Sure you can. I'll treat this time and you can treat next time."

She hesitated then said, "Okay. But I treat next time."

"Deal."

Junior felt a sense of well-being spread through him. The fact that she had agreed to supper had surprised him. He would have preferred to take her somewhere nice like Constantine's or the new Italian restaurant on Government Street, but he knew she would balk at the expense. That's why he had suggested Korbet's. It was nicer than the Dew Drop but still casual and homey. They were just friends, working late, going to supper together, he reminded himself.

In that moment, he remembered that he was supposed to take the cute receptionist from Dr. Fellowes office bowling tomorrow night. He would have to cancel because of the case. He realized he wasn't sorry about the fact.

The only thing that concerned him was that Evie ordered the cheapest thing on the menu. He didn't comment but made up his mind that there was no way he would let her pay for their next meal. Living at the YWCA wasn't as expensive as an apartment on her own would be, but he knew she was very frugal with her money. It probably had to do with growing up in an orphanage. Evie hadn't been lucky enough to have a grandmother who could take her in.

Junior felt a momentary pang of guilt at the thought of his grandmother. She would have something waiting in the oven for him when he got home. But he had been unable to resist the potential opportunity to spend time with Evie. Against all hope, she had said yes and here they were. He ordered his meal accordingly.

"So, tell me about the case," she said.

"It's a real tangled mess. From what we know so far, my guess is a lover's triangle kind of motive."

"That's the buzz around the station."

"Yeah?"

"The Chief isn't happy that everyone's gossiping about it but what can you do? She was sleeping with her boss and everyone at the courthouse knows it. People are going to talk."

"Hear anything useful?"

"I heard that Talbot's wife allows him to wander but not too far. She apparently ran one woman out of town."

"Really?"

"It's just gossip. The woman moved to Biloxi for a job. But the wife is supposed to have famously said no stringy-headed whore was going to step into my shoes."

"And yet she told me her husband's little indiscretions didn't really bother her."

"I don't think they do. I think the possibility that he might get too carried away with the right someone is her concern. Or, in the wife's view, the wrong someone."

"You think Ruby was that someone?"

"I have no idea. Didn't know her. Don't know Davis Talbot other than to recognize him when I see him." Evie squeezed lemon into her iced tea and took a long drink. "That's good. Didn't have lunch today we were so busy."

"With what?"

"A robbery at the new First Citizen's Bank then a battery and rape over in Birdville." She sat back against the high back of the booth. "I don't think my new assistant is going to make it."

"Oh, yeah? What's the problem?"

"He's much too important for the nitty gritty of the job."

"All play and no work."

"Something like that. Knows no one will listen to me if I complain."

"Don't let it get to you."

She smiled at him. "It doesn't. And he won't be my problem much longer. He managed to get himself on the Chief's radar by talking about the scene."

"You're kidding?"

She shook her head. "You should have seen the Chief when he came storming into the basement. Fortunately for my soon-to-be ex-assistant, he was running an errand."

"What did he leak?"

"Talked about her sheer robe that hardly covered what God gave her, for one thing."

"Who did he talk to?"

"Have you read the paper?"

"You're kidding me!"

"Nope."

THE SUN WAS setting over Mobile when Hugo drove down Hwy 31 to the Causeway. A rainbow of colors reflected through a scattering of clouds. It must be nice, he thought, to live on the eastern shore and have this view every evening.

He pulled into the parking lot of the motel. The place was the shadowy purple of twilight except for the lighted entryway. Hugo unlocked the door and entered the foyer. He was greeted by nothing but the distant hum of an air conditioner. In the dining room he flipped on the lights and settled at the desk table, his chair angled toward the chalkboard. Nothing in Junior's scribblings shed any new light on the subject.

At some point Junior had brought the typewriter from the motel office into the dining room and had typed up his notes. Hugo read through them and debated typing up his own interviews but in the end, he wandered into the kitchen in search of food. Except for coffee and a beer, he hadn't eaten anything all day.

First, he started the coffee dripping then looked in the industrial sized refrigerator. It was obvious the motel wasn't planning for a crowd but there was food. All the basics. He decided on steak and eggs. Quick, easy, no real mess. Besides, he reasoned, the steak would go bad and that would be a real waste.

In no time the aroma of searing meat filled the kitchen and Hugo's stomach growled. He added hashbrown to the drippings in the pan and dropped four slices of bread into the toaster.

Then he ate it all. The T-bone down to the bone, the eggs, potatoes, toast; every last bite. He pushed his plate away and leaned back in the chair. He couldn't remember the last time he had truly eaten his fill. Not like this. Not to the point of mind-foggingly stuffed, sated. Hawaii, he decided. That first meal after flying the Freedom Bird out of Tan Son Nhut. Roasted pig and all the trimmings, swimming in beer, hula skirts and tanned skin, hot kisses and—

He stood, stacked his dirty dishes, and placed them in the sink. Then he walked the length of the corridor that served the rooms, opening each door to check them as he went, making sure each was locked after him. Until he came to room number two. He stood in the doorway and surveyed the room and its contents then went to the bed and lay down on top of the covers, his tall frame stretching from the headboard to the foot of the bed. There were dead moths in the cheap glass cover of the overhead light. He felt the weight of his body settle into the comfort of the bed, relished the sensation of a full stomach, and closed his eyes.

Thirteen

GRAMMY OPENED THE screen door before Junior had cleared the front steps.

"It's so late! I was worried to death! Your supper is stone cold. It's the Ruby Stanton case, isn't it? You've been up since all hours. You must be tired to the bone."

Junior kissed his grandmother on the cheek. When she paused for breath, he replied, "Yes. It's the Stanton case. I am tired. And I'm not really hungry."

"Of course you're hungry." She was already heading toward the kitchen "Go along and wash up. I'll have it on the table in a whipstitch."

Junior knew it was pointless to argue. On the drive from the YWCA he had decided he would try to avoid telling his grandmother about dinner with Evie. In part not to hurt her feelings about supper. In part because he wanted to savor the evening, to linger in the afterglow of Evie's presence.

He hung his suit coat on a hanger and gave it a few quick strokes with the brush. In the bathroom mirror he saw his grinning reflection and scowled. Not only had he eaten meat on a Friday, he was being less than truthful with his grandmother. If it came up, he would tell her about Evie. If it came up.

He let the water run hot then held the steamy washcloth to his face. The heat felt good. When he removed the cloth, his expression was under control. He was ready to face his grandmother across the plate of salmon croquettes and extract the gossip going around about the murder.

She started talking as he came down the hallway. "Myrtle is in a state. She really shouldn't listen to the six o'clock news. And the paper! You'll never guess what that Pete Donahue wrote in the paper for all the world to see. Scandalous! A young woman, dead in a motel room in a flimsy nighty. What's the world coming to, I ask you?" She placed the warm plate in front of him and drizzled dill sauce over the salmon. "You know she was up to you-know-what else why would she be in a motel practically on her own front doorstep? It's the talk of the town."

"I imagine it is." A big dollop of melting butter nested on the top of a mound of mashed potatoes. He sighed. "Why is Myrtle in a state?"

"Afraid of being shot in her own house. She's like a cat on a hot tin roof. Couldn't sit still through Mass."

"No one's going to shoot Myrtle. Why would they?"

"You know how she is. Since The War she's been afraid of her shadow. And now, someone she knows is dead. Shot to death."

"She knew Ruby Stanton?"

"Well. I don't think she knew her, actually. But she knew who she was."

"How's that?"

His grandmother waved her hand dismissively and frowned. "Oh, I don't know. But she does know who Buzz Stanton is, so I guess in her mind she knows the cousin." She poured iced tea into a glass and placed it beside Junior's plate. "And that Seth at Six, he just about spelled it all out in detail on Channel 5. Makes me blush to think about it."

Murder and sex, Junior thought. Sex and murder. Nothing like it to stir folks up. "What else is new today?"

"Well, I think this is quite enough news, don't you? A murderer in our midst. What's the world coming to?"

"Ruby Stanton's from Baldwin County. I suspect whatever led to her death will be discovered over the bay. Don't let it worry you too much."

"But a young woman is dead. I lit a candle for her. Poor thing. How could someone do that? And her so very pretty."

In Marilyn Knight's world bad things didn't happen to beautiful people. The rich and famous were somehow immune to tragedy. Except, of course, Carole Lombard. Junior's grandmother and all her friends had felt that tragedy very deeply and still did all these many years later. But Lombard's death in a plane crash while she was selling war bonds in WWII had risen above the gruesomeness of death to a kind of beautiful, sanitized martyrdom in Marilyn's eyes. Not really death at all. But to be shot through the heart in a dingy motel in no-man's land. That was tawdry.

"Yes. She was pretty. And very young."

His grandmother reached across and placed a hand on Junior's arm. "Oh, my dear boy. You had to see it all." She shook her head. "And you've hardly touched your food."

There was such sympathy in her eyes. Junior patted

the hand that rested on his arm. "I'm fine, Grammy. I think I don't have much of an appetite because it's been such a long day. Why don't you save the rest of this for tomorrow night? That way you won't have to cook. You know I love cold salmon."

"Well." She gave him a small smile. "There is the reunion luncheon tomorrow. I'm wearing my Easter hat."

"Perfect. It looks so nice on you."

She beamed at him as she stood and began clearing away his plate. "There's peach cobbler. I've been keeping it warm."

"Who could resist your warm peach cobbler?"

⁂

THE MOBILE PRESS Register had a remarkably detailed account of the death scene. There was a glamor shot of Ruby Stanton on the front page and one of Chief Stanton with a look of thunder on his face that the paper's photographer captured as he was exiting the Spanish Fort police station. No comment had been the party line from all sources. Except one unnamed source, of course.

Junior sat in the armchair in the living room reading between the lines. The fact that Ruby worked for Davis Talbot featured prominently in the story and that she had been engaged previously to a local highway patrolman. Donahue was good at telling all without spelling it out.

He took out his notebook and read through the notes of the case, trying to make some sense of it. Nothing jumped out at him. It was getting on toward nine o'clock and he wanted to stay up for the ten o'clock news to see their coverage of the murder. With a yawn, he turned to the crossword puzzle and took up his pen. The next thing he knew, his grandmother was nudging him, telling him to get to bed and get some proper rest.

RUBY TURNED HER head toward him, her eyes glittered in the low light of the neon sign flashing through the slant of the blinds, her red lips moved. She was whispering to him, telling him something important. He knew it was important, and he tried to lean closer but the more he struggled toward her, the further away she seemed. Then suddenly the red hair turned a pale gold and the face that stared up at him was Bebe. She was speaking to him, but he couldn't hear the words. He watched her mouth, watched her lips move soundlessly. He strained toward her, wanting desperately to understand, to kiss those lips, to hold her in his arms.

Hugo woke suddenly and completely though he didn't open his eyes. He felt the presence of someone in the room. He was at the Thunderbird Inn, he remembered. In number two with no hint of mold in the air. A mental rundown of the space, the location of his gun holstered on his hip, and the placement of the door gave way to an awareness of a fragrance. Slowly, he opened his eyes to see a woman standing in the doorway. A blonde woman.

"Dixie."

"Do you always sleep with the light on?" she asked.

"Not usually." He swung his legs off the bed as he sat up. "What brings you to the motel at this hour?"

"On my way home. Saw the lights."

"Home from where?"

"Mobile."

When she didn't elaborate, he asked, "What time is it?"

"Almost two." She was leaning against the door casing, her arms crossed.

"Late night."

"Not for me. I have trouble sleeping at night." She pushed away from the casing and moved toward the bed. "Feeling restless, I guess." She sat down beside him. "Do you have trouble sleeping?"

Hugo could smell the faint scent of cigarettes mingled with a light fragrance as Dixie leaned in slightly, her hair falling forward as she slanted her head and looked up at him. She had that Lauren Bacall sensuality about her, in her movements, her expressive eyes, in her voice.

"Why this room?" he asked. "When you're not napping under a blanket in the office chair?"

"Because it's next to reception. I can hear the bell at the front desk from here."

"You must have exceptional hearing."

She pulled away. "It's second nature. To subconsciously listen for certain sounds. Like a mother with her baby in the night."

"But not a gunshot."

Dixie stood and moved toward the door. She stopped and looked over her shoulder. "Apparently not."

"Um." Hugo rose from the bed and followed her from the room down the hallway to the front door of the motel.

"How'd you get in?"

She reached into her purse and extracted a key.

Hugo held his hand out and she dropped it into his palm.

"Any more of these floating around?"

"You'd have to ask Dickie."

She started to push the door open. Hugo reached across her and held it closed. "Why did you really show up?"

Her left eyebrow arched, and she gave him a half smile. She lifted a hand to his face and lightly traced his lips with her thumb. "I thought you might be feeling lonely."

He felt the desire rise quickly and urgently. Just as she started to lean in and kiss him, he said, "Like your friend O'Sullivan?"

She lowered her eyelids until her lashes swept the delicate skin of her cheeks as her hand dropped away and she turned her head slightly. "Sully? I wouldn't call him a friend exactly."

"What would you call him?"

"More of an acquaintance."

"A lonely acquaintance?"

"Is that what he said?"

"He didn't have much to say. Seemed to think we were wasting his time."

Dixie placed her hand over Hugo's where it rested on the door handle. "Well, he's a very important man. If you don't believe me, just ask him. Much too busy to be lonely."

Hugo removed his hand from the door and her touch. "For the record, I'm not the lonely type either."

She studied his face and smiled, one eyebrow arched. "You could have fooled me," she said in a husky voice. "A pity." With that she pushed against the door, walked out onto the parking lot with a tantalizing sway to her hips, and got into her little yellow Beetle.

Fourteen

HUGO STARED AFTER the Volkswagen until the taillights disappeared into the night. Why had Dixie suddenly appeared at the foot of the bed at such a late hour? He wasn't deceived by her seductive behavior. Was she really on her way home from Mobile?

He didn't think so.

What had he missed?

Something that mattered enough for her to risk being caught out. A physical something? Or information? She hadn't tried very hard if it was information she wanted. No questions, subtle or otherwise.

He locked the front door of the motel and made his way to the kitchen where he emptied the coffee dregs and went about brewing a fresh pot. The bed in number two had been comfortable, clean. He had slept soundly, even fully clothed and with the light on. It was a learned ability, to drop into deep sleep devoid of dreams. Mostly. To be completely still, and to wake on instinct. He felt wide awake, his mind sharp.

The clock on the wall in the kitchen showed the time as two thirty-five. Hugo took his cup of coffee and returned to the dining room. The chalkboard with Junior's notations was where his gaze settled. Had Dixie seen them? Had she read through Junior's notes carelessly left in a file folder on the table? He sat down and reviewed them as he drank his coffee.

There it was. The thing he hadn't been able to retrieve in the moment. *Sully*. He had read it in Junior's case notes. It had been written in a notebook. In a locked drawer in the motel office. Among Dixie's intimate belongings. Hugo gave a grunt of humor at Junior's use of the word *intimate*.

He closed the file and went to the office. In the lower desk drawer, he found Dixie's things. The notebook wasn't there. Who had removed?

The discovery of the notebook occurred after Dixie left the motel the morning of the murder. Dickie had arrived when she was leaving. He'd spent his time cooling his heels in the office until Hugo kicked him out of the motel and took his key. The green, young Spanish Fort patrolman had been stationed at the motel all morning. Hugo wasn't sure when he had been pulled from his post. Both he and Junior had been off canvassing the area and checking alibis.

And now Dixie had shown up, in the wee hours of the morning, with a flimsy excuse for her presence.

Hugo returned to the restaurant, pulled the typewriter close, and opened his own notebook. Two cups of coffee and fifteen minutes later he had hunt-and-pecked them into three sheets of single-spaced paper.

The process ordered his thoughts. As he re-read the pages, he made notations in the margins. Then he sat back, his hands clasped behind his head, and studied the chalk board.

On the surface it appeared that the mystery of O'Sullivan was resolved. A man with a honey on the side caught in the wrong place at the wrong time. And yet, Hugo wasn't ready to erase his name from the suspect pool. The timing was the issue. And the gunshot. No one claims to have heard the gunshot. With five people on the premises at the time of the murder, someone had to have heard something.

He discounted the couple in number four. The little yellow pills they said they took to help them sleep were probably benzos. They would have slept like the dead. But there was still the issue of Dubya. According to Junior's interview, he claimed to have gone to bed at 12:20 that morning. That he hadn't seen anyone after the cook slipped out of Ruby's room. Why hadn't he heard anything?

It was after three when Hugo left the dining room and wandered through the kitchen and into a back room used for storage. He let his gaze travel over the food items and cleaning products on the open shelves. Nothing caught his eye. Two floor-to-ceiling metal cabinets stood side by side and covered the entire back wall. Each of them had a padlock that dangled from the cabinet handle. The shafts were open on the locks. He opened the double doors of the one on the left. There was nothing inside. He did the same with one on the right. Nothing there either. A six-inch gap existed between the cabinets and the ceiling. Hugo brought a chair from the dining room so he could see into the space. The only thing he found was a deep layer of dust. When he stepped down off the chair, he noticed a pack of Marlboros on the floor almost hidden between the storage unit and the wall. He picked them up, turned them over in his hand. The pack was slightly crushed but unopened. He left them on the kitchen worktop.

Why had Dixie really stopped at the motel? It had to be for the notebook.

Hugo walked out onto the back deck. Fireflies flickered in the tall grasses and the frogs kept up a regular chorus. The night was black with less than a quarter moon hanging in the sky. Low lights near the water line indicated the piers of the houses on Confederate Drive. The occasional speck of light from the top of the bluff pin-pointed the houses. A pair of eyes glowed from the water's edge. Too closely spaced to be a gator, Hugo thought. Probably a 'possum.

He sat in a faded deck chair and longed for a smoke. Curious that he should still have that craving. He thought about that last cigarette on the tarmac at Tan Son Nhut. Until now, he hadn't given any thought to fact it was his last. Had it been a conscious decision? As he sat there in the damp heat of the delta, he realized it had been, after a fashion.

He didn't remember much of that first night in Oahu other than the fact the young woman in the hula skirt at the USO hall had very blue eyes. When he gave her his lighter, she had traced her fingers over the words engraved on it and the smile faded from those lovely eyes.

"Are you sure?" she had asked.

Yes. He was sure.

Hugo closed the door on the memory and stood. He was wasting time at the motel. There was nothing to be learned from wandering the rooms and grounds. The autopsy was scheduled for nine and he wanted a shower.

Traffic was almost non-existent on the Causeway as Hugo made his way toward the Bankhead Tunnel. He passed only one car and a flatbed truck. Downtown Mobile was still asleep as he pulled the Thunderbird onto the empty lot between his shotgun house and that of his neighbor. Once inside he was confronted with the state of his bathroom.

It took some engineering with a wire coat hanger, but he was able to create rings that pierced the heavy plastic of his shower curtain and rigged it so that it functioned. A long diagonal bruise across his left ribcage stood out in deep purple. The hot shower eased the tenderness of his injury. He took a deep breath, felt gingerly along the length of the bruise, and decided nothing was broken.

He was down to his last clean shirt. He examined all three of his ties and picked the one without any obvious stains and placed it with the shirt. It was half past five in the morning, so he sat in the stuffed, faded armchair in his living room in his undershirt, tuned the radio to WABB, and rested his head against the chairback as he listened to Elvis crooning *Are You Lonesome Tonight.*

Fifteen

GRAMMY HAD THE radio tuned to the early news when Junior entered the kitchen with the morning edition of the paper in hand. The Stanton murder was the lead story once again. This time the front page featured Ruby beside an older picture of her mother. Junior was struck by the resemblance. Mother and daughter were almost interchangeable. If not for the age of the photo of Elizabeth, you would assume they were twins.

A quick scan of the newspaper article revealed nothing new. The Chief had apparently squashed any desire to leak further information. Not that they had anything worth leaking. Nothing but loose threads. Junior would be surprised if the motive was anything other than jealousy, but he tried not to let his mind settle there. To do so could lead to assumptions and assumptions most often led down blind alleys.

He gave a nod of thanks and drank the coffee his grandmother placed before him as he quickly scanned the sports section for the baseball scores. The weatherman was predicting another hot day with temperatures in the low nineties. It was only the second week of June.

"Such pretty girls," his grandmother said with a sigh as she picked up the front page of the paper and settled across the table from him. "What a shame."

⁂

HUGO WOKE TO the sound of hammering. The Beatles were singing about Monday's child. He put on his clean shirt and tie. From the bedroom window, he could see his neighbor banging away at his porch step. He pulled on his sports coat and grabbed his car keys on the way out the door.

Maurice stopped hammering as Hugo crossed the empty lot between their houses.

"Heard you were working that murder at the Thunderbird."

"Where'd you hear that?"

"Reporter. Snooping 'round. Askin' questions." He grinned exposing a gold capped tooth. "You famous, you know." Then he laughed.

Hugo grinned. "You know what they say about fame. Here today, gone tomorrow." The grin faded. "Did the reporter have a name?"

"Sho' did. The one made you famous. That Donahue."

The last thing Hugo wanted was a reporter dogging his footsteps. Pete Donahue was tenacious. And very good at his job. "You didn't tell him anything, did you?"

"What I'm gone tell him? That you drink too much and got no style?" Maurice's gaze traveled the length of Hugo. "Everybody know that."

HUGO DISCOVERED JUNIOR was already at the station when he topped the stairs to the detectives' bullpen.

"What's up?"

Junior looked up from the city directory open on his desk. "Looking for Alma."

"Who's that?"

"According to Boo, his girlfriend. Sort of."

"Sort of? He has a girlfriend?"

"It seemed to be a surprise to him, too." He closed the heavy book with a soft thud. "Seems he only realized that was her status when I asked him about her late yesterday." He gave Hugo the details of his interview with Boo.

"So is she? His girlfriend?"

"Don't know. She lives over in Birdville. Got that pearl of wisdom from the dispatcher at Spanish Fort PD this morning. Seems Alma moved to this side of the bay over a year ago. Works at the telephone company. Thought I might find an address but there's no phone listed or anything in the directory."

"Only a year. She won't show up until the next edition. Why did she move from Spanish Fort?"

"The job, I guess."

"And Boo's decision to apply with Mobile."

Junior nodded. "Possibly."

"You think there's something there?"

"I won't know 'til I talk to her, but it seems a little far-fetched."

"You're probably right. It's going to be someone closer to Ruby's orbit."

"I'd say Boo was pretty close."

"But not a maybe, maybe not, girlfriend."

"Jealousy is a strange animal."

"True."

Junior stared off across the bullpen. "I wouldn't discount it."

Hugo glanced up at something he heard in Junior's voice. "I won't. See if you can find out how long Alma's been in the picture. But I think something else is going on."

"Like what?"

"Can't put my finger on it. Something feels off about the whole situation."

"Murder is about as off as you can get."

Hugo grunted. "Dixie came by the motel last night. Late."

"Yeah? How late?"

"About two in the morning."

"What were you doing there at that hour?"

"Fell asleep. Woke up to find her standing over me."

"What did she want?"

"Said she saw the lights on and my car. Just stopped by to say hello."

"Jesus, Hugo! She's a suspect. At the very least she's a witness."

Hugo grinned. "Keep your shirt on. She came for something. I think it was the notebook in the desk drawer."

"Did she get it?"

"It wasn't there after she left."

"Huh."

"Dickie could have taken it. He was there stewing for a several hours."

"Why would he take it? It was personal. You know. Female stuff."

Hugo laughed. "Yeah, I know. A record of her monthly. But what if it wasn't?"

Junior frowned and gave this some thought. "What else could it be?"

"It's a record of something, for sure. Something that happened like clockwork."

"I don't know, Hugo. I think it is what it is. Besides, she wrote Sully under one of the dates. Like a record of— you know."

Hugo caught Junior by the scuff of his neck and gave him a gentle shake as he grinned. "The rhythm method, you mean?" He thought about it. "Could be." He picked up the pink message slips on his desk and read through them. "What's on your agenda today?"

"I'll head over to the phone company and see if I can find Alma. See if that points me in any particular direction."

"On a Saturday?"

"They're open 'til noon."

"Good. It would be nice to eliminate someone from the list of possibles. I'm going to see what I can find out about Dubya. Then I have the autopsy at nine. I'll have my radio with me."

"You think Dubya's involved somehow?"

"I think he didn't hear a gunshot in the dead of night from forty feet away."

IT DIDN'T PROVE too difficult to get the low down on Dubya. The Atlanta police department was enjoying that Saturday morning lull after the usual Friday night bar room brawls, knifings, and domestic violence calls. Things wouldn't heat up again until late in the day.

The detective Hugo spoke with was familiar with W. A. Roth. He ran a pawn shop on Decatur Street at Five Points. There had been the usual brushes with the law over possible fencing of stolen property, but nothing had stuck. The detective was surprised to discover Dubya enjoyed deep sea fishing. He wouldn't have figured him for it.

Hugo had the detective fax him the file on Dubya. Nothing of any significance popped out at him as he read through nearly a dozen incident reports. Atlanta PD hadn't been able to bring a charge in any of them. Hugo leaned back in his chair staring into space. No matter what angle he viewed it from, this new knowledge didn't lend itself to any scenario Hugo could come up with. Still, Dubya was a fish out of water as far as the investigation went. He sighed, glanced at his watch. He figured he had just enough time for breakfast before the autopsy.

Hugo gassed up the Thunderbird at the intersection of Broad and Government before turning west toward Holcombe Avenue and the Tiny Diny. The coffee was hot and the grits and eggs filling.

Chief Goode pulled into the parking lot as Hugo exited the diner. He saw the moment of hesitation when the Chief recognized the Thunderbird.

Hugo waited as the Chief shifted his car into park and climbed out.

"August."

"Chief."

"You looking for me?"

"Not particularly. Just getting some breakfast."

"Anything new I should know about?"

"No. How about you?"

"What's that supposed to mean?"

"Well, I guess it means you're the Chief of Police, you're Stanton's good buddy. I hear one of his men applied for a position with the department last year. You want to tell me about that?"

"News to me. A lot of people apply for jobs with the city. That's personnel's patch."

There was something in the Chief's eyes. A look of satisfaction that almost, but not quite, transitioned into a smile. Hugo lifted his chin in acknowledgment. "Enjoy your breakfast," he said as he opened the driver's door of the Thunderbird and slid onto the seat.

The Chief did smile then as he slammed the door of his car and headed toward the diner.

The exchange confirmed what Hugo already knew. Something heavy was about to go down and Hugo and Junior would be in the crosshairs. He sat with the Thunderbird idling as he watched Goode disappear through the door of the diner. Why had the Chief failed to send promised staff to the motel after the initial search of the crime scene wrapped up? He should have been eager to have eyes and ears in the heart of the investigation. Why was he suddenly so hands off? What did Goode know that Hugo didn't?

He glanced down at his watch and cursed under his breath. It was five minutes to nine.

*

EVIE WAS LOITERING in the hallway outside the autopsy room when Hugo arrived at Mobile General Hospital. He glanced at the clock over the door. It was fourteen minutes after nine.

"He still giving your grief about attending?"

She gave Hugo a rueful smile. "I decided it would save an argument if I waited to go in with you."

"Come on, then." He pushed the door open, and they entered the inner sanctum of Dr. Allen, Medical Examiner.

Allen paused in his dictation as he glanced up from Ruby's body on the autopsy table. His gaze flitted from Hugo to Evie and back. He said nothing but the creases on his forehead deepened in disapproval. He cleared his throat then placed a folded white sheet over the lower half of Ruby's body as he moved on to the gunshot wound just to the left of her sternum.

Before touching the wound, he took several photos from different angles using a high-powered flash. There was very little blood around the entry point. After swabbing it, Allen inserted a thin rod into the bullet hole to measure the depth. The only sound in the stark, sterile room was that of his voice as he continued to dictate into a microphone suspended overhead and the metallic clink of his instruments.

When Allen opened the chest cavity, Hugo stole a glance

at Evie. She was pale, but focused, never turning away from the gruesome procedure.

The bullet, lodged in Ruby's heart, had fragmented. Death would have been instantaneous.

Allen was very thorough with the rest of the procedure, examining organs, taking samples. Once he had finished his examination, his assistant stepped forward to do the closure. As he began to strip off his gloves and gown, Hugo asked, "Anything we should know that isn't obvious?"

Dr. Allen looked over his glasses at Hugo. "There's scarring to the upper vagina. It appears to be old, suggesting trauma at an early age." He glanced at Evie, clearly uncomfortable with discussing the topic in front of her. "The extent of the scarring suggests repeated trauma over time." He stuffed his dirty scrubs into a container. "Whether or not that has any bearing on your case is for you to determine." Then he turned to face Hugo and Evie. "Never be late to another autopsy. I won't tolerate it." His face was as stony as his voice. "The dead deserve better than that." With that, he brushed past them and through the doors of the operating room.

Hugo looked down at Evie. She was staring at the swinging doors still in motion from the force of Allen's departure. Her face was flushed, her eyes bright.

"It's my fault," Hugo said.

Evie swallowed and shook her head. "I shouldn't have been such a coward." She didn't look at Hugo. Instead, she turned back to the autopsy table and waited patiently as the assistant continued working on the corpse.

"Come on," Hugo said. "I'll give you a ride back to the lab."

She shook her head. "I'll wait for the paperwork and the bullet."

He recognized the stubborn set of her jaw. Evie's petite stature and her dark framed glasses made her appear vulnerable, but she was fierce. Her reputation meant everything to her. A wave of regret washed over him. He should have been on time.

Sixteen

ALMA WORKED THE reception desk at the phone company. When Junior showed his badge and asked to speak to her, the color drained from her face.

"Why?"

"You're a friend of Boo Vansant?"

"Yes."

Junior looked around the reception area. "Can we talk somewhere more private?"

She swallowed and rose from her chair. "I'll have to get someone to man the desk."

"You do that."

He waited while she disappeared behind a door to her left. She was back within a couple of minutes. They stepped outside and crossed the street to the bench at the bus stop in front of the Downtown Theater. She sat on the edge of the seat and watched Junior.

"Relax," he said. "I don't bite."

"Is Boo in trouble?"

"No."

"It's about Ruby, isn't it?"

"Yes. She and Boo have known each other a long time."

"Since they were little."

"We're talking to everyone who was close to her."

"He was with me."

Junior didn't say anything for a couple of seconds. "When was he with you?"

"When Ruby died."

"And here I was thinking he was with the Chief."

Alma's face turned pink. Her eyes were bright with the threat of tears.

"Do you know when Ruby died?" Junior asked.

"Thursday night."

He looked across the street at the entrance to Bell Telephone and Telegraph Company, giving Alma a moment to collect herself. "Do you work every Saturday?"

The change of subject caught her off guard.

"What?"

"Do you routinely work on Saturday?"

"Every other Saturday. 'Til noon. Then the office closes until Monday morning."

"How do you like living in Mobile?"

"Okay, I guess. There's a lot more to do and the bus can take you anywhere you need to go. That's nice."

"What about where you live? Birdville, isn't it?"

She nodded and sat back against the bench. "My mama says it used to be a nicer place to live when she was young but it's okay. She worries too much."

"Your mother's from Mobile?"

"Yes. When she and Daddy got married they moved to Spanish Fort."

"So you grew up with Ruby, too."

Alma frowned. "Yes."

"Were you friends?"

"I guess. When we were little. But not since seventh grade."

"What changed?"

"Nothing, really. She just didn't seem to be around anymore. We had different classes starting that year."

"What about Boo? Were they still friends?"

"I don't know. Not that I remember."

"But they had been good friends?"

She nodded. "Yes. He lived down the road from her and they were always together, riding bikes, going down to the creek, fishing."

"What changed?"

Alma sat silently as she stared down at the skirt of her dress where she nervously pleated the fabric with her right hand. "Boys."

"Why did Ruby and Boo fight?"

"She wanted to hurt him."

"Why?"

"Because he loves her."

※

IT WAS A quarter to eleven as Hugo drove across the Causeway. The traffic was typical of a Saturday morning. The parking lot of the Sea Ranch, Judy Fohl's favorite watering hole, was beginning to fill with early diners. He really should talk to her and get the dirt of Dickie Leeton. Why was a member of the Harris clan stuck running a seedy motel in no man's land? If anyone knew, it would be Judy.

He pulled into the parking lot of The Thunderbird Inn and studied the façade. Everything about it looked tired. It wasn't the kind of place that would entice a passing motorist to stop for the night unless he was desperate. Dickie claimed they made money off the bar and restaurant. Hugo didn't see how that was possible. Break-even would be more likely, if that. So what was the inducement to keep the doors open?

The foyer had a staleness to it when he unlocked the door. He went straight to the office and began a search of it, opening the drawers of the file cabinet, searching through all the files, even pulling it from the wall to inspect behind it. Once he had moved all the sparse furnishings and found nothing but dust, he sat at the desk.

He opened the guest register and worked his way back for three months. Occupancy had been a slow trickle. None of the names on the register were repeated over that time frame. He sat back in the desk chair and thought about that for a couple of minutes. Suddenly, he sat forward and paged through the book again. It wasn't what was there that was the anomaly. It was what wasn't there. He looked over the last few days again. Nowhere in the list did he find the name of W. A. Roth. Neither was Ruby or Mr. Smith or any entry that could have fit them.

He could well imagine that the motel didn't worry overly much about recording their guests. It was a place for nooners to slip away from Mobile and dally for an hour or two. Quick and easy and back at work before their absence from the office was noted.

So why did he feel that that wasn't the answer to the niggling sense of something missed? Something out of kelter?

He turned his attention to the desk. He emptied out each of the drawers and examined the contents. He saved Dixie's private stash until last. None of the items held any significance. He lined them up and sat back in the chair. It was the notebook that had been worthy of a locked drawer. Did a woman's cycle dictate that degree of privacy? He didn't think so.

He got up and walked out across the foyer, staring out the glass door of the entry at the roadway and marsh grasses beyond. Was the motel more than a convenience for local businessmen and their mistresses? Was Ruby, in fact, a working girl? Her lover had acted surprised that she'd been at the motel when she was shot. A feigned reaction? Or did she meet men regularly as part of the age-old profession? If so, Dickie and Dixie were involved. Had there been a falling out?

Hugo sighed and returned to the office. He began returning the items to Dixie's special drawer. The last item was the neat row of cigarette packs. Six, all lined up on their narrow sides, the bottoms facing Hugo. That's when it all clicked into place. He got up from the chair and went into the kitchen. The pack of Marlboros was still sitting on the counter. He returned to the office and lined the bent pack up with the others.

Two years in 'Nam had taught him a couple of things.

That the beer in the rear was plentiful and cold. And that the one staple of bush deliveries was the Army's special treat to troops in the field. Cigarettes. All of which lined up exactly like these. Their pristine packaging lacking the little blue stamp of any taxing authority. Uncle Sam didn't have to pay state taxes, but the good citizens of Alabama did.

Dickie was selling untaxed cigarettes. Probably with Dixie's help.

He went to the bar in the restaurant of the motel and let his gaze travel over the bottles lining the shelves. He'd bet his last dollar that none of it had passed under the watchful eye of the tax man.

He could call in the feds but he didn't want them trampling all over his crime scene. Not yet, anyway.

⁂

WHEN HUGO PULLED up to Elizabeth Stanton's house, he saw a Spanish Fort cruiser parked in the driveway on the west side. The scent of fresh mowed grass assailed him as he stepped out of his car. His knock was answered by Buzz Stanton in Bermuda shorts, undershirt, and socks. The top of his socks were flecked with bits of cut grass. He said nothing, simply gestured with a jerk of his head toward the interior of the house, and left Hugo to follow after him.

In the kitchen, Stanton took a pitcher of tea from the refrigerator and topped off a glass sitting on the counter. He lifted the container toward Hugo who shook his head.

"So," Stanton said. "What's happening?"

"I need to speak with Mrs. Stanton."

He shook his head. "Can't. Not today."

"Why not?"

"She's asleep."

"Seems like she's always asleep."

"It's the valium."

"She must take a lot of it."

"What do you expect? Her child's dead."

"That's why I need to speak to her."

"Maybe tomorrow."

Hugo eyed Stanton for a couple of heartbeats. "How about later today."

Stanton shook his head. "I don't think so."

"Well, I do."

Stanton placed the glass of tea on the counter and leaned back against it, his arms crossed over his chest. "I don't think you understand." His expression was as hard as chiseled stone. "I say when and if you talk to Beth."

"If?"

"If."

Hugo touched the knot of his tie. "Ruby's dead. I need to know what was happening in her life."

"I already told you."

"And you know everything going on with her, is that it?"

"Pretty much."

"Huh." Hugo lifted his chin. "Tell me again what your relationship is to Ruby? Her uncle, is it?"

"Cousin, actually. Not that it's any of your business."

"And here I was thinking you wanted to find the killer and bring him to justice."

"Oh, I'll find the killer."

"All by your lonesome?"

"That would be the best case scenario."

"Not a good idea."

"You let me worry about that."

"We'll see," Hugo said as he turned and made his way back along the hallway to the front door. When he slid onto the seat of the Thunderbird, he saw the curtain in the front room on the left side of the house twitch and caught a glimpse of red-gold hair.

Hugo hated being lied to. He *really* hated it.

∗∗∗

ABOUT A QUARTER mile from Elizabeth Stanton's house, the road made a sharp curve. Hugo glimpsed a break in the tree line. A red dirt road intersected the paved street at a sharp angle near the apex. He braked and backed the Thunderbird into the deeply shaded, narrow lane.

Nearly forty-five minutes later he decided Stanton must have taken a different route. He reached for the key to start the car just as the police cruiser came speeding around the curve. It disappeared from view in a matter of seconds. He waited a few minutes to be sure he hadn't been seen by Stanton in the cruiser's rearview mirror.

∗∗∗

ELIZABETH WAS A long time answering the door. Hugo thought his vigil had been for nothing, that she must be in a deeply drugged sleep, when the door finally opened a few inches.

"Yes?"

"Do you remember me, Mrs. Stanton?"

She nodded, her face framed in the narrow opening, her hand tightly clutching the lapels of a floral dressing gown high at her throat, her red-gold hair caught up in a loose knot on top of her head. Damp tendrils curled around her face and neck, the scent of soap perfumed the air.

"Can I come in?"

Beth looked beyond Hugo at the roadway. She blinked slowly a couple of times. "Where's Buzz?" she asked, her gaze fixed on the street.

"I don't know."

Her forehead creased in a slight frown. She seemed to be making an effort to comprehend his words.

"I really need to speak with you. About Ruby."

She studied his face. It was as if she couldn't quite take him in, was struggling to understand what his presence meant. Then she stepped aside as she opened the door. He followed her as she moved slowly in an unsteady path toward the living room where he had previously spoken with Nora Stanton.

"I see the Chief mowed the yard."

"Did he?" she asked as she sat on the sofa facing away from the view out the bay windows. She watched Hugo, her eyelids heavy, her speech slow.

"Why didn't Ruby return to the university for her sophomore year?"

"Henry died."

"Her father?"

The hand clutching the lapels of her gown moved higher, tightening the fabric into a knot. Her gaze wandered around the room never quite focusing. Hugo waited but there was no response. Stanton had been right, after all. Ruby's mother had removed herself from the horror of the past thirty-six hours.

"Is there someone who can be with you, Mrs. Stanton?"

Her eyes brightened with the threat of tears. "There's no escaping. There never has been."

"I don't think you should be alone."

A sad smile briefly touched her lips, and she shook her head. "I'm never alone."

Just then, they heard the slamming of a car door. Hugo's gaze moved from the despair in Elizabeth's eyes to the view out the bay window. Nora Stanton stood staring at Hugo's car then crossed the lawn toward the house. When he looked back at Elizabeth, she had turned and was watching as well.

"She knows."

"Knows what?" he asked.

She made no reply.

⚜

NORA STANTON STOPPED in the opening into the living room and looked from Hugo to Elizabeth.

"Everything all right?"

Hugo stood as she entered the room. "Just asking some questions about Ruby."

"Did you get the answers?"

"You never know what's of value until it is or isn't."

"I see." She crossed the room to the couch were Elizabeth sat. "Here, Beth. Let's get you dressed."

Elizabeth smoothed her hand along the silky fabric of her dressing gown as if suddenly aware of what she was wearing. At the touch of Nora's hand on her arm, she stood and shot a quick side-eye in her direction. "Yes." With her free hand she touched her hair, sweeping the loose damp curls upward. "I should get dressed."

Nora took her arm. "Careful. You know the medicine makes you unsteady."

Elizabeth made no response as she grasped the material of her robe more tightly in her fist and moved toward the doorway.

As they turned into the hall, Nora looked back over her shoulder. "You can see yourself out, Detective August?"

"Sure."

⁂

HUGO STOOD ON the small front porch and stared across the lawn to where his car was parked on a brick apron between the manicured lawn and the street. Abruptly, he cleared the two shallow steps and turned toward the driveway and the detached garage at the rear of the house.

A 1964 Dodge Dart sat off-center of the space allowing a small area about five feet wide with a workbench running the length of wall. The lawnmower was tucked away at the rear. Though it bore the faint scent of cut grass and gasoline, it was free of any debris and dirt. A brown peg-board mounted on the wall above the bench held a variety of tools. They hung like pieces of a puzzle in a maze created with a black marker outlining each one. Nothing was out of place. Every item was polished and neat.

Beside the garage and toward the back, a rusty early fifties Ford truck sat in the shade of an oak tree. At one time it had been red but was now faded to an orangey color. Hugo walked around it. An attempt had been made at restoring it at some point in time, but the effort had given way to the elements. The bed held a variety of odds and ends, tools, old polishing rags, a baseball cap well weathered from the elements. The cab wasn't any neater. Candy wrappers, a baseball, and a bright blue toy sailboat about a foot long. He opened the door and picked up one of the candy wrappers. The scent of cherry clung to the paper. He lifted the sailboat and studied it. Someone had fashioned a sleek vessel with a tall mast. But the paint job suggested a child's project. The bright blue was unevenly applied and a smudge much like a fingerprint marred the bow. He replaced it on the seat of the truck.

Hugo climbed the stairs to Ruby's apartment. The door was unlocked. He stood in the doorway and surveyed the room. The bed bore no evidence that Nelson had been there the day before mourning his friend. All the books were stacked on the bottom shelf of the nightstand, their spines aligned. Ruby's paints and potions on her dressing table had been neatly grouped, her brush and hand mirror angled together just so. The towels in the bathroom were folded and draped to hang evenly. A woman's touch, Hugo decided. But who? Elizabeth? Or Nora?

Nelson was swinging under a pecan tree in his back yard as Hugo closed the door to the apartment. He walked between the bushes of the row of bridal wreath that formed a loose boundary between the two houses.

"Hey, Nelson."

"Hey." He began to twist around and around in the swing.

"Everything okay?"

Nelson lifted his feet and the twisted ropes quickly unraveled spinning him as his head dropped back with the force of the movement.

"That looks like fun."

"Yeah."

"Did Ruby like to swing?"

"She pushed me high."

"You like swinging high?"

"Yeah."

Hugo moved behind the swing and pulled it back. "Hold tight," he said, and he gave it a push.

Nelson laughed and threw his head back as Hugo pushed him higher and higher. Finally, he let the swing slow of its own momentum.

"That's fun. Do it again."

"I can't right now. I have to go to work."

"To find who shot Ruby."

"Yes."

"Will you come back?"

"When I can." Hugo placed a hand on Nelson's shoulder. "Do you swing out here a lot?"

Nelson nodded.

"Do you see people come to visit Ruby?"

He nodded again.

"Who comes to visit Ruby?"

"The police."

"Anyone else?"

"You." Nelson started twisting the rope of the swing again.

"No one else?"

"Sometimes." He looked up at Hugo then lifted his feet to let the swing spin him around and around. He took a contented breath as the motion stopped. "They come in the back. In the dark."

Hugo caught the two ropes of the swing and stilled Nelson's back and forth movement. "Who comes in the dark?"

"The bogeyman."

Seventeen

HUGO CURSED UNDER his breath as he pushed through
the bridal wreath and rounded the garage. The back of
the building came within fifteen feet of a low white picket
fence that separated the Stanton property from a stand
of trees. He stepped over the fence and quickly found the
faint traces of a path leading through the woods.

The property soon began to slope gradually downward.
A hundred yards in he found the creek. At the edge of
the water where the sandy soil was free of dead leaves
and weeds, the imprint of a shoe heel was visible. One
long stride carried him across the stream and the terrain
leveled out for several feet before it began to dip steeply.
He continued to follow it down the bluff until he came to
a small strip of beach where the water emptied into the
delta. A trail on the far side of the little cove quickly began
to climb. When Hugo reached the top of it, he discovered
a dirt road beginning to give way to the encroaching vegetation. Tire treads were clearly visible in the bare soil of
a turnaround.

He walked down the lane about a quarter of a mile,
keeping to the undergrowth on one side. It appeared to

be sparsely used. He identified two different tire treads in the soft shoulders of the road. One of which had definitely been in the turnaround since the last rain. When he came to a curve he looked back. No one would see a parked car until they were upon it. And maybe not even then unless they were looking.

Hugo started jogging. It took him ten minutes to reach the highway. The dirt lane was the same one he had parked in and waited for Stanton to leave Elizabeth's. He followed the paved street back to her house. As he opened the driver's door of the Thunderbird, he saw Nora watching him from the bay window.

❧

JUNIOR LOOKED UP from the typewriter at the sound of the door of the motel closing. Hugo appeared in the entrance to the dining room, disheveled and sweating. His shoes muddy, the hem of his pants damp, covered with briars and beggar lice.

"What happened to you?"

Hugo took a couple of paper napkin from a stack on a table by the door and wiped perspiration from his forehead and along the back of his neck. "There's a hidden trail to Ruby's apartment through the woods behind the garage. Someone's been coming and going that way regularly."

"How do you know?"

"Nelson. The kid next door. He says the bogeyman comes in the dark."

"Who's the bogeyman?"

"That's what I plan to find out. Do you have that map?"

They spread the map of Spanish Fort across one end of the table they were using as a desk. With his finger, Hugo traced Hwy 31 up the hill from the Causeway then a hard left onto Spanish Main. Confederate Drive and Rebel Road were the only streets marked on the map that forked off toward the water. He placed a mark on Confederate Drive.

"This is Ruby's house right along here." He followed an unmarked ribbon of blue running through the area. "And this has to be the creek that runs down the bluff."

Junior tapped the map a short distance from there on Blakely River Road. "Boo has his camper set up about here."

"You don't say." Hugo said as he straightened.

"We already have motive, and this is clearly opportunity. Not only can Boo spy on Ruby, but he could easily take a boat across the river to the motel. The girl friend said he lived close to Ruby's house when they were kids. I doubt it was in the travel trailer, but it looks like he's been set up there for quite a while."

"I'd bet someone in Boo's family owns the land."

"That would be my guess." Junior frowned, his arms crossed, as he stared down at the map.

"What?"

He gave a dismissive shake of his head. "Nothing."

"But?"

"Don't know. Just don't get that kind of vibe, you know?" He sighed. "If you love someone so much, how could you kill them?"

"This isn't about love. I think we're dealing with a

narcissistic little bastard who can only see himself. What he wants. The kind of man who won't be denied."

"That's a little too heavy for me." Junior took his gun from his side holster and checked it. "I say we go see if Boudreau Vansant is ready for company."

"You think you'll need that?"

"Who knows. He's a cop so he's carrying. And Grammy has cold salmon croquets for supper."

"Wouldn't want to miss that," Hugo replied.

"Or the peach cobbler."

"Definitely not that."

⁂

JUNIOR TOOK THE lead down a dirt road barely wide enough for their cars to pass through the tall grass and saplings that bordered it. There wasn't a vehicle anywhere in sight. Fifty feet beyond the camper appeared to be the end of the line for this little pig trail off Blakely River Road.

The camper was vintage, to put it kindly. The sun reflected off the aluminum as they rounded it from opposite ends. The only sound was the chirping of crickets.

Both men scanned the open landscape before them. Someone, at some point in time, had cleared the land to where it began to slope toward the delta affording a breathtaking view.

Hugo approached the door from the right as Junior approached from the left. No one responded when he banged on it. After a second knock, he tried the handle. It wasn't locked. With a nod to Junior, he stepped through the door.

"No one home," Hugo said.

Junior stepped up into the cramped space. "It sure is small."

"I guess it doesn't really matter if you live alone."

The whole of the camper was, at most, six by ten feet. A bench seat with cushions ran down one side. It served as the bed. At the foot of the bench, a square table of the same depth was squeezed into place. A couple of beer bottles, a Coleman lantern, matches, and a checkbook with no checks in it littered the top. Otherwise, the place was fairly clean.

"I wouldn't really call this living." Junior opened a cupboard over the bench. It was filled with papers, books, candles.

Hugo peered into the toilet cubby. It obviously hadn't been used in a long time. Boo's clean uniform hung from a peg in the space. A box holding underwear and socks sat on the toilet lid. He let his gaze travel around the confined space.

Alone, isolated, a steady diet of beer, if the empty bottles were anything to go by. The perfect picture of a lit fuse, Junior thought.

"Where does he bathe?" He tried the faucet in a tiny sink next to a hot plate covered in dust. It didn't even gurgle. "There's no water, no power."

"The jail, maybe. Or the would-be girlfriend."

Nothing caught their interest inside the camper, so they walked down to the folding chair that faced the delta. It looked no different than the previous evening except maybe a few more beer bottles added to the collection in a bucket beside the chair. About forty yards from the chair a tree stump rose three feet. On closer inspection they discovered Boo had been using the beer bottles for target practice.

Hugo looked up at the sun. It registered about two o'clock. "This way," he nodded toward the southwest. "The creek should be in this direction."

They quickly found Boo's water source. As they followed the westerly flow, there was no evidence that anyone had traveled this way routinely. The banks of the creek became steeper and more impassible as they got deeper into the surrounding foliage.

"He must have cut across the woods. If he's lived here all his life, he knows the lay of the land." Hugo stopped in a briar thicket, seemingly oblivious to the swarming insects and the choking undergrowth.

Junior swatted at the gnats and mosquitoes buzzing around his ears, nose, and eyes. "It's a jungle in here."

"This isn't a jungle." Hugo pulled his coat sleeve free of a long twisting briar. "This is a cake walk." He turned back along the way they came. "We need a tracking dog."

Junior slapped a mosquito on the side of his neck. His mood had turned sour about a quarter of a mile down the slope. But nothing bothered Hugo. Nothing penetrated his self-containment and there were times when Junior resented it. Like now. He might not have been in the jungles of Vietnam, but this was, by God, a damn jungle. The mosquitos were eating him alive, and he was ruining his good shoes.

They forced their way back through the undergrowth.

When they reached the clearing, Junior asked, "Should we try the station?"

Hugo glanced at him, an assessing look, then leaned against the Thunderbird. He stared off toward the delta, sweat running down his face, a breeze blowing from the water. "I don't want to tip our hand. Not yet. Stanton isn't exactly anxious to do things by the book." He fell silent.

"You think he knows who did it?"

"I think he *thinks* he knows."

"So we're just chasing our tails and he's biding his time." Junior picked a briar from the sleeve of his coat and examined a long run in the fabric. "Shit."

Hugo remained silent. Finally, he said, "There should have been a path following the creek."

Junior took a pack of Marlboros from his inside sports coat pocket, lit up, and blew smoke at the gnats and mosquitos. In the clearing near the camper, the breeze severely reduced their numbers. "Wouldn't Stanton already know how close this set-up is to Ruby's house? And that the garage can be approached from the woods?"

"Yeah. He knows. He's right a home at Elizabeth's. Cut the grass this morning."

"In the middle of a murder investigation?"

Hugo grunted. "Like you said, biding his time. I think he has his sights set on Boo. That's why he told us there was nothing to see there."

"Don't *we* have our sights set on Boo?"

"Let's talk to the girlfriend again. We need a better handle on Boudreau Vansant." Hugo took off his sports coat and threw it onto the back seat of his car and checked his watch. A gust of breeze swept in from the delta, scattering the remaining insects that swarmed both men. "I need a shower. Meet me at my place in an hour. We'll double team her and see what she really knows."

"We've got weather coming."

Hugo watched the black clouds rolling in from the bay. "Then we'd better get ahead of it."

Eighteen

HUGO SLIPPED OUT of his muddy shoes on the front stoop of his house and began peeling off his sweat-soaked shirt as soon as he cleared the doorway. He was hot, tired, and frustrated. It was the let-down of knowing you'd been chasing down a rabbit hole. He felt the urgency of time lost. Time wasted. He'd been sure they were on the right track but now he didn't think so. Boo Vansant lived a solitary, lonely life, but the state of his camper hadn't been much different than Hugo's own residence. As his gaze traveled around the living room of the shotgun house, he realized anyone could draw the same conclusions about him.

As he waited for the water in the shower to heat up, he examined the welp across his ribs. His left side had turned into a spectacular array of colors from yellow to almost black. The march through the jungle hadn't helped.

But it wasn't the jungle, was it? Overgrown, full of briars, mosquitos, saplings and vines, but no bamboo that formed an impenetrable wall. No spiked pits deceptively camouflaged. No elephant grass cutting your clothes to shreds. No leeches in the stream. No land mines strategically placed on the edges of a trail. He pulled back from the image. Wouldn't let it take root.

He'd offended Junior. What had he said? He couldn't remember exactly. It hadn't been intentional, wasn't meant to be a slur on the fact Junior hadn't been in Vietnam, that he didn't know that panic of never finding your way out, finding your way home. The Arch Bishop had been right to wrangle a deferment for Junior. He hadn't lied when he stated that Junior's grandmother couldn't manage without him. Marilyn Knight was fragile. Maybe not physically, but in so many other ways. She had needed Junior. And so had the police department. No, Hugo was glad his friend had been spared.

He'd have to be more careful.

There were so many things that couldn't be said, couldn't be understood. No one who hadn't experienced it would believe it anyway. And he didn't want to visit that horror on anyone, didn't want to be pitied. None of them wanted to go there, to stir the memories, except maybe the guys in the rear with the beer with their tales of hoochie mamas and cookouts, ticking the boxes, climbing the ranks. Those men needed the war, wanted the war. But then, none of them had had to hump the boonies. None of them had tried to scoop a man's guts back into a hole in his stomach. None of them had watched a buddy disappear into a mist of blood.

Hugo stepped into the shower and pulled the makeshift curtain across the opening. The water flowed over him, washing away the sweat and grime, washing away the memories. He held the soap to his nose and inhaled.

The scent of it, the heat of the water, the sense of being clean, of being human, allowed his subconscious to sift through the day. Waiting for the thread to emerge. But today it wouldn't surface; it remained elusive, teasing at the edges of his mind.

⁂

A FORK OF lightning, followed by a loud thunderclap, pierced the sky above the huge cranes rising from the shipyard on Mobile River a few blocks east of Hugo's house on South Cedar Street. As Junior pulled up to the curb, the wind kicked up considerably. It was almost five and the weather had been threatening since he left Spanish Fort. Just as he was about to tap the horn, Hugo came out the front door and down the steps wearing an untucked shirt with a stand-up, narrow collar.

"Nice shirt," Junior said as Hugo slid onto the passenger seat. "All you need is for the collar to be white and anyone would think you're a priest."

"Nehru. The latest fashion in San Francisco, I'm told."

"Yeah? Who told you that?"

"A girl with flowers in her hair." Hugo looked in the direction of the river and another lightning flash. "It was either this or my Hawaiian shirt."

"Good decision." Junior shifted the car into gear. "I have Alma's address. Let's hope she didn't decide to go to the movies or off somewhere else once she got off work."

They hadn't traveled three blocks when large droplets of rain began to smack against the windshield. Within seconds, visibility dropped to near zero and the spray from passing cars washed against the sedan and into their path. Junior slowed to a crawl so as not to drown out the car's motor in the high water creating a river of the poorly maintained streets in this part of town as the downpour drummed against the roof.

They pulled up in front of one of the two-story apartment buildings that were known as Birdville. They'd been constructed during WWII to house personnel at Brookley Air Base and were now low rent public housing. The rain did nothing to improve the drab, tired façade of the structures or the neglected appearance of the area.

Then the rain stopped in that sudden way it had here in the subtropics. It was as if a spigot had been turned off. Water swirled along the street seeking an outlet in the old, decayed infrastructure of the city. Hugo stepped out on the passenger side onto the raised curbing. Junior opened his door and looked down into the ankle-deep flow. With a sigh, he stepped out as far as he could toward the center of the street. It didn't help. His shoes instantly filled with water. This was turning into a thoroughly shitty day, he decided.

Alma lived in the second-floor apartment in building D. Junior could hear music playing as he tapped on the door.

"You're early—," Alma swung the door open. The smile disappeared from her face and her hand went to the pink foam curlers in her hair. "Oh. It's you again."

"Yes. Me. Again."

She stepped back and gestured for Junior to enter the apartment. "I thought—" She saw Hugo.

"This is my partner, Detective August."

"I—I recognize you. From the paper." She touched her hair again and began to blush. "I wasn't expecting—well."

"You were expecting Boo," Hugo said as he stepped into the small living room. The aroma of spaghetti sauce permeated the apartment, "for supper."

She looked from Hugo to Junior and back. "Yes." Her chin came up and she directed her words at Junior. "You said he wasn't in trouble." Her tone was accusatory.

"He isn't," Hugo answered. "Yet." He looked into the tiny kitchen and lifted the lid on the pot of sauce.

"Hey!" Alma cried. "You can't do that!"

He ignored her protest and opened the refrigerator. "What's this?" He lifted out a bottle of Boone's Farm. "Celebrating?"

Alma cast a pleading look in Junior's direction.

He stood with his hands in his pockets and let Hugo do his thing. Which was probably a little more heavy-handed because of the comment about the newspaper article from their last murder case, but it wasn't quite time for him to come to the rescue.

For his lack of sympathy, Alma gave him a scowl and snatched the bottle of wine from Hugo. She returned it the refrigerator with a slam of the door, all thought of the pink curlers apparently gone from her mind as she placed her hands on her hips and glared at each of them in turn.

"How long have you and Boo been dating?" Hugo asked as he brushed past her and took a seat in the armchair in the living room.

She shrugged and crossed her arms at her waist. "A while."

"Six months? Six Years?"

"We've known each other forever."

"But?"

Alma glanced at Junior then sat on the only other chair in the room. "It's hard to say exactly. We dated a while in high school. He took me to the prom." She looked down at her hands clasped in her lap. "It's been kinda on and off."

"More off than on would be my guess."

Her eyes brightened with the threat of tears. "Why do you have to be so mean?"

"It's the truth, isn't it?" Hugo's voice was emotionless.

Junior squatted beside Alma's chair. "That's enough, Hugo."

Alma gave him a side eye glance. "Yes. It's true." Her lip trembled.

"I know what that's like," Junior said, "to love someone who doesn't love you back. To know that they love someone else. To see each glance, each longing look. It's like an arrow to your heart every time."

A tear rolled down her cheek and she turned her profile to him. "He does love me. In his own way. He just can't see it because of her."

"Ruby?"

She sniffed and straightened her shoulders. "No one could ever be happy because of her. Not Boo, not me, not her fiancé. Not even Chief Stanton. What kind of life is that? She was like—" Alma gestured wildly with her hands, "like a praying mantis, eating their hearts out but leaving them alive."

Alma looked Junior in the eye. "Don't you see? She had to die. As long as she was alive, no one could ever be happy."

No one spoke into the silence. Finally, Junior took her hand in his, gave it a gentle squeeze. "What do you mean, Alma?"

She drew a deep breath then pulled her hand away and stood. "Oh, I didn't kill her, if that's what you're thinking. Neither did Boo. He loved her too much. But I'm not sorry she's dead and that's the truth." With that, she crossed the room and opened the door. "Now, I have plans for this evening and I'd like you to leave."

Junior and Hugo did as she asked. As she was about to close the door, Junior said, "I'm sorry."

Alma's brown eyes glistened. "There's no escaping her. Not even now."

A long-remembered verse sprang to his mind, *"She has a lovely face; God in his mercy lend her grace, The Lady of Shalott."* Was Ruby Stanton the unknown curse? Or was she cursed?

☙

HUGO AND JUNIOR rode in silence as they left Birdville. After a couple of blocks, Hugo said, "Well played."

Junior gave a small grunt and kept his eyes on the road.

"Drop me at home. There's a storm in the Gulf and the weather's only going to get worse from here. There's not much more we can do tonight."

Rain began to pelt the car again and Junior turned off Broad toward Hugo's house. He cleared his throat. "I found the woman Lissa Talbot supposedly ran out of town. Her version of the gossip was very different. Said Davis tried to pick her up at a function for the Chamber of Commerce held at the Club. Lissa was drunk and caused a scene. Said she never dated him. Only knew him through a program of coastal towns promoting tourism. And she's never lived in Mobile. She's from Biloxi. Can't even recall having seen him since that event two years ago."

"The jealousy doesn't square with what Lissa told you."

"Depends, I guess. Was she just warning her off, marking her territory?"

"Either way, the question is, how far would she go to keep her husband and her lifestyle."

Junior thought about that and said, "My money says she'd do what she had to for the sake of the lifestyle. Since the husband is part of that, then we have a lot of motivation."

"And we have opportunity. She's still in the frame."

"So is the ex-fiancé. I ran the route for the emergency call Thursday night. Spoke to the staff at the hospital in Atmore. They confirm his timeline but that still leaves opportunity. He knows the territory well and he had plenty of time if Ruby was shot around two. We only have his word that he didn't swing by the Thunderbird and put a bullet in her heart."

"Risky."

"True but who would take notice of a patrol car in the early morning hours on the Causeway? That's the job."

"True."

"You interviewed him. What's your take?"

"He loved her."

"So did Boo."

⁂

HUGO SPRINTED FROM the car as the wind picked up and drove the rain at a sharp slant. The small stoop of a porch offered no protection. He dripped a trail of water to the bathroom where he peeled off his shirt and hung it over the shower rod. The towel was still damp, but he managed to get relatively dry. He returned to the living room, tuned the radio to the weather, and sat in his only chair, his head against the high back. The tropical depression had traveled up from Cuba leaving a path of flooding and high winds.

He closed his eyes as the announcer switched back to spinning platters. The Young Rascals were *Groovin'* as he tried to settle into the overstuffed, faded armchair. It had been a rough, physical day but what had him feeling restless was Junior's words to Alma. He couldn't pretend he didn't know what was at the root of Junior's compassion and understanding. Since high school Junior had been infatuated with Evie. He hadn't had the talent to hide his feelings back then and even now Hugo knew he still longed for her. The guilt of being the object of Evie's desire ate at Hugo. He had never acknowledged an awareness of her feelings and had studiously remained friendly but distant with her. None of that changed anything. The heart wanted what the heart wanted. Junior wanted Evie, Evie wanted Hugo, and Hugo wanted Bebe. No one was happy because love was cruel that way. And now, Alma wanted

Boo who had wanted Ruby who had wanted... Who had Ruby wanted?

I'VE BEEN LOVING you too, too, long to stop now... Otis Redding was bearing his soul to Hugo as the rain pounded on the tin roof. Her fragrance drifted on the air. Had he summoned her from the black pit of his loneliness? He should open his eyes. But what if it was just another hallucination, his mind once again deceiving him, teasing him with the illusion of the thing he most wanted?

Hugo slowly opened his eyes to find Bebe leaning over him, her perfume intoxicating, tendrils of her long blonde hair curling with the damp of the rain, the blue of her eyes piercing him through the heart. He reached up and pulled her forcefully to him, kissing her deeply as he pulled her into his lap, ignoring the slight resistance on her part. Running his fingers into her hair, pulling her into the kiss, tighter into his arms. Then she was kissing him. Kissing him. Kissing him.

At last, at last. They were whole, they were one. His heart sang with the feel of her, the touch of her hand on his face, the deep moan of pleasure that rose from her throat. For so long they had been apart and now, in an instant, all was right again. She was here. She had come to him. She was in his arms. It was as though they had never been apart.

The phone began ringing. It barely registered. Hugo

could think of nothing beyond her presence, here, now, in this moment. Then she was pulling away.

"Hugo—"

He kissed her again, holding her tight, ignoring the ringing. Willing it to go away. Desperate to hold on to the sensation of her.

Bebe pulled her head back. "Hugo, please. We can't—"

"Ignore it. It isn't important. Whoever it is can wait."

"Please." Bebe pushed against his chest creating a small space between. "This isn't right. We shouldn't—"

"Shh." He kissed her gently on the lips. "You're here. That's all that matters."

"We need to talk, Hugo."

"Later. We'll talk later."

Tears began to well up in her eyes. "We have to talk now." She attempted to rise from his lap, but he pulled her close.

"I've missed you so. I've missed us. Everything will be all right now. We'll work it out. But later. Now I just want to hold you. To be with you."

The phone stopped ringing.

A tear ran down Bebe's cheek. "Oh, Hugo."

"Shh." He pushed her hair back from her face, studying the curve of her lips, the arch of her brow, the slight shadows beneath her eyes. He wiped away the tear with his thumb and kissed her gently again. "Everything will be all right. I promise."

Bebe shook her head just as Hugo's police radio squawked to life with the dispatcher's voice. "Twenty-one, do you copy?"

Hugo made no move to respond.

"Hugo—"

He shook his head. "Ignore it. Someone else will respond."

"Twenty-one, do you copy?"

"You should answer," Bebe said.

"If I answer, I'll have to go."

"Twenty-one, do you copy?"

Hugo swore silently. The spell had been broken. Bebe, the dream of her, was suddenly here, in his lap, in his arms, and yet he couldn't ignore the call. It would be about the case. There was no other reason for anyone to be looking for him at this hour.

With a sigh, he eased Bebe from his lap and crossed the room to the radio. "Twenty-one," he replied.

"Request assistance to Spanish Fort police. Missing person alert."

Hugo's thoughts were instantly of Elizabeth Stanton. "That's a matter for the locals."

"Negative. Request from subject's mother. Said you'd want to know. Name of Gorton."

"Nelson." Hugo looked out the bare window at the driving rain. "How the hell did he go missing?"

"No additional details available. Only that you're needed."

"Ten-four."

Hugo looked at Bebe standing there, a touch of wind-swept glamor against the backdrop of his drab, poorly furnished room. He wanted nothing more than to stay with her. The need was a physical tightness in his chest. "I have to go."

"This can't wait, Hugo. I have to tell you."

There was something in her voice, in her eyes. He swept a lock of hair behind her ear. "Nelson will be frightened. He's slow. Mentally. He could be out in this weather. Alone." Hugo was already headed toward his bathroom, glad for the excuse while, at the same time, resentful of the need. "I have to find him." He took the damp shirt from the shower rod and pulled it on. From the armoire in his bedroom, he grabbed an old army camouflage jacket.

When he returned to the living room, he took Bebe gently by the chin and gave her a quick kiss. "We'll talk after I find him."

Bebe threw her arms around his neck and buried her face against his shoulder. "It'll be too late."

"My darling. We'll have all the time in the world." Did they? He hugged her tight, running his hands the length of her. "But right now, I have to find Nelson."

"I'm sorry." Her voice caught on a sob.

He reached up and drew her arms from around his neck. The tears on her cheeks caused a small knot of fear to settle in his chest. "Don't cry. Everything's okay now. We'll sort it out." He slipped the coat on. "I have to go." With that, he ran through the rain to the Thunderbird parked on the vacant lot next to his house. The powerful engine sprang to life and Hugo glanced at the clock. It was after midnight. The water on South Cedar Street was ankle deep when he pulled off on his way to the Bankhead Tunnel.

Nineteen

THE RAIN CAME in intermittent squalls of intensity. Waves slapped against the embankment of the Causeway spraying the side of the Thunderbird as Hugo drove through the high water over the roadway. If this kept up, it would soon become impassable.

He thought of Bebe as he fought the pull of the water on the car's tires. He should have told her to wait, to be there when he came home. The tightness had settled in his chest along with a sense of impending doom. He told himself it was because of Nelson. In his heart he knew the cause to be the look in Bebe's eyes.

Time was the problem. It had been a steady fight against the weather as Hugo topped the hill at Spanish Fort. The rain suddenly relented to a steady drizzle. He glanced at the clock. The twenty minute drive had taken twice that long. There was no need to stop in at the police station. The Gorton house would be center of the search. He turned down Spanish Main and drove straight there. It was lit up from every window as was Elizabeth Stanton's house next door. Adele Gorton opened the door before Hugo could clear the steps. Her hair and clothing were wet.

A long red scratch slashed across her cheek. She held the scruffy little dog in her arms. Both of them shivered visibly.

Hugo wiped his feet perfunctorily on the mat but there was no need. Wet footprints tracked into the foyer and all through the house. He took her elbow and steered her into the living room and the uncomfortable sofa.

"What happened?"

Adele was white around the lips. Her eyes dilated with panic. "He wasn't hungry at supper. It's the weather. The thunder frightens him. I settled him in his bed with the lamp on. He had one of his books. It helps calm him when he has something to focus on."

"What time was this?"

"About six."

"When did you discover he was missing?"

She turned her profile to him, her mouth gaping down in a grimace of pain and remorse. "It's my fault. I knew he was upset. What with Ruby—"

"Don't go there, Adele. We need to focus on finding him."

"I was reading. Trying to finish the book. Then the power went." She wiped her eyes with the back of her hand and cleared her throat. "It does that sometimes. The high winds make the pine trees rub against the power lines."

She fell silent, mindlessly rubbing the dog's ears.

Hugo waited, allowing her time to gather herself.

"I sat there in the dark. Listening for Nelson. The house was silent, so I decided he had fallen asleep."

"How long was the power out?"

She shook her head. "I don't know exactly. I hadn't been paying attention to the time. But it wasn't long. Maybe fifteen minutes. Twenty at most. I didn't bother to get the candles out. Just sat there in the dark."

She bent forward on a sob, clutching the little dog to her chest. "I should have known something was wrong. I should have felt it. I always know when Nelson's in danger." She started rocking back and forth. "But I just sat there, enjoying the quiet, that peace that comes with complete darkness."

Hugo placed his hand on her shoulder, and she looked up at him, pleading in her eyes.

"Find my boy, detective. Please find my boy."

"When did you realize he wasn't in his bed?"

"Twenty past ten. When the power came back on, I went to check on him. He's afraid of the dark." She compressed her lips tightly together and took a deep breath. "He wasn't in his bed. I checked the bathroom. All over the house. That's when I decided he must be in Ruby's apartment. He goes there sometimes. Even though I've told him he shouldn't, he still does. But he wasn't."

Silent tears began to trail down her face. "There's nowhere else he would go."

"What about next door? Would he go to the Stanton's?"

"Never. He'd be too afraid to go there."

"Why?"

She gave a small shake of her head. "He's developed an irrational fear of the Stanton house. It started a couple of years ago. He never goes there."

"But you checked?"

She nodded. "Every inch of the house, the garage. Everywhere. Buzz has had his men checking every house in the area, the woods behind us, down to the creek." She buried her face in her hands. "Everywhere," she cried on a low sob.

Where would Nelson go? Hugo thought back over his conversations with the man-child. He loved Ruby. That would be the logical place to hide if he was afraid. He would seek refuge there. But he was afraid of the thunder. And the dark. And the bogeyman.

What would make him leave the safety of his bed? Of his home?

Ruby.

But Ruby was dead.

⁂

IN NELSON'S ROOM, Hugo found the copy of *The Tales of Br'er Rabbit* which told him Nelson had been in Ruby's apartment at some time after noon on Saturday. The urgency of the situation made him take a deep breath and slow down, study the room. Toy planes, trucks, and trains were scattered about the floor. Other story books lined the shelves of a bookcase in a haphazard fashion. Nelson's tennis shoes were behind the bedroom door.

A deafening clap of thunder followed by a lightning bolt drew Hugo's attention to Nelson's bedroom window. The sky above Ruby's apartment lit up for a long, drawn-out moment as the lightning danced in the night sky above the garage. Hugo found himself staring straight into the lighted interior of Ruby's apartment through the open lacey curtains. This, then, was Nelson's view. Had something he saw there drawn him from the safety of his bed?

In the hamper in the bathroom, he found the clothes Nelson had been wearing when he played on the swing in the back yard. The room held the scent of soap and shampoo.

Adele hovered in the hallway as Hugo made his way throughout the house.

"When did Nelson take his bath?"

"Before the rain came. A little after five, I guess."

"What was he wearing?"

"Pajamas. Blue, with sailboats on them. His favorite."

"Shoes?"

"His sneakers, I guess." Adele went into Nelson's room and checked the closet. "His Sunday shoes are here, and he doesn't like slippers."

Hugo closed the bedroom door behind them as they returned to the cramped hallway. "Let's keep the room undisturbed, okay?"

Adele's face went white. "Why?"

He chose his words carefully. "The book he was reading. It's from Ruby's apartment. There may be other clues that can lead us to where and why he left the house. I don't want anyone moving anything."

"But Buzz and his men have been through the room already."

"Sometimes you don't know what you're seeing until events reveal their significance." He didn't want Adele to discover the sneakers. It would only increase her fear for Nelson to know that wherever he was, he was barefooted.

"I'd like to keep the room exactly as Nelson left it until we bring him home."

He could tell his words didn't reassure her, but it was the best he could do. He didn't want further contamination of the evidence because in his gut, he knew Nelson hadn't left the safety of his bed of his own will.

⁂

HUGO STOOD IN the drizzling rain looking through the open door into Ruby's apartment. Two sets of wet shoe-prints were clearly visible on the wooden floor. The smaller one he decided would be Adele. The larger boot prints led straight across the wooden floor to the bathroom. They were much too big to be Nelson's. Hugo followed them. The toilet seat was up with wet prints on either side of the bowl. Whoever had left them had then crossed the room to the armchair and sat. Stanton? He would be the one to search Ruby's apartment, not one of his men. He would be the one to take a piss in her toilet then make himself at home in her armchair. Why had he done that? Taking the time to sit in her chair, in her space. Marking it. Especially under the circumstances and the urgency of the moment.

Hugo felt the rage building. He surveyed the room. Everything else was as it had been the day before except for a slight misalignment of the children's books on the bedside table. Nelson hadn't lingered in the room. He had taken the book, his favorite book, and returned home.

From the apartment, Hugo went to Elizabeth's house. Nora answered his knock, her damp hair combed back from her face, the shoulders of her blouse darkened by the rain.

"I want to see her," he said as he pushed past her. "Where is she?"

Nora closed the door and followed him down the hallway. "In the kitchen."

Elizabeth sat at the table, a half empty cup of coffee before her. "What news?"

She was fully dressed, and the most clear-eyed Hugo had seen her. He shook his head. "Nothing yet."

"Poor little simple boy."

"Nelson is a man, full grown, and all that implies. Did Ruby ever feel threatened by him, did he ever make any sexual advances?"

"No!" Elizabeth drew back at the thought. "He would never."

"Are you sure? Would she tell you?"

"Yes, I'm sure. Whatever his urges might have been, Ruby knew how to handle him. She could tell him things, make him understand."

"Did someone else misinterpret their relationship? Would he be jealous?"

"What are you asking?"

"I want to know who would take a simple boy from his bed in the dead of night in this kind of weather knowing he was terrified of the dark and the thunder." Hugo fought to keep the rage from his voice. "I want to know who would terrorize him this way."

"No one. He ran away. Maybe he was upset because

of Ruby. I don't know. Something made him go out into the night."

"That's a lie." This time he made no attempt to reign in his feelings. "You've lived next door to him his whole life. He was Ruby's shadow. You know he wouldn't go willingly. I'm sick and tired of being lied to. I want the truth."

Nora abandoned her stance by the doorway and advanced into the kitchen. "That's enough. Beth can't possibly know what would motivate the boy to run away. No one could know what was in his mind. Have you ever talked to him? He was simple."

Hugo ignored Nora. He kept his eyes squarely on Elizabeth. "You see him from this window. See him playing in the yard, on the swing. Know that he goes to her apartment." He studied her. "What else do you see? Huh? Who else comes and goes in the night? Who's the bogeyman?"

"Now just a minute." Nora moved behind Elizabeth's chair. "You can't come in here and badger her like this. She's just lost her child. Another is missing. This will get us nowhere."

"Get your raincoat," he said to Elizabeth.

"What? No." Nora placed a hand on her shoulder, keeping her in her chair. "That's enough. She's not going anywhere. The medication, it makes her unsteady. Buzz won't allow it."

"Buzz isn't here. And Mrs. Stanton appears to be feeling quite clear headed." He rounded the table and caught Elizabeth's arm. "We'll manage without the raincoat. It's barely a drizzle now."

Nora grabbed his arm. "You can't take her out in this weather."

"Watch me."

Elizabeth had yet to say a word. She rose to her feet and leaned on Hugo's arm as they left the kitchen.

"I'm calling Buzz," Nora yelled after them.

Hugo ignored her. At the front door, he took off his jacket and placed it around Elizabeth's shoulders. Still supporting her, he guided her around the house and up the stairs to Ruby's apartment.

She hesitated in the doorway, then stepped over the threshold. "It's so pretty. So like Ruby."

"When was the last time you were in the apartment, Mrs. Stanton?"

She gave a faint shake of her head. "Not since Henry died. April. 1967."

"Over two years. That's a long time. Why?"

Elizabeth blinked rapidly several times. "She needed her privacy. She'd been away at school. His death—"

Hugo felt a tremor run through her and he guided her to the armchair.

She sat but didn't release her grip on his hand as he knelt beside her. "I wasn't myself. Not for a long time. The medicine—" her voice trailed off.

"Is that when you started taking valium?"

"My guilty little secret." She looked at him then away. "Why did you bring me out here?"

"You said you were never alone. I thought you might like to be. Just for a bit."

"And you could ask your questions in private."

"Yes."

"Then you had better ask them while you have the chance."

"Tell me about Nelson."

She sat back in the chair. "He's always a sweet boy. Ruby loved him, protected him from the bullies. He never went to school after his first year. Nora tried to help him, but his abilities are so limited. It's difficult for him to focus, to retain things no matter how many times you go over them. He loved Henry. When he was about seven, his father left them. Adele has had to cope on her own all these years. I think that's why Nelson followed Henry around like a puppy." She gave Hugo's hand a light squeeze. "Poor, poor little lost boy. But he always has a smile on his face, loves animals. His pet chicken died the year after— After Ruby came home. It broke his heart."

"Did you see him yesterday, after I left?"

"It's yesterday already?" Her brow furrowed and a vacant look settled over her features.

"Mrs. Stanton."

She looked at him and blinked.

"Did you see him?"

"Yes. I went to the kitchen for a glass of water. He was swinging all by himself in their back yard."

"Did you see anyone else come and go yesterday afternoon?"

Her shook her head slowly, a look of concentration on her face. "No. Nora was here. Buzz came late in the day. Before the storm but he didn't stay."

"Has Nora been here the whole time?"

Again, her brow furrowed. "Yes. I think so. I had a nap in the afternoon then Buzz gave me my medicine." She gave Hugo a quick glance. "I didn't swallow it, just pretended to be asleep so I could be alone in my room. I lay there, listening to the storm."

"Does Buzz always give you the medicine?"

"No. Just sometimes. When he knows I need it."

"But you take it at other times?"

"Yes."

"Why didn't you take it this afternoon?"

She remained silent for several seconds. "I have decisions to make. I'll have to be careful now. Nora knows."

"Why don't you just tell Buzz you don't want the medicine?"

She turned her profile to him. "I can't do that. It would upset him."

Hugo studied her a moment. "What happens when Buzz is upset?"

She made no reply then they heard the slamming of car doors and the baying of hounds.

Twenty

"WHAT THE HELL are you doing here," Stanton demanded as Hugo came down the stairs of Ruby's garage apartment.

"Nelson's mama called me."

Stanton glared at Hugo. "Why?"

"Maybe because I like Nelson and he likes me." Hugo kept his voice level, bit back the desire to lay the Spanish Fort Police Chief out flat of his back with one raging upper cut. The man was a bully. Elizabeth Stanton was afraid of him. His wife probably was as well. Had Ruby been fearful, too?

The tracking hound pulled at the lead Stanton was holding, baying loudly.

"I can't see how you'll be any help. You don't know the lay of the land."

"The more searchers, the better the chances."

Stanton looked like he wanted to object to this logic but after a moment he turned his attention to the dog and the tee shirt one of his men brought from the Gorton house.

Hugo saw Adele standing on her porch, her little dog still clutched in her arms. He knew what she was feeling. The guilt of being weary of the constant care of a man-child like Nelson, the regret of having given in to the relief of the quiet darkness, of having relaxed in her constant vigil. And if the search for him ended as Hugo feared it would, she would be crushed under a lifetime of self-flagellation because of that single lapse in vigilance.

The only thing he could do for her was find Nelson. He didn't intend to be left out of the search. He couldn't let his gut feeling that Nelson hadn't left the safety of his bed on his own cloud his thoughts.

Where would he go if something had frightened him or enticed him? Mentally he ran through all he had gleaned about the young man.

The apartment was the obvious first choice. If not there, then where? What had Alma said? That he followed Ruby and Boo everywhere they went when they were kids. They were the three Musketeers.

Hugo scanned the small gathering of men until his gaze fell on Boudreau Vansant. He sprinted the twenty feet between them in a few long strides and grabbed Boo by the front of his shirt.

"Where would he go?" he growled.

"Hey!" Boo pulled free as he fought to maintain control of an agitated hound. "What the hell's wrong with you?"

"If anyone knows what Nelson would do, it's you. He was your shadow."

"We were kids! That was years ago. He always wanted to tag along, and Ruby let him. Around the neighborhood, in the woods, down to the creek."

"To the bay?"

"Sometimes. His ma didn't like him near the water."

Hugo stared at the Gorton house. What had he seen? Something tickled at the edge of memory. The toy boat in Henry Stanton's old red pick-up. Nelson's pajamas.

"He liked the boats, didn't he?"

"Yeah. Got all beside himself, squealing and running up and down the beach."

Thunder rumbled in the distance. Hugo glanced around at the chaos of dogs, men, the bobbing of flashlights in the darkness. The dogs seemed to be caught in a loop of the Gorton's yard, porch, a path to Ruby's door, and then repeat.

"Bring the hound. We need to see if we can track him to the creek."

"He wouldn't go there. Not on his own. At night." The hound whined and tugged on the lead. "Besides, we've already searched there."

"In the rain and dark. He could have fallen; he could be hurt. Or hiding."

Boo looked to where the Chief was directing men with dogs, setting them out in different directions.

"Forget the Chief. We're wasting time." Hugo grabbed the lead and pulled the hound in the direction of the garage. He didn't bother to look to see if Boo followed. The dog jumped the low fence at the back of the property and put his nose to the ground, all business.

Hugo gave the dog his head and they tracked back and forth in the sparsely wooded stand of trees behind the Stanton garage. Boo had a flashlight, but it was pretty useless in the storm darkened night. Occasionally the dog would obsess over a spot but couldn't pick up a trail.

"It's the rain," Boo said. "He can't find the scent. If Nelson even came this way."

The occasional flashes of lightning alleviated the dense black of the night but even this was already trailing away to the east in the path of the storm. Hugo felt the heaviness of the air, the building sense of urgency. Daylight was hours away.

"Can you find you way to the bay from here?"

"I could, I guess, but we should wait for morning. The bluff's steep. Lots of hidden sink holes and downed trees. No point in breaking a leg. Or worse."

"The creek, then. Can you lead me to the creek?"

Boo didn't respond.

"He's alone and he's scared."

"Shit." Boo used the flashlight to check his bearings. "He always was a little pain in the ass." He set out on a southwesterly course through the trees.

The hound seemed to understand their actions. He followed the path Hugo had traveled the previous day at a pretty good clip. In just a few minutes they were at the creek bank and the dog set to baying. He had found the trail.

Hugo's hopes evaporated as the hound tracked in and out of the creek, sniffing along the bank and along the lower trunk of a tree growing almost in the water, seeking the scent in a confused circle. He took Boo's flashlight and examined the area. The rain had obliterated any evidence of any prints other than the dog's.

He almost missed the small patch of fabric. The few strands of bright baby blue thread were caught about a foot up the rough bark of the tree. Nelson had been here. Had he crossed the creek?

With only one flashlight between them, they were running blind. The rain had stopped with occasional, fleeting breaks in the cloud cover. They forded the creek. It was only about four feet across at this spot even though the water was running high. Hugo gave the tracker free reign and ten feet along he found the scent. Hugo slipped the lead and let him run. He knew where they were going.

Hugo decided to use the creek as a footpath. Tree branches slapped and grabbed at him as he felt his way toward the sound of the distant baying of the hound, long since lost to the night. His water filled shoes were a dead weight as he fought his way toward the edge of the bluff.

The moon broke through as they reached the steep drop toward the Blakeley River. Both he and Boo were panting heavily.

"Stay to the right," Boo said. "The going will be easier."

The baying call of the hound was louder now, reaching them from the bottom of the bluff.

Hugo slipped and slid down the depression of the creek. He heard Boo fall and swear. The breeze pushed the clouds east and the moon broke through and bathed the water below in ripples of dancing light. He climbed over the roots of a downed tree, lost his balance, and tumbled several feet before catching a low branch about fifteen feet above the little shoal of a beach.

The hound was frantic, pacing back and forth as Hugo ran the rest of the way to a small wash that eddied around a tangle of sea grass and debris.

Only it wasn't debris.

It was Nelson, face down, in the flowing creek, his baby blue pajamas an eerie white in the moonlight. The images of small rectangles of sailboats struck Hugo like an accusing finger.

Boo stumbled the last few feet of the incline and came to an abrupt halt beside Hugo.

"Shit."

The scene was a mess. Rain and runoff had obliterated any evidence of how Nelson came to be so far from the comfort and safety of home. Hugo used Boo's flashlight to examine the area as well as he could in the pre-dawn hours of the day. The weather had created the perfect accomplice for whatever foul deed had brought the young man to his death.

Nelson's body curved around the clump of sea grass not fifteen feet from the turbulent lapping wash of the Blakeley River. The wind had died down to occasional gusts.

In the cone of the light from Boo's flashlight, Nelson looked more boy than man. Without touching the body Hugo knew there was no hope. Only the back of Nelson's head was above the rush of water in the creek bed. His right arm wasn't visible. His left hand was splayed against the sand, half buried.

He had struggled against the pressure, tried to lift his torso out of the flow of water.

"Don't touch him," Hugo said as Boo reached down. "We'll wait for the photographer."

Boo stared at Hugo. "We can't leave him like that! He might be alive."

"No." Hugo clenched his jaw. "The sand has silted in all around him. There's nothing we can do now but preserve the scene."

"Preserve the scene! He drowned! We—His ma—This ain't decent!"

"Go for help."

"I ain't leaving him."

"Neither am I."

The two men stared each other down for a long moment. Then Hugo spoke. "This is about Ruby. You know it."

"Why would it be? He was just a kid." Boo looked away but Hugo had already seen the realization in his expression. And the grief.

"My case. My call." But his tone held a note of sympathy.

Boo shook his head as he gave Hugo an accusing look. "Someone has to tell his mama." He swore softly. "I guess it had better be me."

Hugo held the flashlight out toward him. "Take it. You need to travel fast. Call MPD for the forensics team. We need them here as soon as possible."

"The Chief won't like it."

"Are you really worried about what the Chief likes right now?"

Boo gave Nelson's body one last look. "The little shit," he said in a soft voice. Then he turned and headed up the bluff at a jogging run.

Hugo followed his progress until the bobbing flashlight disappeared over the top of the incline. He squatted beside the body. With no light source he could do nothing else. A glance at his watch showed it was 3:12 a.m. Sunrise would be about 5:30. Another two hours, give or take. He closed his eyes for a long count then opened them. His vision adjusted to the night. In a few minutes, the last of the trailing clouds scuttled east leaving a clear view of the river bathed in moonlight.

"What did you see, little man?" Hugo had no doubt that somewhere in Nelson's disjointed world view was the killer. A policeman? Ruby had taught him to be afraid of policemen. Chief Stanton? Boo Vansant? Sam Hollingsworth? All three wore the uniform. Was one of them the bogeyman?

Time seemed to slow down as Hugo waited but, in truth, Boo made quick time back to Adele's. Hugo saw the lights bobbing down the slope of the bluff from the opposite side of the creek and the access road beyond.

The Chief was the first on the scene.

Hugo stood as he approached.

Stanton placed his hands on his hips and stared down at Nelson's body. "Drowned," he said.

"Yes."

Two of Stanton's men came to stand on either side of him.

"Get him out of there."

"No," Hugo said.

The officer to Stanton's right took a step forward.

Stanton stared at Hugo. "It's a simple drowning."

"There's nothing simple about it."

Stanton narrowed his eyes to that crocodile look Hugo had seen before. "You want to explain yourself?"

"Not particularly but in this case, I'll make an exception. There's no way Nelson left his bed to go out into the night, through the woods, and down the bluff where he somehow managed to drown. He was either forced or lured by an incentive so strong it overcame his terror of the wind and lightning."

Stanton crossed his arms and cocked his head to one side. "Why would anyone do that?"

"Because Nelson knew something. Or saw something. He just didn't know what it meant."

"So, you think this had something to do with Ruby's death?" Stanton glanced at the officer beside him with a look-at-the-boy-genius quirk of his lips.

"I know it did."

"And you plan to do what? Leave him in the creek till daylight? That's not happening."

"I plan to do my job. Which is to preserve the evidence."

"Evidence? Look around you, man. The storm has destroyed any potential evidence."

"A crime scene unit is on the way with lights and a photographer." Hugo watched the stoney set of Stanton's expression. "Since your department doesn't seem too familiar with the process, they'll assess whether or not there's any evidence."

"And who gave you the authority to step into my business?" he asked.

"You did."

The officer beside Stanton took another step closer to Hugo.

"Leave it," Stanton's eyes betrayed the indifference of his words. "He's the hot shot detective. Thinks he'll get his name on the front page of the paper again. Let's give him what he wants. And we'll let him answer to Nelson's mama as well." With that, he turned from the scene, crossed the small patch of beach, and started up the bluff.

"Have someone on the look-out for the crime scene team," Hugo said to the last of Stanton's men.

The policeman gave Hugo an up and down look then turned to follow in the Chief's footsteps. Neither man was in a hurry.

⁂

BOO HAD FOLLOWED Hugo's instructions. Forty-five minutes after the departure of Stanton and his men, he saw Evie struggling with her heavy case as she picked her way down the rough path from the bluff. A uniform patrolman trailed after her, making no effort to assist her in any way.

Hugo had returned to a squat beside Nelson's body when Stanton left the scene, his men in tow. A lone cop had been stationed about fifty feet away. He had watched Hugo while Hugo watched Nelson, his thoughts turned inward.

As Evie approached, he rose and stepped across the creek. He took the heavy case from her and for once she didn't protest.

"Sorry about this," he said as he placed the case well away from the body.

"It's the job," she replied as she pulled on gloves then took a tripod with lights from the case.

"Where's your assistant?"

"Good question. My guess would be applying for a job as a lifeguard at mommie and daddy's country club."

"Why a lifeguard?"

"The sun, the daughters of the equally well-to-do, the ambience."

"Ouch."

Evie shrugged. "Makes life easier for me." She adjusted the light to fall full on Nelson. His skin was paper white. The water moved slower now in small rivulets around him. She started with the body, studied the positioning and the flow the creek. After scavenging about for a bit, she found two fairly straight pieces of driftwood. With a strip of cloth from her case, she created a break for the run-off. It was the best she could do. With a high flash camera, she worked her way out in widening circles. Finally, they lifted Nelson from the creek bed and laid him on his back. She continued to photograph him, zooming in on his face, neck, hands, and down the length of his body. When she was done, they placed him in a body bag and Hugo carried him up the bluff to the ambulance that had just arrived.

Hugo felt the fatigue in his limbs. He wanted nothing more than to rest, to return home to find Bebe waiting for him. Instead, he made his way back down to the water's edge. Daylight had finally arrived. In the early gray light, he examined the place where Nelson had died. There was nothing to be learned from the site. He doubted the sieve Evie had rigged up would contain anything of use. The steady flow of water had already obliterated any evidence long before Nelson was found. At least they would have the photographic evidence of the position of the body.

He stared off across the water toward Pineda Island on the other shore of the Blakely then wearily walked the length of the small beach. It was at the far edge where the wild growth from the bluff blocked any further passage that he saw it. The toy sailboat from the cab of Henry Stanton's old pick-up, caught in the debris of the river, bobbed gently against the shore.

Twenty-One

HEAT ROSE FROM the sidewalk as Junior reached down to retrieve the Press Register from a rain puddle. The plastic sleeve had done little to protect it from the deluge of the tropical storm. He glanced at the sun barely cresting the treetops that lined North Carlen Street. He felt the humidity in the air with each breath. It would be a sweltering day.

Grammy dropped bread into the toaster as he separated the sections of the newspaper and spread them over the backs of the kitchen table chairs. The front page was unreadable but some of the interior sections had fared better. The news announcer on the radio was giving the forecast for the day. The temperature was expected to be in the mid-nineties. He wished he had picked up his seersucker suit at the dry cleaners, but the case had derailed his to-do list for Friday. Myrtle Crum would have to take his grandmother to mass. She didn't need to be walking in this heat. Although, riding with Myrtle behind the wheel might be just as dangerous.

These thoughts were running through Junior's head as the weatherman droned on about the dissipation of the storm over Georgia and the relief it would bring the peanut farmers from the near drought conditions they had been enduring. He was deciding what course of action to take in the investigation at this point when the words of the newscaster penetrated his mental ramblings.

His grandmother had stilled, the spatula motionless in her hand, as she looked from the radio to Junior. He reached across the counter and turned the volume up.

"There has been no official identification, but the body is believed to be that of a young man who was the neighbor of recent murder victim Ruby Stanton. The drowning..."

Junior snatched up the receiver of the wall mounted phone near the kitchen door and began dialing. Dispatch quickly informed him of what little information they had. They had not had any contact with Hugo since the initial request in the early morning hours for assistance in the search except a call from a Spanish Fort officer for the forensics team. Last report from them was that Hugo was still at the scene.

He looked across the room at his grandmother as he hung up the phone. "I have to go." Then he disappeared down the hallway to his bedroom. It took him less than ten minutes to finish dressing for the day. As he headed for the front door, his grandmother stood in his path, her face pale, her hand, which held a section of the damp newspaper, trembled.

"Oh, Junior," her voice was wobbly. "What are we going to do?"

"Grammy," Junior took her arm and sat her in a chair near the door. She was frightening him. "What is it?"

"Oh, my poor boy. My poor, poor boy." She pushed the newspaper into his hands.

It was the society page. It was basically intact in spite of the rain. The image and the article jumped out at him. His expression turned grim, and he squatted beside his grandmother. "I'll take care of it, okay?"

"How?" A tear trailed down her cheek. "This can never be fixed. How will anything be right again?"

He patted her hand and tried for a soothing tone, but he felt the anger deep inside. "It'll be all right. I'll deal with it. I promise. You go to church with Myrtle, okay? Light a candle."

She patted his cheek and brushed at her tears. "You're such a good boy. How would we manage without you?"

He kissed her cheek and stood. "I have to go."

"I know." She gave him a watery smile. "Don't worry about me. I'll say a prayer for both of you. And that dear boy."

⁂

THE MOMENT HE got into the car, Junior started trying to reach Hugo on his police radio. When there was no answer, he decided to go straight to the station before heading across the bay. Even though the hour was early, he found Goode at his desk. The Chief motioned for him to enter when he tapped on the door.

"What's happening?" Junior asked.

"Don't know much. This kid, Nelson, disappeared from his room when the power went out last night. They discovered his body on a small beach along the Blakeley. Drowned. August thinks it's tied to the murder. He also thinks this isn't an accident." Goode sat back in his chair as he studied Junior. "I think he's gone rogue, looking for connections that aren't there. You need to reign him in."

Junior chose his words carefully. "Nelson lived next door. Had a bird's eye view of Ruby's apartment. It's not unreasonable to think he saw things that might be helpful to the case."

"He was an idiot. Couldn't even go to school." Goode sat forward, his forearms resting on the desk. "Move on. Even if he saw anything he didn't have enough gumption to realize what it meant. I want this case wrapped up. If August can't handle it, I'll put someone else on it."

Junior jangled the change in his pocket. This was the second time the powers that be had insisted Nelson was irrelevant to the case. "I'd better get over there." He turned for the door, but the Chief wasn't done yet.

"You've got to look out for yourself, your career. Don't let August drag you down with him."

Junior gave a small grunt in acknowledgement. The Chief had always had it in for Hugo. He had piled the crap calls on him from his first day on the job. In the beginning, Junior thought Hugo would chuck the whole thing, but for some reason he had stuck it out. Goode had taken Hugo's success in the Camden case as a slap in the face. Never mind that it reflected well on the whole department and the killers had been brought to justice. There was something personal about the situation. What that was, Junior had no clue.

One thing about Hugo was a certainty. He invoked strong feelings from the people in his life. You either adored him or you resented him. Maybe even hated him. As Junior made his way to the forensics lab in the basement of the building, he admitted that sometimes both sentiments were at war within him.

Evie was bending over a large flat tray of sand as he entered the lab. A bright light made the quartz in the mixture glitter. She was moving inch by inch over the surface with a large magnifying glass mounted to the workstation.

"From the scene?" Junior asked.

She looked up. "Yeah. I thought there might be something there but it's a longshot."

"What do we know?"

"The body's with the coroner. But I did a pretty thorough on-site examination. His feet are all torn up, so we know he walked. Scratches on his face and hands, his pajamas snagged and filthy. The position of the body suggests he was held down. Right now, that's just speculation. We'll have to see if the coroner finds any water in his lungs. If so, then the scenario is very ugly."

"Someone held him under."

She nodded. "The natural tendency would be to lift your face out of the water, even if you were injured or constrained. He was face down. Sand had silted around his body. The placement of his left hand suggests he struggled. It was planted palm down, almost covered by sand."

"He could have been unconscious."

"Possible."

"But you don't think so."

"He'd been in the water a long time when I got there but, no."

"And Hugo?"

"Still at the scene when I left. He looked like Jacob after wrestling the angel."

Junior thought she wanted to say something more, but she didn't. Her hair was still damp. It curled around her face. She didn't have on any make-up, and she had dark circles under her eyes. "You okay?"

She picked up a fine-grade sifter and began filling it with sand from a bag sitting on the counter. "Sure."

"Okay."

They both were silent as Evie began to slowly sift the sand onto a clean area of the tray.

"Let me know if you find anything. I'll have my radio."

She didn't look up, simply nodded.

⁂

JUNIOR SKIRTED AROUND debris of marsh grass, driftwood, a mangled crab trap, and the usual trash that the storm had washed over the roadway. The water had mostly receded from the roadbed of the Causeway. The wind buffeted the car even though it was a heavy Crown Vic.

He topped the bridge over the Apalachee River and the Thunderbird Inn came into view. On impulse he turned onto the parking lot. All the lights were on in the foyer. He climbed out of the car. The motel door was unlocked. The acrid smell of burnt coffee greeted him as he entered. A stack of the Mobile Press Register papers sat on the registration counter. The binding cord had been cut and a good four inches of the wet soggy stack of newsprint lay to one side exposing the relatively dry interior papers. His heart sank.

In the kitchen he unplugged the large coffee maker. The contents had burned down to a dark stain in the bottom of the pot. In the dining room he found the newspaper scattered across their worktop. The front page of the society section was on top. Bebe's face stared up at him. Captured in the photo with her was Trey Whitehall, heir apparent to the family banking empire. It was their engagement photo. And Hugo had seen it. Where would he go? What would he do?

❧

HUGO FELT SOMETHING on his face. He opened his eyes to blue sky overhead. He reached up and captured an ant crawling across his cheek. His heart jumped as his brain kicked into gear. In one swift motion he sat upright, crushed the commie ant between his finger and thumb, and crabbed backwards into the protective lee of a huge tree trunk. Wildly he scanned the area for an instant until realization settled in. This wasn't a field of elephant grass. No coolie hats wended their way through a rice paddy. He took a deep breath, and the thumping of his heart began to calm.

The sun was well above the tree line of the bluff of the eastern shore of Mobile Bay. A trio of sandpipers dug in the sand of the little beach below the Paradise Inn searching for periwinkles. Cigarette butts and the occasional beer can dotted the shoreline. A woman with a mesh bag walked toward him as she picked up the detritus of a stormy night and an uncaring public. When she saw him, she paused then turned back in the direction from which she had come.

Yes, he thought. Best to be wary of the beast. He watched her glance over her shoulder as she reached the footpath leading up to the bluff. She would remember, he decided, but the thought held no significance, no bearing on his existence. Goode would use it against him if it reached his ears. So would Stanton. None of it mattered. Nothing really mattered anymore. He would get fired or not. But he would finish the job. Ruby would be avenged. Nelson would have his justice. There was nothing left that anyone could take from him, not even the dream of something. Except maybe his life. But it wasn't really a life anymore without the hope of Bebe, was it?

Why had he gone back to the motel? To wash up before he went to tell Adele that her son was dead. He should have gone straight to her. But she would have known already. Boo would have told her.

He should have never cut open the bundle of newspapers. There was no time for curiosity about what Donahue had to say about the case. But he had given in to the urge and with that one decision he had cut himself adrift from the only thing that still mattered.

His life was full of decisions he never should have made. And now, here he was, filthy, gritty, exhausted on a beach below a juke joint. He looked around at the empty beer cans and cigarette butts floating in the wash at the edge of the water. How had he gotten here?

Hugo brushed at the sand on his face and clothing as he climbed up the bluff. His shirt was a tattered mess, dirty, torn and snagged by the trek through the woods behind the Stanton house. The stubble of his beard rasped against his palm. He needed a shower and clean clothes.

He expected to see his car parked at the Paradise Inn as he came through the straggly growth near the top of the trail. It wasn't. But the white Caddy was. There was another car as well. It was a big, black, imposing Mercedes. Not a common sight in the area. Hugo crossed the parking lot and checked the tags. As he suspected, the Caddy had Georgia plates. The other car was local. Baldwin County, in fact. What was Dubya doing at the Paradise again and at this early morning hour? There was no doubt that this was the same car Hugo had seen two days ago. He started toward the side door of the bar near where the cars were parked then realized what a wreck he was. He looked around for his car.

How *had* he gotten here? Surely it was close by. The blackouts had been few and far between since the resolution of the Camden case with only an occasional instance of too much beer, too little caring. Lost time that hadn't meant anything. But this felt different. Like the lapses in San Francisco. He couldn't go back there. Wouldn't allow himself to be derailed before he found his killer. He backed away from the building and turned to looked up and down Hwy. 98. There was a layby a few yards up the highway, he remembered. He set out in that direction. Up a small rise in the road he saw it, his front right tire edging dangerously close to the ditch. The keys were in the ignition, his notebook and radio on the front seat.

He slid behind the wheel and fired up the engine. It took some jockeying back and forth on the narrow road to turn the car around. As he started to pull out, he saw Chief Stanton driving Elizabeth's Dodge Dart up the highway. It turned into the Paradise parking lot.

Hugo sat with the motor idling, trying to make sense of what he was seeing. The clock in the Thunderbird read 7:52 in the morning. A Sunday morning. An unusual time for a gathering at the local bar. He needed to know who the Mercedes belonged to. And he knew just the person who could tell him. He flipped through the pages of his notebook and found the address, then he pulled out the map and found the location.

⁂

THE SMALL WHITE house was located down a winding county road near Malbis Plantation. The yellow Beetle stood out against a dark green hedge of camelias in the side yard. Dixie answered the door on his first knock. She had a fluffy white robe tied loosely at her waist, her blonde hair brushed back from her face in loose waves, and no make-up.

She leaned her hip against the door frame. "Well, well. Don't you look a sight."

He thought the same about her but in a quite different way.

"Got a minute?"

"Sure." She stepped back as he entered the clean but untidy living room. "I just made coffee. Want a cup? You look like you could use one."

"Sounds good." He followed her through an archway into a tiny kitchen with a table under the window that barely accommodated two chairs.

"Cream? Sugar?"

"Black."

"Good choice. I think the cream's gone bad." She filled two mugs and sat across the little bistro table from him. "Now tell me, Detective, what has you on my doorstep at this early hour? And looking like you've been wrestling a gator?"

"I thought we'd have a little chat about your acquaintance."

"And who's that?"

"O'Sullivan. Or does he prefer Sully?"

Dixie shook a cigarette from a pack on the table and lit it. She exhaled a plume of smoke toward the ceiling and let her gaze settle on Hugo. "He really is just an acquaintance."

"Someone seems to think it's more than that."

"You shouldn't listen to self-serving gossip."

"Smoke and mirrors?"

"That would be my guess."

"Why?"

"The pot. Squatting. Who knows."

"Is he dealing?"

"Don't ask me."

"Because you don't know?"

"Because I keep my nose out of other people's business."

"Is it other people's business?"

"I don't know what you're talking about."

"The cigarettes. And liquor."

She made no reply, simply watched him across the table.

"Does O'Sullivan drive a black Mercedes sedan?"

Dixie crushed out the cigarette in a small tin ashtray on the table, took a sip of her coffee, then looked Hugo in the eye. "Yes."

"How often does Dubya make a haul from Atlanta?"

When she didn't reply, he said, "We know about the book, the times, the dates. That's what you came to the motel for wasn't it? To retrieve it?"

She sat back in her chair, studying him. "Suppose there was a book? How would I know anything about it?"

"Because you're always there. The night shift? Moving untaxed contraband is a job best done in the dark of night, don't you think?" He gave a shrug. "And because it was in your personal drawer."

She looked away from him then. After a moment she said. "I don't know what you want from me. I just work there. I don't see anything; I don't know anything."

"And you don't hear anything."

When she didn't reply, he picked up the pack of cigarettes from the table and turned them over to study the bottom. "I'm looking for a killer. Someone cold enough to shoot a woman through the heart without blinking an eye. Someone cruel enough to drown a senseless man-child to keep him from telling what he saw."

"What?" Her eyes rounded in horror as she abruptly

sat forward. She ran a hand through her hair. "Nelson? Nelson's dead?"

Hugo saw the fear though she tried to hide it. It was there in the shallow quick breaths, the refusal to look at him directly, the jump of her pulse at her throat.

"Tell me! Is he dead?"

"Yes."

"It has to be an accident."

Hugo shook his head. "It was deliberate. And vicious. You're playing a dangerous game, Dixie."

She stood and turned her back to him, cinched the belt of her robe more tightly, and shook her hair back from her face as she straightened her shoulders. "I don't know anything."

Hugo drained the cup of coffee and stood. The motion left him a little dizzy. The sleepless night was catching up with him. "I'll find out, you know. Don't make it harder on yourself than it has to be."

She didn't look around at him. Instead, she crossed the kitchen and made for the front door which she held open. "I think you should go. There's nothing I can tell you."

"I think there's plenty you could tell me. I hope you realize that before it's too late."

She looked at him then, her face pale. "Don't worry about me, Detective. I've been taking care of myself for a long time now." She gave him a hint of a smile. "You really should get some sleep. Tidy up."

"Don't worry about me. I've been taking care of myself for a long time, too."

"Then aren't we a pair."

"Who are you afraid of, Dixie?"

She made no reply, simply closed the door softly behind him. He heard the lock slide home.

Twenty-Two

PEGGY SUE WAS alone in the Spanish Fort Police station when Junior entered the building. Dark circles bruised the flesh beneath her eyes and her nose was red. She'd been crying. The resentment and animosity he had felt from her before was gone.

She filled him in on the events of the night, the fact that Nelson had been taken to Mobile for an autopsy, that an exhausted department had dispersed to clean-up, catch a bit of sleep, and regroup later in the morning.

"And Stanton?"

Peggy Sue shrugged. "Couldn't say. He wasn't happy about the body being taken out of his jurisdiction, but Bay Minette isn't really equipped to handle this kind of thing. Especially with your detective insisting it was murder and that it had to do with Ruby. The only other solution would be Montgomery."

"And where is my detective, do you know?"

"No. They were down at the scene 'til well after daylight. Can't imagine he'd still be there." She glanced at the clock on the wall. It was a few minutes past eight. "I mean, how're you going to find any evidence after the storm we had? Everyone says it's hopeless."

"Everyone?"

"They were all down there at one time or another. There's only five of us. And the Chief. Spanish Fort's a small town. I mean, we have problems. Accidents, boat crashes, fights. This is different." Tears began to well up in her eyes and she blinked rapidly. "This is evil. Everyone knew Nelson. He was just a harmless little guy who loved orange soda."

"You said fights. Anyone in particular?"

Peggy Sue's demeanor became more guarded. "Drinking, raising hell. The usual."

"Raising hell about what?"

Her brows shot up. "Everything. Football, property lines, screwing around."

"Who's screwing around?"

"Who isn't? There's nothing much to do in a place like this except fool around and gossip."

"That seems like a risky cure for boredom."

"And that's probably why they do it. For the thrill, the danger of getting caught."

"Any of these thrill seekers having an affair with Ruby?"

"How would I know?"

"You're sharp, observant, you've got the catbird seat of what's happening in town."

That pleased her. Junior could see in her eyes the calculation of how far she was willing to go. Secrets were only powerful if people knew you had them and the only way anyone could appreciate your power was if you told.

"It wasn't Ruby's affairs that raised eyebrows. Everyone's known about her since she was a teenager."

"A big fish, then?"

But Peggy Sue had decided to forego the satisfaction of the telling. "Couldn't say. It's all rumor and gossip."

"It could be important. Two people are dead."

"Just because someone's cheating on his wife doesn't mean anything. And I have to live here once all is said and done. Airing dirty laundry isn't going to help you find who killed Nelson. And Ruby."

"You never know."

She shook her head. "Not this."

⁂

HUGO STOOD ON Dixie's stoop of a front porch and tried to marshal his thoughts. Two people were dead. Whatever was going on at the Thunderbird Inn was beginning to unravel. Had it led to Ruby's death? If so, how did Nelson fit into the frame? The fatigue pulled at his limbs, muddled his thoughts. Where was the pattern? The murders were related. Had to be. And he had to find his killer before anyone else died.

But first, he needed to see Adele Gorton. She would be devastated. Nelson, by his very existence, had become her whole world. There would be heavy guilt on her part. Guilt that she hadn't protected him; that she had survived him. And if he was any judge, there would be guilt at the sense of relief from a life of unending duty and responsibility. He had seen it at Letterman General when the sweet young wife of his army buddy had made it to his hospital bed in time to hold his hand as he died of wounds that left him unspeakably scarred and maimed. That sense of relief and shame that she had escaped the long dying of them both. Because that's what it was. The slow death of meaningful life with each passing day stretching out across a lifetime.

He glanced in the rearview mirror as he drove along Hwy 31 toward Spanish Fort. His hair was wild. There was still sand from the beach behind the Paradise trapped in his whiskers and his eyes were bloodshot. He would have to make the time for the drive to Mobile to clean up and find something to wear. His police radio squawked to life.

"Twenty-one," he responded.

"Hugo. Where are you?"

It was Junior. Hugo heard the relief in his voice.

"Headed to the Gorton's."

"I'll meet you there."

"No. I won't be long. Need to swing home to clean up. I'll meet you at the Thunderbird on my way. We need to review the case."

"Something specific?"

"When I get there."

"Ten-four."

✻

JUNIOR SIGHED AS he got behind the wheel of the Crown Vic. Everyone knew and no one was talking.

✻

ADELE GORTON WAS alone when she opened the door to Hugo. She stood in the doorway a long moment as she assessed his appearance. He, in turn, noted the purple shadows beneath her eyes, the swollen eyelids and redness. Everything about her was diminished from her stature to the blue of her eyes. They somehow seemed faded, clouded.

Finally, she turned from the door and headed to the back of the house and the kitchen. Hugo followed in silence. Her little dog wagged his tail and looked up at him with soulful eyes from a pillow beside the refrigerator. She made a weak gesture toward the table and opened the cabinet for a cup. The black, strong brew she poured for him tasted as bitter as her heartache.

"I'm sorry," he said as she collapsed into a chair across from him.

She nodded.

"Where's everyone?"

It was several seconds before she answered, her reply seeming to have traveled a long circuit from his question to the part of her that could analyze what he had said and formulate a response. Without looking at him she said, "Gone. I sent them away."

He didn't ask why or suggest she didn't need to be alone. He understood her grief. It was a pain best suffered in private. She didn't need the platitudes that time would heal all wounds, the murmurs of false sympathy, the patronization of understanding the unfathomable. Adele now existed on a different plane than the world around her, an existence that left her looking inward, numb to everything except that inner reality.

"Is there anything I can do for you?"

"No. Nelson's gone. Everyone he loved is gone, too. Except me. Henry dying in that awful way. Ruby murdered. Nothing matters now." She studied his face. "But if it makes you feel better, I wish you luck." She sighed from the depth of her soul. "There's no luck to be found around here."

"He didn't go on his own."

She nodded.

"And he wasn't forced. You would have heard something."

Tears formed in her eyes as she looked up at him. She nodded again.

"Who would he go with?"

Silence settled over them. Finally, she said, "Only Ruby."

"Not Elizabeth? Not Stanton?"

"No. He might have at one time but not since his chicken died. Something about that made him fearful." She shook her head. "Maybe because it happened so soon after Henry died. Only Nelson knew the logic behind his thoughts. His fears."

Hugo let his gaze travel to the kitchen window and the view of Ruby's apartment. The sun's rays slanted through the window, washing Adele in a patch of light that only served to emphasize the lines of her face, the ashen color of her skin. "Boo."

She started to shake her head but hesitated. "I don't know. When they were kids he loved Boo, followed after him, would do anything Boo said."

"What kind of things?"

"Climbing trees, playing with a knife."

"Swimming in the bay?"

She clasped her hand over her mouth and squeezed her eyes shut as the tears seeped slowly from behind her closed eyelids.

Hugo clenched his jaw and swallowed down the rage swelling in his chest. "I'll catch him, Adele. I'll catch him and I'll punish him." He stood and placed a hand on her shoulder. "Call me if you need me. For anything. The dispatcher will find me."

She made no reply, simply sat with the tears flowing soundlessly down her cheeks, locked in her own private world of grief.

⁂

JUNIOR WATCHED FROM the window of the motel restaurant as Hugo pulled into the parking lot. He looked totally gutted as he climbed out of the Thunderbird.

The Sunday newspapers were in the garbage can in the kitchen beneath the scorched coffee pot. Junior had the case file open before him as Hugo strolled into the room in that loose, deceptively casual gait of his. His gaze traveled swiftly across the table before settling on a spot to the left of Junior.

"You know about Nelson?"

"Most of it."

Hugo sat heavily in the chair across the table and ran a hand through his hair. "He was held under, his face buried in the sand."

"That's Evie's opinion, too."

"We have another problem."

"Yeah?"

"Untaxed cigarettes and booze. I figure Dubya is bringing them in, using the motel as a hub for local distribution."

"Right under Stanton's nose?"

"He's involved. Has to be. O'Sullivan's probably the money."

"Dickie?"

"Takes care of the day-to-day would be my guess with Dixie keeping the books."

"How does Ruby fit into the scheme of things?"

"Don't know. If she's meeting Talbot here regularly it could be an inconvenient coincidence."

"Coincidence?"

"Yeah. I don't like it either."

"And two out of the four of them were here when Ruby got shot. Is that why she's dead?"

Hugo rubbed his eyes with the heels of his hands then leaned back in the chair and stared at the ceiling. "Hell if I know. It would be an amazing stroke of bad luck if she just happened to decide to have a roll in the sack on delivery night."

"Do you think Stanton was here when things went south?"

"Before last night I would have said no. His shock seemed real. Now I'm not so sure."

"But she's his niece."

"Cousin, actually."

"Do we bring Chief Goode into the picture?"

Hugo sat in silence, then shook his head. "Not yet. We

need something more than half a dozen untaxed packs of cigarettes."

"So, what's next?"

"Good question. Dixie more or less confirmed my suspicions. She insists that O'Sullivan wasn't here to see her."

"Covering her backside. You think she's involved?"

"Has to be. She kept the delivery schedule. Always works the night shift."

"And Dickie?"

"Without question. O'Sullivan's the bank, Stanton the protection, Dubya the supplier. Someone had to manage the distribution. My guess would be Dickie."

"With Dixie's help and possibly the cook."

"Don't know where Chapman fits in other than I'm sure he's aware of what's going on."

"That leaves the question of Ruby."

Hugo sat with his arms crossed, his chin almost touching his chest, as his eyes drifted closed. Junior studied him as silence settled over them. He cleared his throat.

"You need sleep. Go crash in one of the rooms."

Hugo struggled to lift his head and open his eyes. "Can't. Too much to do."

"You won't do any of it asleep on your feet. A couple of hours will help you think straight."

Junior thought he would refuse again but instead he got to his feet, gave a brief nod and staggered out of the restaurant to make his way to room number two. He knew that feeling; the spaghetti legs and mental shutdown that came in the wake of the long chase, the adrenaline rush followed by the crash of the body's physical limits.

Once the door to room two closed behind Hugo, Junior turned to the chalkboard. He picked up the piece of chalk and turned it over and over in his hand, then he stood and used a napkin to erase everything. He bounced the piece of chalk in his hand as he stared at the blank slate. The faint sound of water running through pipes in the quiet building told him Hugo had gotten into the shower. No amount of fatigue would keep him from being clean. Two tours of the jungles of Vietnam had done that. Junior knew that it was more than just the dirt and sweat that Hugo needed to wash away. But some things couldn't be dispelled with mere soap and water.

With a sigh, he brought his attention back to the task at hand. He drew a line down the center of the chalkboard. The left side he captioned GREED. The right side, SEX. Next, he listed all the players. The field was growing rather than shrinking. When he finished, he realized that all the contenders except Dixie would qualify for either motive. That assumed Hugo was right about O'Sullivan and Dixie.

If O'Sullivan didn't have a relationship with Dixie, did he have one with Ruby? Surely with the lawyer in the picture that couldn't be the case. Unless O'Sullivan was the new man in Ruby's life.

Junior erased the board again. Alibis, he decided. That was the only way to narrow the list.

Davis Talbot had the best alibi. Two lawyers and a banker had told the same tale of the poker game, including who had won. William, the ageless doorman at The Club, had supported their story. But, of course, he would. He had held the job as long as anyone could remember. Which meant he saw nothing and heard nothing. Ever. The drive time from The Club would have been tight if Ruby was shot when they believed but it was doable on a quiet, late, week night.

The wife had ample opportunity both in the hours around midnight and after Talbot returned home to a separate bedroom. He thought back over his interview of her. Separate bedrooms would be the norm for them, he decided. She wouldn't fear being caught. The lack of concern about her husband stood out in his mind, not her sense of betrayal. There was no passion there. But there was greed.

Boo Vansant had arrived on the scene with Stanton just before three in the morning. Junior shuffled through the pages of notes for the exact time. It lined up with Dixie's statement that she had called at 2:45. Before the call, Boo had been on duty patrolling the area. That left plenty of opportunity.

Why would O'Sullivan shoot Ruby? To protect his identity. If she stumbled onto what was happening at the motel, she could be a danger to his reputation, not to mention the threat of prison on a federal charge. Dubya had so far managed to avoid anything beyond suspicion in his past criminal activities. That gave him motive. And he certainly had opportunity.

Could Stanton possibly be in the picture? Junior didn't feel it, but Hugo had been the one to interact with the Spanish Fort police chief. Something had changed in his assessment. Something in his gut, perhaps. It didn't pay to ignore those feelings.

Would Stanton shoot Ruby? Had she gone too far? According to Peggy Sue, she knew how to push his buttons. And he had a temper. He was a big man. Powerful. Authoritative. Junior considered this then shook his head. He wouldn't use a gun. He would use his hands. A moment of rage, lost control. He would punish her, and he would want the physicality of it, need to show her who was in control.

Everyone knew Ruby was a friendly girl. Would Stanton go off the deep end because of who she was meeting? If it was O'Sullivan, that would complicate their smuggling operation. Assuming Stanton was involved. Hugo thought he was. But what if Boo was the protection? He was on patrol that night.

How did any of this square with the murder of Nelson? He was as far removed from the activities at the Thunderbird Inn as he was from the moon. Half the people on the list probably didn't even know of his existence. Greed and sex. Could there be another motive?

Junior threw the piece of chalk at the board and dug a pack of Marlboros from his inside coat pocket. As he drew a cigarette from the pack, he left the restaurant, crossed the foyer, and down the hall to Lucky Number Seven. He opened the door and stood looking into the room. The pool of blood had soaked into the worn carpet. There wasn't much of it. Her heart had stopped pumping almost instantly. With a bit of clean up, no one would ever know a murder had been committed there.

After he made a circuit of the room and adjoining bath, he went outside and smoked his cigarette. The motel was a dead end. So, where to start? He flicked the half-smoked cigarette onto the oyster shell parking lot. With the kid, he decided. There had to be something that connected Nelson to Ruby's murder.

Twenty-Three

JUNIOR DEBATED KNOCKING a third time on Elizabeth Stanton's front door when it suddenly opened a crack. The eye that stared at him through the two-inch opening was startlingly blue.

"Mrs. Stanton?"

"Yes?"

He pulled his shield from his inner coat pocket. "Junior Knight. Mobile Police Department."

"What do you want?"

"To talk about Nelson."

She hesitated. "It really isn't a good time. I can't help you. I don't know why he would run away."

"But you knew him well, didn't you? He was Ruby's friend. She loved him."

She glanced down, obviously warring with the desire to refuse and a sense of obligation, or guilt. Finally, she stepped back and opened the door.

"Thank you. I won't take much of your time." Junior realized the photograph in the newspaper hadn't done her justice. The image of her that had run with the breaking story of her daughter's murder had been of a young beauty.

That beauty was so much more in life and in maturity. Perhaps it was the hair paired with the blue eyes. The blouse she wore matched those eyes perfectly. Unlike Hugo's description of a woman heavily sedated, Elizabeth Stanton was alert, nervous, perhaps. Why, he wondered? The thought of more questions?

As he followed her into the living room, she discretely pushed a small overnight bag behind an armchair with her foot. She sat in the chair as she motioned for him to have a seat on the sofa across from her.

Her hair was done up in a French twist, her make-up subtle. A pearl necklace accentuated by a ruby encased in gold nestled at the small indenture above her collar bone. It partially hid a small dark bruise on the right side of her throat.

"Are you okay, Mrs. Stanton?"

"Yes. Of course." Her hand went to the necklace as she turned her profile toward him. "I'm just going out. So, if you could be quick." The floral print of her skirt held hints of the blue of her eyes, and she wore high heels of a darker shade. Church, Junior thought. He was keeping her from church. And on this Sunday of all Sundays.

"What do you want to know? I rarely see Nelson except when he's out in his yard. He hasn't been around much since—" the pulse at her throat jumped. "In a long time."

"Why is that do you think?"

She looked down as she smoothed the pleats of her skirt. "I couldn't say. Maybe because Henry isn't around anymore. Ruby went away to school for nearly nine months and that's a long time for someone like Nelson." She shrugged. "I guess there was nothing to draw him here."

"But he would have visited once Ruby came home from college?"

Her gaze settled on the view out the windows that were to his back. Initially, she didn't reply.

"Things were different then. Ruby wasn't his playmate anymore. Going away, living as an adult. I guess that changed things. Their relationship.

"She didn't have time for him anymore?"

"That, I suppose, and her sorrow about her father."

"Was Nelson sad about that, too?"

"Oh, yes. He followed Henry around like a little puppy. Loved pretending to drive that old truck while Henry tinkered with the engine." She looked down at her hands and clasped them in her lap. "I felt sorry for him, living with only Adele, never growing up, always a child."

"How limited was he? Could he understand directions? Make decisions on his own? Do simple tasks?"

"Henry was always tying his shoelaces for him, but he could dress himself, do easy things in the kitchen like make a sandwich and get a glass of milk. Nora tried to help him. Even after they decided he couldn't be in a classroom setting Adele had her work with him in the afternoons for a time. It didn't help. His mind was like..." she shook her head, "it's hard to put into words. A bumble bee comes to mind. It seemed his thoughts jumped constantly from one thing to another, bumping into things, jerky, disconnected.

"He could be sly sometimes. When he really wanted something. There was a time when he would slip away to go to the service station at Confederate and 31. He loved orange soda, and Adele couldn't keep it in the house because he would drink it all up. But he knew there was a Coke machine at the station. He actually made it all the way there a couple of times. But all of that was in the daytime. Usually when Ruby or Boo were off doing something. He wanted to be brave like Boo but each of those attempts left him and Adele frightened and unsettled for days."

"So, what made him slip out into the night in the middle of a raging storm?"

"Fear, I suppose." She returned her attention to Junior.

"Of what?"

She gave a small shake of her head. "I can't imagine."

He saw her eyes glisten with the hint of tears.

"It had to be a powerful fear."

"A fear in the mind, perhaps." She looked down at her hands. "Aren't those the most terrifying fears, detective? The ones we can't hide from behind locked doors? The ones that invade our dreams in the night and the shadowy corners of the day?"

Junior leaned forward, his forearms resting on his knees, his voice quiet. "Do you have such fears, Mrs. Stanton?"

She touched the ruby centered in the pearl necklace, her fingers worrying the beads. "Don't we all?"

Junior sat back. What did Elizabeth Stanton fear?

"He spent a lot of time here, didn't he?"

"Once. Before Ruby went off to college."

"But since then, he didn't come around?"

"Not really."

"Why's that?"

Elizabeth's gaze traveled past Junior to the windows again, her eyes tracking right to left along the roadway. "I don't know. Soon after Henry died, he quit coming at all. He would swing under the tree in his back yard and sometimes walk the property line where the bridal wreath grows and watch the house, but he wouldn't come into the yard."

"Not even after Ruby moved back home?"

"He would visit her in her apartment. But after a while she was gone a lot of the time." She frowned and turned away from Junior's steady gaze. "He watched for her car. Her little Mustang. I would see him hurry up the stairs almost before she could get in the door." She shook her head as she twisted her fingers together into a tight knot of a fist. "I didn't even realize what was happening at first. I wasn't myself. Nora pointed it out to me one day as she watched him from the kitchen window."

"It sounds like he was afraid."

"Maybe he was."

"Of what?"

"I don't know." Her brow creased briefly as she considered his question. "It might have had something to do with Henry's death. And his pet chicken died soon after the funeral. Everyone was emotional, not paying attention, I guess. Maybe he didn't understand about death, or he was frightened by it."

"Did Ruby ever say anything about Nelson's behavior?"

"No. She rarely mentioned him at all."

"Had he ever done anything like this before?"

"Like this? No. Never." Elizabeth rose from the chair. "I really can't be late."

Junior stood and followed her to the front door. As she opened it, he asked her one last question.

"If you don't mind, could you tell me how your husband died?"

Her face paled and she physically pulled back from him. She blinked a couple of times and turned her profile to him. "It was an accident," he saw her throat work as she swallowed, "a hunting accident."

⁂

HUGO WAS BEING pulled under, couldn't move. The red-gold tendrils held him in a crushing grip, curling around his torso, his throat, weaving through his hair. He fought for breath, strained to lift his arms, to tear through the tightness in his chest. As he struggled the silky vines changed to the palest gold, a soft yet painful caress that held him immobile, unable to break free. The trap had appeared out of nowhere. How could he have been so careless? Better to die than be taken prisoner. He fought, reaching for his gun. It wasn't there. He felt the panic rising as he thrashed out.

Hugo opened his eyes, instantly awake. He stared at the ceiling and the moth filled light fixture. He was breathing heavily, his heart thumping against his ribcage. Room number two. That's where he was. How long had he slept? The blinds were partially open, and the room filled with light. He swung his feet off the bed and stared out the window. Close to noon, he decided.

The motel was silent. He lifted his pants from a puddle on the floor where he had dropped them. They were a filthy, bramble-torn mess. He shook them fiercely then slipped them on. His shirt hadn't fared any better. There was nothing for it but to make the drive to South Cedar Street and find something clean to wear.

It was a quarter past noon according to the clock behind the registration desk. He had slept nearly three hours. The restaurant was empty. Junior's list caught his eye. Stanton had been added to it. All the known occupants of the motel on the night of the murder were on the left. Except the vacationing couple.

He picked up the chalk and added their names. Six people. *The dog in the night-time.*

Who were they protecting?

He marked through the couple. It was time to drill down and get some answers.

⁂

HUGO SETTLED FOR the Hawaiian shirt. He had no other choice. The pants he'd been wearing during the search for Nelson were beyond repair. He threw them in the garbage and pulled on a pair of old tan slacks. The armoire held very little because he owned very little in the way of a wardrobe. His shoes were a muddy mess and still damp. They were only six months old. He tossed them into the corner and dug his Army boots from under the bed. Laundry and everything else would have to wait. There were more pressing matters to deal with.

With keys in hand, he headed across the small living room of the shotgun house. The overstuffed, fading armchair sat in a shaft of sunlight filled with dancing dust motes. The image of Bebe in his arms, saying his name, kissing his lips, formed in a trembling mirage, bending the air, gathering the dust, giving form to an ethereal specter. He closed his eyes to the illusion, fought the memory of Trey Whitehall leaning into Bebe at the cemetery when they laid her aunt to rest, the sight of his hand on her waist on the tennis court of The Club. The Press Register society page with Bebe's photo staring at him swam on the lids of his closed eyes. She was smiling as she announced their engagement. He felt a momentary swaying, his world crashing. The pull of his grief strong as he placed a hand on the door frame to steady himself, to resist the blackness swirling around, the subconscious desire to let go, to embrace the lost moments, hours. That would have to wait, too. Besides, it no longer mattered, did it? Bebe had slipped through his fingers. Again. He wouldn't let that happen with this killer. That he could control.

He forced his mind to turn to Junior's list. It was time to get some straight answers and he planned to start with Davis Talbott.

⁂

IT WAS TALBOT'S wife who answered the door at the house in the heart of Spring Hill. It took her a long time to appear down the hallway from the depths of the house. Her long blonde hair was loose around her shoulders, and she wore white shorts that showcased her long, tan legs. A halter top in a tropical print completed the outfit. She gave him an assessing once over then glanced at his badge.

"You must be Hugo August," she said. "Not that I've ever had a policeman show up on my doorstep in a Hawaiian shirt."

"Exigent circumstances," he said.

"My husband isn't here."

"You'll do."

Her brow shot up at his remark. She gave him a hint of a smile as she stepped back for him to enter. She closed the front door then headed across the foyer toward the back of the house. French doors were open onto a deep covered porch that spanned the length of the home. Other French doors opened onto other rooms all along the expansive living space. Another woman sat on a cushioned wicker lounger, her bare feet pulled up and a half full martini glass in her hand. She, too, wore shorts and a halter top in scarlet red. Her lipstick matched the top.

"Well, well. What's this?" Her left brow lifted as she smiled at Hugo.

"Don't get excited, Boots. It's the cops."

Boots let her gaze travel the length of Hugo's tall frame. "I hope you brought handcuffs." She gave a deep chuckle and winked.

Lissa Talbott gestured toward a chair and settled on a love seat. "Martini, detective?"

Hugo shook his head and sat. "I just have a few questions."

Boots sat slightly forward, an avaricious look on her face.

Lissa took a sip of her drink. "I've already answered the other detective's questions."

"But not mine."

She studied him, shook her hair back over her shoulders and smiled as she lifted her glass in salute. "I guess you'd better ask, then."

"Ruby was different from the others, wasn't she?"

Lissa Talbot turned her profile to him. "Well, she was his first redhead. And she may have been a better than average lover. Who's to say? But other than that, she was just another distraction. Something to amuse him for a while until the excitement faded."

"He wanted a divorce, didn't he?"

Hugo had her full attention now.

"He couldn't afford a divorce. This house," she made a sweeping gesture with her hand, "has been in his family for over a hundred years. On his mother's side. The membership at The Club," she shrugged, "a birthright. Mardi Gras and all it entails; he'd never give that up. And he'd have to if he divorced me. I'd get it all."

"Are you sure about that? Old family, old money. Well-connected friends all the way up the food chain. You really think you could win against all that?"

Lissa crossed her legs and swung a bare foot nonchalantly. "My husband has something of a reputation in case you haven't heard." She smiled across at her friend. "His affairs are known far and wide. Legendary, you might say. And while it's true I might not get the house, the fight would

be long and nasty. And very costly. I'd make sure of that."
She emptied her glass in one long drink. There was the
glint of steel in her eyes when she looked at Hugo. "You see,
detective, I've been very careful. Very proper. There are no
skeletons in my closet. The picture of propriety. But Davis.
Well," she poured herself another drink from the pitcher,
"he has an expensive lifestyle and while his mother might
be willing to bail him out, his father controls the money.
A moral, upright pillar of the church, that's Davis, Sr. He
won't tolerate the family being at the heart of a scandal."

Hugo let his gaze travel around the porch, as nicely
furnished as any interior room, and the immaculate yard
and flower beds. Everything just so. He studied Lissa as
she watched him over the rim of her glass. She came across
as a tough cookie. He had no doubt she'd fight until she
either won or destroyed Talbott's life.

"Do you own a handgun?"

"Yes."

"I'd like to see it."

"You'll have to ask my husband."

"He has your gun?"

She smiled. "No. But he's a lawyer. A lawyer in hot
water. And he'd advise me to let him handle everything."
She shrugged again.

"Tell me about Thursday night."

"I already told the other policeman. I have nothing
further to say."

"You had motive and opportunity."

"You're wasting your time with me, detective. Davis
wasn't going to leave me. I knew he'd get bored. He always

does. I'm not worried about gossip, but I can't say the same for his father. You might want to ask him where he was when Ruby was killed."

She rose from the chair and Hugo glanced at her friend as he stood. Boots ran her tongue across her deep red lips and winked at him. He had no doubt this conversation would be the topic of the hour among their social set before the sun went down.

"You'll find Davis at The Club playing a round of golf," Lissa smiled as she held the door open, "with his father."

⁂

BUT DAVIS TALBOT wasn't at The Club. Neither was his father. Hugo had just missed them according to William. Neither was Hugo able to make any headway with the ever-present doorman. His answers to the questions about the activities of Thursday night were monosyllabic and in line with his initial statement to Junior. With one exception.

"This poker game, is it a regular thing?"

"Yes, suh."

"Always the same night? Thursday?"

William nodded.

"Always the same players?"

William hesitated. "Mostly."

"Mostly? Who doesn't show up regularly?"

William stood with his hands clasped behind his back and stared at the pea gravel of the horseshoe driveway. Finally, he said, "This one or that one."

"Is Davis Talbot this one or that one? Or one and the same?"

A frown creased William's forehead. "I couldn't say."

Thursday was Davis' night to prowl. A regular event at the Thunderbird Inn with Ruby. Unless they went to Diamondhead. That would be a bit of a drive to do every week. Maybe he saved that for the occasional weekend or a special treat. Hugo stood staring across the driveway of The Country Club. Dixie would know their schedule. So why had Dubya made the delivery on a night when there was a good chance of being discovered?

"Suh?" William said.

Hugo pulled his mind back to the moment. He gave William a grunt then headed to his car. Ruby and Davis knew about the smuggling. And Ruby was dead. He paused with his hand on the door handle. Did that mean Davis was in danger? Had there been a falling out among thieves?

❧

THE DAY WAS slipping through Hugo's fingers with nothing accomplished. He now had a better feel of Lissa Talbott. Junior had been right. She was a bulldog with a bone. No one would take it from her without a fight. A vicious fight.

He didn't have a clue as to where Davis had scurried off to, but Lissa had planted a seed and now he had to chase it down.

Colonel Dixie sat at the intersection of McGregor and Old Shell Road. The burger joint was closed on a hot, lazy,

Sunday afternoon, but it had a phone booth. He found Talbott, Sr.'s address on Tuthill.

The residence of Davis and Elaine Talbott was impressive in the extensiveness of the real estate it garnered on the most exclusive street in Spring Hill. The creole cottage looked small in that massive lawn until Hugo came to a stop at the apex of the long horseshoe drive.

Hugo saw the strong resemblance when Davis's mother answered the door. She gave him a scarcely veiled once over before raising her chin a notch.

"Yes?"

"Is Mr. Talbott in?"

She didn't respond for a couple of seconds. "And you are?"

He showed her his shield. "Hugo August, Mobile Police Department."

"It's Sunday. What do you want?"

"I'd like to speak to Mr. Talbott, Sr. Or to Junior, if he's here."

"About what?"

Hugo wasn't in the mood for the attitude. "Junior's dead mistress."

Elaine Talbott pulled back as if she'd been slapped. "Well, *really!*"

"Yes," Hugo replied. "Really."

Talbott, Sr. appeared in the doorway beside his wife at that moment. "Detective August, it's Sunday. Is this really necessary?"

"A murder investigation is a ticking clock, Mr. Talbott. And now there are two bodies."

Talbott, Sr. frowned. "What do you mean? Two bodies?"

"Someone else has been killed and the murders are connected. If you'd like to spare your wife the unpleasantness of this conversation, we can discuss it downtown."

"Oh, for pity's sake—" Talbott, Sr. glanced at his wife then glared at Hugo.

"Two murders, Mr. Talbott."

Elaine Talbott's indignation had turned to a hard anger. "Well, you should be out there doing your job then instead of harassing innocent people."

"If I were doing my job, your son would be in a jail cell."

She inhaled a sharp breath, "How *dare*—"

"How dare I follow the evidence to your doorstep? Means, motive, and opportunity? Your son had all three. He has no alibi for the time of death, and he feared a costly and very public divorce. Stop me when you think I've got something wrong."

Talbott, Sr. gave his wife a dismissive lift of his chin and motioned for Hugo to precede him across the foyer. There, behind double doors was a book lined study. And Davis Talbott. He turned from the view out the window to stare sullenly at Hugo. His face looked like a punching bag.

"Ouch," Hugo said.

Davis turned his face back to the view from the window.

His father closed the study doors firmly then rounded his desk to sit. "Now, let's deal with this mess once and for all."

"You say you were at the poker game then went straight home." Hugo asked Davis. "Why did you stand Ruby up?"

He sat in a worn leather armchair, took out his notebook, but didn't open it.

Davis glanced at his father then turned his attention to Hugo. "I didn't. She called and said there was a change of plans."

"What change of plans?"

"I don't know. The message said forget tonight. Change of plans. That's all."

"You didn't talk to her?"

"No. She left a message with Betty. I tried to call her several times over the course of the afternoon, but she never answered." He came to sit across from Hugo. "So, I went to dinner at the club then joined the poker game."

"Why wasn't she at work that day?"

"She had been. In the morning. But she didn't come back to the office after lunch."

"What time did she go to lunch?"

He shrugged. "It was late. Close to two o'clock, I think."

"Does she do that often?"

Davis glanced at his father. "She sometimes left early."

"Or came in late?"

He made no reply.

"She made her own hours. One of the perks of being your mistress?"

Davis turned his profile to Hugo and remained silent.

"Had you argued?"

He shook his head.

"Anything unusual happen in the days leading up to Thursday? At the office or otherwise?"

Davis focused on his wedding ring as he turned it around and around on his finger. "No."

"I want your wife's handgun."

Davis didn't respond immediately. He sighed. "It's at the house. I'll bring it by the station tomorrow."

Hugo reached across the desk and turned the telephone toward Davis. "Call your wife. Tell her a patrolman will be by in a few minutes to collect it."

Davis clenched his jaw then released it. He dialed the phone and spoke to his wife. The exchange was short and to the point. The moment he hung up, Hugo called the dispatcher to have a car sent to the house on Yester Place.

Then he focused on Davis. "Tell me about the cigarettes and alcohol."

Talbott, Sr. had been trimming his nails with a small pen knife. His head jerked up at Hugo's question.

The glance Davis shot in his father's direction was quick but not quick enough. "I don't know what you mean."

"At The Thunderbird. The untaxed flow of illicit goods. Brought in from Atlanta."

Davis sat back in his chair and laced his fingers together. "I don't know anything about that."

"Thursday nights. Delivery night. Dixie kept a record. It lines up once a month with your little trysts with Ruby. Thursday is your *poker night*, isn't it?"

Talbott, Sr.'s chair creaked. "What in the hell's going on?" He stared at Hugo and then his son.

Davis shrugged. "Whatever's happening has nothing to do with me. I don't know anything about it."

"Ruby knew." Hugo opened his notebook and flipped

through the pages. He stopped and stared at a page as if reading a notation. "It's hard to believe that you wouldn't notice all that going on right beneath your nose. Or are you really that dumb? Can't think beyond the zipper in your pants? Is that why you needed money? Too focused on Ruby to take care of business?"

Talbott, Sr. leaned forward, his forearms resting on his desk. "Now just a minute, August. In case you haven't noticed, Davis isn't exactly destitute. Whatever this *woman* was up to, my son had nothing to do with it." He leaned back and turned toward the window overlooking the side garden. The room fell silent, the only sound the ticking of a clock. With a sigh, he turned back to Hugo. "This sounds like a fishing expedition to me and it's obvious you haven't been able to come up with a legitimate suspect so you think you can bully my son. I would press charges against Stanton for the beating Davis has taken if I didn't think his poor judgment brought it on. His moral depravity aside, you have nothing on him. This conversation is at an end." He stood. "If you want to speak to Davis again, call his lawyer."

Hugo stood also as he returned the notebook to his back pocket. "You know what I think, Mr. Talbott? I think this is going to be a bigger scandal than the airing of the Haywood-Prescott dirty laundry."

Talbott, Sr.'s face reddened but he said nothing as he opened the door of his study.

Hugo crossed the foyer and stepped out onto the wide front porch, a deep sense of satisfaction at the stony expression on Elaine Talbott's face as she watched him from one of the floor-to-ceiling windows of the living room. But what next? The dog's body.

He put the Thunderbird in gear and headed down Old Shell Road toward Midtown.

Twenty-Four

ADELE GORTON HADN'T answered Junior's knock on his
initial visit after leaving Elizabeth Stanton's, so he spent
a good deal of the morning tracking down Sam Hollingsworth. He found the highway patrolman at the local VFW.
Going over his earlier statement revealed nothing new.
Hollingsworth was aware of Nelson. Had seen him a couple
of times in the Gorton's back yard and actually met him
once at Ruby's apartment. The only other thing he knew
about Nelson was that Ruby was fiercely protective of him.
He claimed he hadn't seen him in nearly a year.

He had no better luck rousing anyone at the Gorton
house on his return visit. An older model station wagon
sat in the carport to the right of the house but not so much
as a curtain twitched. Junior felt like he had wasted most
of the day spinning his wheels, revisiting dead ends. He
decided it was time he talked to Buzz Stanton. It was time
he took his own measure of the man.

As he made his way down Confederate Drive, Junior

tried to think who else might have interacted with Nelson. From everything he knew, the boy led a quiet, lonely life with his mother. He had no friends other than Ruby, and even that had become a distant relationship over the past year. He sat with the motor idling at the intersection of Hwy 31 and Spanish Main and let his gaze travel over the buildings crowning the top of the hill. On impulse, he turned into the Gulf station.

The ancient proprietor had a face that was ravaged by sun and a permanent squint. He looked up from the Sunday paper as Junior came through the door.

"Hep ya?" he asked.

"Marlboros," Junior said.

The old man swiveled his stool around, pulled a pack from the dispenser, and laid them on the counter. "That it?"

Junior nodded.

"Thirty-nine cents."

Junior looked up from counting the change in his hand. "Thirty-nine cents?"

The man shrugged. "Take it or leave it."

Junior laid the coins on the counter, made note of the tax stamp on the bottom of the pack, and tore the cellophane from the cigarettes as his looked around the station. In a cooler near the front door a hand-written sign advertised wigglers, shrimp, and crickets. An oak barrel held cane fishing poles and a couple of cheap rod and reels. An assortment of lures, corks, and hooks were displayed nearby. That was pretty much it aside from a rack of chips, peanuts, and what promised to be stale cookies and crackers and the Coke machine.

"You the owner?" Junior asked.

"Yep."

The view from the service station was of a new Texaco station on the opposite corner of Spanish Main and of the city's municipal offices across Hwy 31. Two cars were at the pumps of the Texaco, the attendant bustling between the two, filling their tanks and washing the windshields.

"Business seems kinda slow."

"It's Sunday."

Junior didn't think the day of the week had much bearing on the matter, but he didn't comment. "Been in business here a while, have ya?"

The good eye squinted almost as much as the bad one. "Just ask your questions and be done with it," he said.

"You know Nelson Gorton?"

"Yep."

"I heard he liked to come here for orange soda."

"His Ma brings him."

"He didn't walk here sometimes?"

"Not since he was a kid. Got lost once. Scared him, I reckon."

"But everyone around here is familiar with Nelson, right? Everyone knows him?"

"Well, I imagine they recognize him. Don't know how many would say they know him."

"Ruby Stanton?"

"Sure."

"Boo Vansant."

"Yep. They played as kids. Live close by."

"You haven't seen Nelson out on his own lately, have

you? He hasn't been to the new service station for a soda, maybe?"

"Not that I know."

"And you'd know, wouldn't you?"

The old guy stared at Junior. "I reckon I'd know."

"It's just you running the station, right? No hired help?"

"My daughter helps on Monday and Tuesday til three."

"When do you close?"

"Ten."

"And when do you open?"

"Six."

"Long days."

"Got nothing better to do."

Junior looked pointedly at the Texaco where a third vehicle had pulled up to the pumps. "And business has dropped off lately would be my guess."

"What's your point?"

"That you don't miss much. You see who comes and goes. You're kinda in the catbird seat."

The old man made no reply.

"Tell me about Thursday night."

"Not much to tell. Besides, I already told Buzz."

"Tell me anyway."

He looked out the wide plate glass window of the station and thought for a minute. "Ruby stopped in just before eight. Topped off her tank. Then headed south toward Daphne. A few locals came and went down to the Causeway and back up. Going into Mobile for this or that I reckon. It was the usual weeknight."

"Did you recognize any of them?"

"I recognized most of them. Dixie, on her way to work, for one. That was about six. And Nora Stanton. A little before ten that motorcycle come whizzing past. He likes to throttle it up Spanish Main. Boo stopped in just before closing. Gassed up the patrol car. Hung around while I closed up."

PEGGY SUE WAS at the station when Junior arrived, manning the switchboard. Boo was there, too. Neither of them knew the whereabouts of the Chief so Junior decided it would be a good time to review Boo's activities on the night of both Ruby and Nelson's murders.

He sat across from Boo at one of the two desks in the pit and opened his notebook. "Who else was on patrol Thursday night?"

"Harold. At least he was back-up. We generally have only one car cruising at night. Especially during the week."

"One car for the entire area?"

"Two on weekends. It's generally quiet. Mostly rural. Unless there's an accident or a bump in the night, we just cruise around."

"Any bumps in the night on Thursday?"

"A teenager caught sneaking back in late. The mother called."

"Why?"

"Because the father went nuts. Beat the crap out of her."

"Where was this?"

"Out 31. Almost to the county jurisdiction."

"Give it to me in miles."

"Sixteen, eighteen. Something like that."

"Did you ask for back-up?"

"No need. It's not the first time. And probably not the last. The father's an asshole and the kid's wild. She'll probably be pregnant or gone in short order. Or both."

"Did you bring him in?"

"What for?"

"Beating his kid."

"That would just open a can of worms. He'd argue he had a right to discipline her. Sneaking out, drinking, wouldn't tell him who she was with. It was nearly midnight. The Chief has spoken to him before. I imagine he will again. Besides, it's like she wants to provoke her dad. How you gonna keep them from going at each other? The whole family's like that."

"And you didn't have any concerns about stepping into that situation without back-up?"

Boo shrugged. "He knows not to take it too far."

"How far is too far?"

Boo looked across the station to where Peggy Sue was on the phone at the switchboard. "She'll be all right."

"Did you take her to the hospital?"

"No need. It wasn't that bad, really. Besides, her mother's a nurse. Doesn't want everyone knowing their business. Like they don't already."

Junior drew a line under the notation of the time of the incident in his notebook. "About midnight. Can you be more specific?"

Boo looked away from Junior, flexed his jaw, then stared

at him with an unblinking, hard glare. "I didn't kill Ruby. I loved her."

Junior watched him, unfazed by his attitude. "Time? When you received the call?"

"Ask Harold. He'll have logged it in." Boo nodded in Peggy Sue's direction. "Or have her show you the logbook."

"How long were you on the scene?"

"Half an hour. Forty-five minutes, tops." He leaned back, tilting his chair. "You can ask the mother. I reckon she'll remember."

"Help me out here. I'm trying to figure out why Nelson was murdered. It has to have something to do with Ruby's death. Has to." Junior studied the young policeman. "He was an innocent. Whatever was going on, he shouldn't have paid the price for it. You know he was terrified, forced through the briars and undergrowth, barefooted with a storm raging. He was afraid of the dark, for Christ's sake. He would have been confused, in a panic."

Boo brought his chair upright and lowered his gaze to the desktop. "I wish I knew." He looked up at Junior. "I honestly wish I knew 'cause I'd kill the S-O-B."

"Then tell me what Nelson could have known. Someone was threatened by him. We both know he was incapable of making a connection to an event that happened at the motel."

They sat in silence, considering the possibilities.

Finally, Boo spoke. "It was something he heard," he looked up at Junior, "or something he saw. Someone didn't want him to tell. The killer knew people would make the mental leap, place him at the scene. That has to be it."

"I think you're right. But how would Nelson know who was at the Thunderbird? That's what? Two miles away? Would Ruby tell him about what was going on there? About who she was meeting?" Junior shook his head. "I can't imagine she'd do that. So how did he know this *something*?"

"It was someone he saw."

"Which means it had to be someone he recognized. Someone who came to Ruby's apartment."

Junior and Boo looked at each other and spoke in unison, "The bogey man."

"Someone doesn't want us to know he visited Ruby at her apartment in the night because—" Junior tap-tap-tapped his pencil against the desk. Why? What made those visits such a deep, dark secret? "Because of *who* he was. Not why he came, though I think we can figure that one out, but because of who he was." He watched Boo from beneath slightly lowered lids, saw the subtle change as realization dawned. He knew. They both knew.

Boo turned his head slightly, guarding his expression. He glanced at his watch, cleared his throat, then stood. "I need to make a round. We're light today because of last night."

Junior stood as well. "We could be wrong."

Boo focused on his gun belt, adjusting the fit. "About what?"

"We have nothing to back up our suspicion."

Boo looked at him then. "That someone visited Ruby in the night and didn't want to get caught out about it? I think that's a solid."

"But we don't know who."

"If you say so."

With that he crossed the police station and out the door.

JUNIOR HURRIED TO his car and tried Hugo's police radio. He got no response. Dispatch informed him that they hadn't heard from his partner and that the Chief was looking for both of them. That was never good news. So, what now? If he was right, then Boo Vansant was about to alert their prime suspect that they were on to him. And possibly get himself killed in the process.

He went back inside the Spanish Fort police station. "Can you raise the Chief for me, Peggy Sue?"

She studied his face a moment. "Sure." But her radio call went unanswered.

"Can you ring his house?"

"What's going on?"

"I need to bounce some thoughts off him about the case." He gave a slight shrug. "The clock's ticking."

Peggy Sue rang the Chief's house. "Nora, I'm looking for the Chief."

She listened briefly then hung up and turned back to Junior. "Not home. Thinks he might have gone with Beth to the funeral home."

"O'Sullivan's?"

"Where else?"

"Right."

HUGO FOUND BETTY'S residence on the second floor of the Warwick Apartments on Government Street. She answered the door in a pair of shorts and a sleeveless blouse tied at the waist. Her short hair was pulled away from her face and neck by a twisted configuration of a pink bandana that allowed the curls to form a pretty crown on her head. He realized that she was more attractive than he had first thought. Perhaps it was the absence of her glasses. Or the shapeliness of her legs.

An oscillating fan stirred the hot, humid air but did little to cool the room. She looked surprised to find him on her doorstep.

"Detective." She glanced beyond him into the hallway then returned her attention to him. "What do you want?"

"To talk about Ruby."

"I heard about the boy."

"News travels fast."

"News at Noon. He drowned they say."

"Could I come in?"

"Oh. Sure." She stepped back and Hugo entered the pleasant room with dark hardwood floors and tall windows.

"Nice place."

"I like it." She hesitated. "Would you care for something to drink?"

"A glass of cold water would be nice."

She gave a dip of her chin and motioned toward an armchair. "I won't be a minute."

He heard her breaking the ice in a tray and the tinkle of it as she filled a glass. She returned from the kitchen with two glasses in hand. The cold felt good to the touch and he took a long swallow.

"That hits the spot."

Betty made no comment, simply settled in the chair on the other side of the window from him and waited.

He looked out at the view of Government Street. "The tree keeps it nice and shady here."

"But cold in the winter."

"The traffic noise doesn't bother you?"

"You get used to it."

He drained the glass of water and placed it on a coaster on the small side table. "Tell me about the phone call from Ruby Thursday afternoon."

A blush traveled up Betty's throat to her cheeks. "What about it?"

"There wasn't one, was there?"

"Why would you say that?"

"Because it's true. You wanted him to stand her up, didn't you?"

She didn't respond, simply stared at the glass in her hand.

"He was going to file for divorce so he could marry Ruby. You knew, didn't you? Because you're the one who does everything. The filing, the typing."

The threat of tears rose in her eyes, but she blinked them away. Still, she remained silent.

"Even with all that that would cost him, he had made up his mind. She was the one who was worth the sacrifice. You couldn't let that happen."

Hugo waited but still no response.

"You knew Ruby had a temper. That it would cause a fight between them. Maybe even end their relationship."

They sat there with only the Sunday afternoon traffic breaking the silence.

"Where were you Thursday night?"

"What?" Her head came up and she stared at him, a look of fright on her face.

"Between midnight Thursday and 2:00 a.m. Friday morning?"

"Here." Her hand trembled and she set the glass on the side table. "Asleep."

"Anyone vouch for you?"

"What? No!"

"Do you own a car?"

She shook her head, the tears threatening once again.

"How do you get to work? Run errands?"

"The bus. There's a stop on the next corner."

Hugo turned his attention to the view and the stately homes on the other side of the broad street. Love. What would Betty do for love? Sabotage Davis's relationship with Ruby? Yes. Murder Ruby? How would that change her situation? It wouldn't. He was married to Lissa. Maybe not happily but comfortably. He would still be married to her if Ruby went the way of all his other mistresses. But he hadn't been willing to give up his cushy life for any of the others, had he? Would that be enough to cause Betty's jealousy to rise to the level of murder? Would she be willing to go that far to keep the status quo? What kind of life was that?

And yet he knew. An empty one filled with the

monotonous passing of days and weeks. A life teetering on the hope of the impossible.

Twenty-Five

HUGO SAT IN the idling Thunderbird flipping through the pages of his notebook. Something was teasing at the edge of his mind. Davis was off the hook—for now. Without Betty's interference, he would have been at the motel. And maybe Ruby would still be alive.

The question was, had Lissa known about the divorce filing? She and her friend had been in a celebratory mood. Ruby's death had solved her problems. In the short term. Davis didn't strike Hugo as the kind of man who would inconvenience himself with a messy divorce with no reward in sight.

His police radio squawked to life. It was Junior.

"What's happening?" Hugo asked.

"It's not about the murder."

"What?"

"Nelson. He was killed because of what he saw—or rather who he saw—at Ruby's. Someone who didn't want his visits known."

"Because of the scandal."

"Not O'Sullivan."

"No." Hugo put the car into gear and pulled out of the parking lot of the Warwick Apartments. "Stanton."

"Bingo."

"Where is he?"

"With Elizabeth, I think. I hope."

"Because?"

"Boo came to the same conclusion."

"Where are you?"

"On the Causeway. She's at the funeral home. With Stanton. I'm headed there now."

"I'll meet you there."

⚜

HUGO FORCED HIMSELF to drive the speed limit from the top of Spring Hill down Old Shell Road to O'Sullivan's Funeral Home. He could hear the pounding of his blood. Junior's suspicions dovetailed nicely with the picture that had been building over the course of the investigation. He replayed the interviews with Hollingsworth and Boo. His conversations with Adele, Elizabeth, and Stanton. He wanted to punch the dashboard of the car.

He was the first to arrive. Four cars were in the parking lot. He didn't recognize any of them. The receptionist informed him that the funeral director was with a bereaved family. It would be Elizabeth, he decided. They must have come over in Buzz's car. He would wait, out of deference to a mother who had lost her only child. He would control his reaction out of sympathy for that bereaved mother. He would.

Junior arrived about ten minutes into his wait. He brought Hugo up to speed on his thinking about the bogey man.

Hugo focused on a standing spray of flowers as he listened. He could feel Junior's watchful eye. He reached for the knot of his tie only to remember he wasn't wearing one.

Subdued voices reached them, and Hugo looked up to see O'Sullivan escorting an elderly man and a young woman along the central hallway of the funeral home.

O'Sullivan glanced from Hugo to Junior then back again as he turned the couple over to the receptionist. He settled his attention on Hugo.

"Detective August."

"Where's Chief Stanton?"

O'Sullivan's brow creased fleetingly. "I have no idea."

"Elizabeth Stanton?"

"She was here earlier."

"When?"

"Just before ten."

Hugo checked his watch. Four hours. He looked at Junior who shrugged.

"How long was she here?"

"Less than an hour. She knew what she wanted. Signed the contract and asked me to co-ordinate the services with the Methodist Church in Spanish Fort."

Junior spoke up. "Was she alone?"

"Yes."

The two detectives exchanged a glance.

Hugo pinned O'Sullivan with a look sharp with contempt. "We'll want a formal statement about your activities on Thursday night. Say, ten o'clock? Tomorrow? Feel free to bring your lawyer." He didn't wait for a response but turned and, with Junior, walked out of the building.

Hugo and Junior stood beside their cars in the parking lot.

"Are you sure she said Stanton was with Elizabeth?"

"She said probably."

"And that they were coming here this afternoon?"

"Yeah."

"Why would she lie about that?"

"Maybe it wasn't a lie. Maybe she thought it *was* this afternoon. It's Sunday, after all."

"Umm." Hugo stared into space, lost in thought. Finally, he spoke. "Strange, isn't it?"

"What?"

"Elizabeth's every move has been carefully monitored until now. Always someone with her. And suddenly no one knows where she is or what she's doing."

"She's at home by now, I'd expect."

"We should make sure."

"What about Stanton?"

"Until we have some evidence, there's nothing we can do about him. Right now, our only hope is that Elizabeth will tell us what she knows."

"You don't think she knew? Surely, she would have done something—her husband would have done *something*."

"People don't always see what's in front of them. Especially when they don't want to."

"I can see Henry not knowing. Men don't notice things. But Elizabeth. She's her mother. She would know." The depravity of what his words implied seemed to fully register with Junior. He frowned and shook his head. "She didn't just turn a blind eye. Who would do that?"

"Let's not get the cart before the horse. We don't really know."

"And yet, we do." Junior's face looked cast in stone.

"Elizabeth. We need to find her." Hugo gave his partner a gentle slap on the shoulder. "We'll leave your car at the motel. If we're right, then the only other person who knows Stanton's secret is Elizabeth."

"You don't think—"

"Let's find her. Then we'll find him."

"Boo may have already beaten us to the punch."

"That wouldn't hurt my feelings one little bit."

"He's running on his anger. Setting himself up for trouble."

Hugo touched the collar of his shirt again. "Don't worry about Boo. I expect he can take care of himself. Even against Stanton. And if we're right, Stanton deserves whatever Boo gives him."

"That could jeopardize the case."

Hugo opened the driver's door of the Thunderbird. "On this, I'm with Stanton. I'm not overly worried about taking it to court. My guess is, neither is Boo." He slid onto the seat of the car and roared out of the parking lot headed toward downtown and the Bankhead Tunnel.

⁂

JUNIOR PULLED ONTO the oyster shell parking lot of the Thunderbird Inn and parked the drab city issue sedan beside Hugo. He grabbed his police radio and got into Hugo's idling car. He'd barely closed the car door when the tires caught rubber out onto the Causeway. Within five minutes, they were staring at Elizabeth Stanton's house.

"Car's here," Junior said.

"Umm."

Junior let his gaze travel across the yard and over to the Gorton house. Adele's station wagon was still parked in the carport. Both houses had a shuttered, closed-in look. The only sound was the buzzing of a bumble bee circling the honeysuckle vine growing on the mailbox. The air felt heavy. The June sun beat down with an afternoon hazy heat. It felt off somehow. Too quiet. His heartbeat quickened. Something wasn't right.

Hugo was already halfway to the front door of Elizabeth's house. Junior pushed his sports coat back from the gun holstered under his left shoulder and followed after him.

There was no answer to Hugo's knock. He tried a second time then turned the door knob. It opened easily and silently. Junior turned and looked left to right along the roadway with a sweeping glance at the Gorton's, then he stepped into the house behind Hugo.

"Elizabeth," Hugo called out.

He gave Junior a lift of the chin and the two split up quickly covering both sides of the house. No one was home.

"Where would she be?"

Hugo opened the closet door in Elizabeth's bedroom.

Everything appeared to be in order. The bathroom was neat and tidy. Nothing out of place. In the kitchen, an army jacket hung on the back of a chair.

"Someone's been here. They left their coat," Junior said.

On the table was a photograph. Hugo picked it up. "I did."

"You?"

Hugo ran his thumb over the faces in the picture then he slipped it into the pocket of his Hawaiian shirt. "We should check Adele's," he said. "And Ruby's apartment."

A large pecan tree shaded the back yard between the house and the garage apartment. Hugo went up the stairs as Junior checked the Dodge Dart parked underneath. The hood of the car was cool to the touch. Tire tracks leading in and out showed little activity in the damp soil of the driveway, evidence she hadn't taken the car out since her trip to O'Sullivan's.

Hugo came down the stairs with a shake of his head. They crossed the lawn to Adele Gorton's house.

She answered on the first knock. She didn't greet them, simply opened the door and retreated down the hallway toward the kitchen.

Hugo and Junior followed her. A photo album lay open on the kitchen table.

She sat and waited.

"We're looking for Mrs. Stanton," Hugo said.

"Which one?"

Hugo and Junior glanced at each other.

"Elizabeth."

Adele nodded and slowly turned a page of the album.

She traced a finger along one of the photos. It was of Nelson in the tree swing. "She left right after you were here." She nodded toward Junior. She turned another page. "Came back about two hours later."

"She's not home."

"No? Umm." Another page turned. "Maybe she left with him. Or her."

"Stanton?" Hugo asked.

She nodded. "Showed up as soon as she got home. Stayed about an hour, I guess. Didn't see when he left but heard the truck start up."

"And Nora Stanton?"

"Not long ago. Close to three o'clock, maybe. In and out. Didn't stay."

"Did Elizabeth leave with her?"

"Couldn't say. I was trying to take a nap, but I heard the car door."

Hugo sat down across the table from Adele. "We need to find her. Do you know where she might go? To the Chief's house?"

Adele looked up from the album. "I doubt that."

"Why?"

"Because of Nora."

"What about Nora?"

"She doesn't like Elizabeth."

Hugo sat back in his chair. "Why?"

"Who knows? Jealous would be my guess. They didn't have any kids, you know. Her and Buzz. And he was crazy about Ruby. Always over there hanging 'round with Henry, cooking out, tinkering with one old truck or another. And

Beth, doing stuff around the house for her. Painting the kitchen, screening the back porch. Just an excuse to be 'round the child, if you ask me." She turned toward the kitchen window and the view of Ruby's apartment door. "Nora quit coming with him years ago. Can't say I blame her. It was like they were his family and she was an outsider. And after Henry died? Well, Buzz couldn't do enough for Beth, could he? Cutting the grass, fixing the leaking faucet. Popping in all the time." She shook her head. "Nora was a teacher, did you know? Always looking after other folks' kids but never one of her own. Sad, really."

"If that's the case, I'm surprised that Nora's been over there all the time since Ruby's death."

"He would have told her to, wouldn't he? Grieving mother. His cousin's widow. Family. Love 'em or hate 'em, you put on a caring face when trouble comes 'round."

"How did Henry die?"

Adelle looked up from the photo album. "Don't you know?"

Hugo shook his head.

"Shotgun. Hunting accident. Tore up a major artery. Bled out before Buzz could get him any help."

Hugo stood abruptly, his chair scraping violently against the linoleum floor. "Stanton was with him?"

Adele sat back in her chair, startled, a concerned look on her face. "I thought you knew."

He looked at Junior.

"I just found out this morning. All Elizabeth said was a hunting accident. I didn't know that Stanton was with him."

Junior saw the flare of Hugo's nostrils. This put paid

to any doubt. Another piece in the puzzle, another nail in the coffin. Ruby's behavior, Elizabeth's retreat into a drug induced stupor. The threads weaving together in a twisted tale of obsession and control. Stanton was their man. And he had Elizabeth. Junior no longer had any doubt that she knew. That she knew it all.

Hugo was already turning for the hallway. "Stanton's truck. What does it look like?"

"Red. Ford, I think." Adele said.

He was halfway down the hall. "He's got at least two hours on us."

Twenty-Six

"WHERE WOULD HE take her?" Hugo asked as he sped around a sharp curve on Confederate Drive. He banged his palm against the steering wheel. "We're at a disadvantage. We don't know enough about the area, about him and his habits."

They were flying along Spanish Main toward the intersection with Hwy 31.

"Turn in here," Junior gestured to his right.

It was the Gulf service station.

"The owner's nosey. Business is slow. Maybe he saw which way Stanton went."

Hugo braked and made a hard turn onto the paved apron of the gas station.

The owner looked from Junior to Hugo as they entered the store.

"You been here all day?" Hugo asked.

The owner sucked on his teeth and nodded.

"You know the Chief's truck?"

"Yep."

"Seen it today?"

He nodded again.

"When?"

"'Bout two hours ago."

"Anyone with him?"

He shrugged. "Don't know. Didn't see nobody."

"Which way was he headed?"

"Over to the station."

Hugo and Junior looked through the large storefront window across the intersection to the southeast corner where the Spanish Fort Police Station stood.

"But he didn't stay long," the attendant said. "Quick in and out. Then south on 98."

"Where does he live? The Chief?"

"Just over the way. 'Bout a quarter mile." He nodded south. "Take a right off 98 on Patrician Drive. Don't know the number."

"We should check at the station," Junior said as they hurried back to the car. "He may have told Peggy Sue where he was going."

Hugo pulled across the intersection against the red light and slid to a halt at the front door of the station. "Be quick. She's the key. We have to find her."

Junior was in the station less than five minutes. "Don't know," he said as he climbed onto the passenger seat of the Thunderbird. "He's not answering his radio or the home phone. Thinks he might have been headed home but that was two hours ago. Got the house number. Three oh eight."

But when they arrived, there was no red pick-up parked in the drive. The carport sheltered a Ford station wagon. No one answered the door but as they were getting back into Hugo's car, Nora Stanton walked around the corner of the house carrying a canvas bag. She frowned and stopped.

"We're looking for the Chief," Hugo said.

"He's not here."

"Do you know where he is?"

"Haven't seen him since this morning. Early. He came back from—down the bay and got a shower. Left right after. You should check with Beth."

"He's not there. Neither is she."

She opened the back of the wagon and put the bag inside then turned to Hugo and Junior and gave a small shrug. "Well, I can't help you."

"Where would he go? Any idea?"

Nora shook her head and moved to the driver's door of the vehicle. "Couldn't say. He doesn't feel the need to keep me informed of his whereabouts." She got into the car.

"Where're you going, Mrs. Stanton?"

"Sailing." She closed the door and rolled down the window.

"Kinda late in the day to set out, isn't it?"

"This is the best time, actually. The most peaceful time of day." The engine sparked to life. "Sorry I can't help. Is it important?" She sat there with the engine idling.

"Two deaths. So, yeah, it's important."

"Check with dispatch. Beyond that I don't know what to tell you."

"If you see him, have him call Mobile. Our dispatcher will patch him through on our channel."

"I won't see him anytime soon. I'll be out on the bay til dusk."

"Where's your boat?"

"Fairhope Yacht Club."

"How can we reach you if we need to?"

She frowned. "You can't. That's the point." She studied Hugo. "Why would you need to?"

"No reason."

She nodded, put the car in gear and backed out of the carport.

⁂

THEY WATCHED HER pull onto Patrician Drive and disappear around the corner.

"What now?" Junior asked.

"Hell if I know. Spanish Fort is so spread out, he could be anywhere."

They fell silent. Junior focused on the sun slowly lowering. It was a couple of hours above the treetops. He focused his thoughts, sifting through the odds and ends of information gleaned in his many conversations with potential witnesses. Finally, he spoke. "Peggy Sue. She knows the dirt on everyone. If anyone can tell us where the Chief would disappear to, it would be her."

"We've got nowhere else to start so let's see what she says."

⁂

"BACK SO SOON?" Peggy Sue asked as Junior and Hugo walked into the police station.

"No luck at the Chief's house. Mrs. Stanton doesn't know where he might be," Junior replied. "Boo been back since this morning?"

She shook her head. "Called in a couple of times. Wants to find the Chief just about as bad as you two. What's going on?"

"Elizabeth Stanton's missing," Hugo said. "Considering all that's happened, we're concerned." He leaned an elbow on the high counter that served as a reception point as well as housing the dispatcher apparatus of the department. "No one has seen Stanton or Elizabeth since the early morning. We figured they might be together."

Peggy Sue dropped her gaze to the switchboard. "I suppose they could be."

"Where would they go?" Junior asked as he dug a Marlboro pack from his coat pocket. "They're not at the funeral home. Not at the Chief's." He looked up from worrying with the cellophane on the cigarettes. "Any idea?"

"How would I know?"

"Everyone is fooling around with everyone, isn't that what you said? Someone important. That someone probably has a hidey-hole somewhere. The motel is a possibility but too public. All the cars lined up out front for the world to see." He gave a little *meh* movement of his head. "Better for the Mobile nooners, would be my guess. He'd want someplace else where the locals were less likely to see."

"You know of any place like that, Peggy Sue?" Hugo asked.

Peggy Sue looked uncomfortable. "I never said it was the Chief."

"True. I'm not saying it's the Chief either. Just jogging your memory of any place where the locals feel safe from prying eyes, is all."

"Why would he take Elizabeth to such a place? What's really going on?" Peggy Sue's gaze darted back and forth between Junior and Hugo.

"Two deaths," Hugo said. "The Chief might have been concerned about Elizabeth's safety. Both victims are connected to her. We don't have a motive. It's like chasing a ghost. He might feel the need to keep her out of sight. Out of harm's way."

"Wouldn't he have told you?"

"He's not real happy with our involvement in the case. You know that. Wants to dispense his own brand of justice is my guess. But we have to talk to Elizabeth. She's what links the two deaths. The answer has to be with her."

"But, why? Beth is the least likely person I know of that someone would want to harm. She's lived here her whole life. Married Henry within six weeks of graduation. Quiet. A housewife and mother. You hardly ever see her except for church or the grocery store."

"She's a very striking woman. I imagine she attracts attention wherever she goes."

"Yeah, sure. But everyone knows, don't they?"

"Knows what?"

"That you don't go there. The Chief wouldn't tolerate it."

"Interesting," Hugo said.

Peggy Sue stared at him.

"You said the Chief. Not Henry."

"Well, both, I guess."

"But the Chief was the one who came to mind at the thought of someone showing too much interest in Elizabeth."

"You're putting words in my mouth." She glared at Hugo. "It's just that Henry is—was—always quiet. I guess with the Chief being his cousin, it was the obvious thought. That's why it popped into my head. And the Chief has always been close to Beth. Even before she married Henry."

"They dated, didn't they? In high school?"

"Yeah. She was a cheerleader. He played football and basketball."

"Let me guess. Star of the team?"

She frowned. "Well, yeah. When you think about it, he kinda was."

"So, what happened?"

Peggy Sue shrugged. "I don't really know. The end of school. Things change. I went off to teach summer camp down Mary Ann Beach Road after graduation. Didn't come home except on Sundays. Everyone was getting jobs or off on family vacations. I didn't see much of anyone. When I came home in August, Henry and Beth were married."

Junior lit up a cigarette and squinted through the smoke at Peggy Sue. "There has to be some place."

Peggy Sue started to shake her head then stopped. "Maybe the shack. But I can't see him taking her there."

"Why not?"

"That's where Henry died."

Junior glanced at Hugo, saw the subtle straightening of his stance, the sharp focus on Peggy Sue.

"Tell me about the accident," Hugo said. His voice calm, void of emotion.

"Not much to tell. Henry had a bit of land down along D'Olive Creek. Liked to go deer hunting. They'd gone to shoot quail. Apparently, there're a couple of small but open fields. Used to have cows down there when the previous owner had it. They were climbing through the barb wire fence when it happened.

"Henry leaned his gun against the post and as he was climbing through, it dislodged and went off. Tore a hole in his groin. Must have been the movement of the barbed wire. The post was mostly rotten." Peggy Sue became pale as she talked. She swallowed. "It was awful. Hard to think about even after two years."

She sat back in her chair and stared out the window. "The Chief couldn't do anything about the bleeding. The wound was too torn up." She shook her head. "He had to come all the way back to the highway for help. There was nothing anyone could do."

"Where's this shack?"

Junior heard the steel in Hugo's voice.

Peggy Sue frowned and looked down at the desk blotter. "Off 98 just over the bridge at D'Olive Creek. It's not much more than a logging road. Got a metal gate to keep out trespassers. A 'do not enter' road sign on the gate." She looked up. "But I really can't think he'd take her there."

"Get Boo on the radio. Tell him it's an all-out search for the Chief's truck. That he's to call it in if he finds them. Get some more help in here. Call up everyone."

"I can't do that!" Peggy Sue pushed her chair back as if

she would stand but didn't. "I mean, it's—the Chief has to say what's to be done. I can't just call everyone in like that." She snapped her fingers for emphasis. "Besides, if she's with the Chief, she's safe."

"Do you really believe that, Peggy Sue?" Hugo locked eyes with her, his voice not unkind. "Do you?"

After a long moment, she looked away, switched on the mic and called out to Boo.

Hugo and Junior didn't wait for her to initiate contact. They were out the door of the station and headed down the hill on Hwy 98.

⁂

IF HUGO HADN'T known what they were looking for they would have missed the road. It was a single track, deeply rutted, the metal gate and sign partially obscured by a low hanging branch of a sweetgum tree. Wild growth had overtaken the fencing on either side of the lane.

Junior got out of the car to open the gate. He checked for tire tracks.

"Someone's been in and out of here since the rain stopped," he said, as he got back into the car. He checked his gun as they bumped along with the occasional tree branch slapping at the roof and sides of the car.

Sun glinted off the metal roof as they came around a curve. The building before them was made of rough, sun-bleached boards, the metal roof scarred with patches of rust. It was low to the ground with the roof extending over hard packed earth that provided an outdoor space protected from rain. A pock-marked aluminum glider and matching rocking chair sat in the shade of the overhang.

There was no sign of the Chief's truck. The only vehicle on the premises appeared to be an ancient John Deere tractor with a flat tire, the grass growing up around it.

Both men got out of the car and waded through the knee-high weeds toward the shack. They approached from opposite sides of the door. Junior reached across and turned the doorknob. As he pushed, Hugo swung into the opening with his gun pointed into the dim interior.

"No one home," he said as he stepped across the threshold into the one room building. He holstered his gun as he and Junior stood just inside the door and took stock of the space.

There was a window on each end of the building. A pot-bellied stove stood in one corner. A metal coffee pot sat on top of it. An old kitchen hutch stood to the right of the stove and held a bit of china and cutlery as well as a cast iron skillet. Two mismatched chairs and a wooden table stood in the center of the room. On the far end wall an iron bed occupied most of the space.

Sitting on the bed was the overnight case.

"They were here," Junior said. "That's Elizabeth's bag. I saw it at her house this morning."

A thick layer of dust on the floor showed evidence of someone walking all around the shack, overlapping, scuffing previous footprints. But Hugo could tell by the size and shape that they had been made by two different people.

Junior started toward the bed and Hugo caught his arm.

"Leave it," he said. "We need to preserve the footprints."

Junior looked at Hugo and clenched his jaw. With a curt nod, he stepped backward out the door. Hugo followed.

Under the overhang they surveyed the dense growth that began about thirty feet from the shack on all sides. Gnats and mosquitos swarmed in the air.

"Why would she go with him?" Junior took his cigarettes from his pocket. "The bag doesn't fit. I thought maybe it was Ruby's things. For her burial. Why would it be here?"

"We won't know until we see what's in it. We know she went to O'Sullivan's. That Stanton showed up soon after she got home, stayed for an hour. Somehow he convinced her to leave with him."

"But why the bag? Why bring it here?"

They fell silent, each thinking his own thoughts.

Finally, Hugo spoke. "Because it never contained Ruby's things. She was afraid. She packed to leave but he got there before she could."

Junior lit a cigarette and blew the smoke at the gnats. He cleared his throat. "She had a bruise. On her throat. Almost hidden by her necklace. Small. When you think about it, it was about the size of a thumb print."

Hugo lowered his gaze to the hard packed earth but said nothing.

"I should have known. I should have done something," Junior said.

"Did she seem frightened?" Hugo asked.

Junior shook his head. "Not really. Maybe. We talked about fear, about what made Nelson go out into the storm. But mainly I thought she was just in a hurry. She kept watching the road through the living room window. I should have known."

*

THEY MADE A circuit of the house. As the ground sloped away from the building about a hundred feet at the back, they found a trail that led through an opening in the hedge of wild growth. The tall grass showed no sign of having been disturbed recently.

"No one's been this way. It looks like they came to the house and nowhere else. We won't find her here," Hugo said.

"Do you think she's dead?"

"No. But I think we've got to find her. And soon."

Hugo needed Junior to keep his head and focus on the search, so he kept his thoughts to himself. The facts were leading them straight to Buzz Stanton, a man who had very good reasons to silence any potential witnesses. And if he was eliminating witnesses, Elizabeth was already dead.

But why leave the bag? Had Junior gotten it right? Maybe the plan had been to go to the funeral home in the afternoon as Nora suggested. He should have asked O'Sullivan. If that was the case, what made Elizabeth change her mind? They needed forensics to process the shed. He needed to know what was in that overnight bag.

Twenty-Seven

HUGO PUT A call through to Mobile's dispatcher requesting forensics at the shed as they made their way back to the Spanish Fort police station. He hoped Evie was still on call. He trusted her to do the job right. And he needed to see what was in the over-night bag sooner rather than later.

Boo and two other patrolmen were at the police station when Hugo and Junior arrived. With Peggy Sue, they comprised the entire force except for the chief.

The officers who had been with Stanton after the discovery of Nelson's body glared at Hugo. He knew they could be more hinderance than help if they chose to be, but he needed their eyes and knowledge of the area. If he requested men from the Mobile force they would be as much in the dark as he was.

"I know this is unusual, but Elizabeth is missing, and I think she's in danger. This search is as much about finding where she isn't as it is about finding where she is. So, I really don't care how you feel about it. I'm in charge of the case because Stanton didn't want the sheriff involved but if you don't think you can put Elizabeth's safety ahead of your hurt feelings, I have no problem calling him in."

No one spoke into the silence that followed Hugo's statement.

"Right. It's important we establish if she's with the chief. No one has seen either of them since early this morning. If he came to the same conclusions we have, she could be with him. That makes locating him a priority." Hugo moved to a map of Spanish Fort mounted on the wall. He studied it then parceled out a search grid to each officer.

"I've programmed our radios to your channel. I want to know the minute you spot Stanton. We believe he's in his truck."

No one made a move.

"For Christ's sake!" Boo said. "Ruby's dead. Nelson's dead. Do you want to risk Elizabeth, too?"

With that, the two men exchanged a glance then grabbed the police radios Peggy Sue handed them. Without a word, they made their way toward their patrol cars.

"Can we trust them?" Hugo asked.

Boo watched them through the glass door of the station. "Yeah. Harold's dumb as a post but both of them are good men. Everyone likes Elizabeth but they'll give the Chief a heads up if they find him first."

"I don't doubt it but if she's with him, he'll know what we're thinking. Hopefully that will keep her safe for now."

Hugo watched Boo who remained stoney faced and wouldn't meet his gaze. "Junior says you've made certain assumptions about the case."

Boo made no reply.

Hugo motioned with a lift of his chin. The three men moved outside and out of Peggy Sue's hearing.

"It's crucial we find Elizabeth and separate her from Stanton. Without her, we have no proof. Ruby's dead. Nelson's dead. She's all we have. Understood?"

Boo looked him in the eye, clenched his jaw, and nodded.

Hugo and Junior watched as Boo drove out of the parking lot.

"What now?" Junior asked.

"Dixie," Hugo replied. "O'Sullivan might not be anything to her, but someone is."

"The naughty nighties."

"Um. I have a strong suspicion it might be Stanton."

Junior frowned. "But what about Ruby?"

"Sleight of hand. Keep the gossips focused on a distraction so they don't see what you really want to hide."

"By gossips you mean Peggy Sue."

"I'm sure there are plenty of others. As she said, there isn't a lot to do in a small place like this. I don't imagine much happens without everyone knowing. Come on. I'll take you to your car." Hugo glanced down at the gas needle. He would need to tank up soon but not now. They didn't have any daylight to waste. "You go check Dixie's. If his truck's there, drive past and call it in."

"Where are you going?"

"The Paradise. I'm pretty sure it's one of their customers for the cigs. And they have rooms. If he's hiding out with her, they could be there."

"But that's for blacks."

"Exactly. Who would look there?"

THE THUNDERBIRD WAS off at speed as soon as Junior slammed the passenger door. He put the key to the city issue sedan into the lock as he swatted at a fly, then hesitated. He looked at the entrance of the motel. It would only take a quick minute to give Grammy a call. He knew she would have been worrying all day about Hugo. At the very least, he could ease her mind.

As he opened the front door of the motel, the fly zoomed past him.

His grandmother answered the phone on the third ring.

"Oh, Junior. I've been worried sick."

"He's all right, Grammy. At least outwardly. The case has his full attention."

"Well, that's a small blessing. It's the talk of the town, you know. Everyone says they'll probably move to Birmingham after the wedding. That's where his family is."

"Maybe so, Grammy."

"It would be for the best. For Hugo, I mean."

"Could be. Look, I have to go. I just wanted to let you know," Junior said as he watched the fly buzz through the door of the restaurant then back out and across the foyer of the motel. "Grammy, I have to go."

He hung up the phone and hurried to the foyer. It was a blowfly. It zigged and zagged down the hallway and bumped against the door to room seven. It buzzed and bumped as Junior came to stand before the door, his heart thumping in his chest.

Junior opened the door.

Late afternoon sunlight filtered through the partially open blinds. Elizabeth Stanton lay on the bed in perfect stillness. A blowfly walked on her pale cheek. He didn't need its presence to know that she was dead. The rage rose up through him in a vicious growl as he swatted at the carrion fly.

There was no visible mark on Elizabeth other than the old bruise at her throat. She wore the skirt and blouse he had seen her in earlier in the morning. Her body lay perfectly straight with her hands flat against her stomach, one above the other, her eyes closed serenely. The dark blue shoes sat side-by-side on the floor at the edge of the bed as if she had lifted her feet straight out of them as she lay down.

The room was hot, and he turned on the window air conditioner to the lowest setting. Evie would probably complain but he couldn't bear to think of her body decomposing minute by minute in the heat of this dingy, sordid room. He swung again at the fly, trying to herd it out of the room. His mind raced.

Hugo needed to be first on the scene. He couldn't have gotten very far in the few minutes it had taken Junior to make his phone call. He hurried from the room, closing the door behind him. His police radio sat on the dining table where he had laid it. For a moment, he hesitated. Hugo's radio would be set to the Spanish Fort channel. The call would have to go through Peggy Sue.

He pushed the talk button. "Spanish Fort, this is Knight."

The radio squawked. "I'm listening," Peggy Sue said.

"Change of plans. Forensics has been diverted from the shed."

"Why?"

"A body was found. It'll take priority. Let August know and tell him Goode got his message and needs him to check in without delay."

"Will do."

Junior felt sure Hugo would understand the hidden meaning behind his words. If Peggy Sue delivered them exactly as he said them. They needed to assess the crime scene before Spanish Fort arrived to bluster and obstruct. He switched his radio to the channel the Mobile department used. He told the dispatcher to divert the forensics team to the motel. All he could do now was wait.

He walked out of the motel and stood beside his car. He let his gaze travel over the oystershell parking lot. The coarse texture of the shells, broken and crumbling from the many vehicles that came and went, obscured any distinguishable tire tracks. On the paved apron under the portico of the building a powdery white web of prints overlapped, each one obscuring earlier foot steps.

The prints faded as they trailed in all directions across the industrial brown carpet into the interior of the foyer of the motel and down the hallway. It would be impossible to find anything useful in the maze.

He examined the door of the motel. The lock was scarred and scratched from years of coming and going. Junior thought back over his arrival first thing that morning. The door had been unlocked. It had been left unlocked all day because he and Hugo had been in and out as the investigation took them in search of leads. There was no mystery as to how Elizabeth gained access.

To insure he didn't further contaminate the scene, he went outside and waited.

JUNIOR FELT A calmness, almost a detachment, as he leaned against the car, his hands in his pants' pockets.

The pill bottle, her shoes aligned just so, the Sleeping Beauty positioning, it all painted a picture of suicide.

Why hadn't any of them realized the possibility? They knew her husband had died two years before. Now Ruby. The death of a child was devastating but the manner of the death unbearable. They should have known about the hunting accident. He could understand why Elizabeth had been so carefully watched. Did she have a history of suicidal attempts?

Why had Stanton kept all of it from them? Pride? An attempt to keep them at arm's length to protect himself?

The Thunderbird plowed into the parking lot and slide to an abrupt stop with a cloud producing application of the brakes.

"Where?" Hugo asked as he got out of the car and made for the door of the motel.

"Number seven," Junior said as he pushed away from his car and followed.

Hugo opened the door of the motel room but didn't step across the threshold. Junior saw the effort it took him to control his rage. He watched him mentally cataloging the details of the scene.

The cruelest blow, Junior thought, was that the look of death had already settled over Elizabeth's features; a subtle slackness in the porcelain skin, a waxen look and hue. Her beauty, so fragile and fine in life, now a pale imitation.

Hugo's gaze settled on the pill bottle on the nightstand. "What made you check the room?"

"A feeling, I guess. And the blowfly." Junior watched the compression of Hugo's lips, the flare of his nostrils. "It looks like suicide."

"No," Hugo said. "No glass. The cap on the bottle. It's *meant* to look like suicide."

Junior nodded. "And no car."

"She was drugged most likely. Unable to resist when he forced her into his truck. Then he finished her off once he got here."

"How?"

Hugo stepped into the room and went to the bedside. He studied Elizabeth's face, let his gaze travel down to her hands so perfectly folded at her waist. "More drugs probably. Or he smothered her."

"Wouldn't she have fought him?"

"Possibly. It couldn't have been much of an effort. She's been posed. We won't know how he did it until the autopsy."

"It's all too tidy."

"Haven't you noticed? He's a tidy man. Elizabeth's lawn, the tools in the carport, Ruby's apartment. A control freak." Hugo let his gaze travel around the room then return to the picture-perfect death scenario before him. "He needs that control, that perfection. It's his tell."

"He took a risk. Either of us could have driven up at any time."

"It was worth it to him. The need too strong to resist."

"How long has she been here, you reckon?"

"We haven't missed him by much would be my guess. Adele heard the truck. He arrived at the house over three hours ago now. Gave her enough Valium to make her docile. She was accustomed to getting it from him. Afraid to refuse. He would have walked her to the truck in case anyone saw them."

They both fell silent. Then Junior asked, "Why the overnight bag, then?"

Hugo didn't reply immediately. He watched as a second, and then a third, blowfly buzzed over the body. "I don't know."

Another fly flew into the room. The air conditioner was making little headway against the oppressive, muggy heat. From the parking lot came the sound of slamming doors. The forensics team had arrived.

✺

EVIE BEGAN WITH photos. She had a new assistant, an older man who remained in the hallway until she put the camera away.

Oscar Rhys, the coroner, strolled through the door of the motel and came to stand beside Hugo.

"Jesus, August. This makes three bodies. Tell me you have a clue."

"I have a clue."

Hugo hadn't intended the remark to be humorous.

The look on Rhys' face said he got the message. He stood in the doorway of Lucky Number Seven and watched Evie and her assistant processing the room.

"Can we take the body?"

Evie looked up from applying print powder to the medicine bottle and nodded.

"When's the autopsy?" Hugo asked.

"We've got the boy scheduled for eight in the morning. We'll do her right after."

Hugo wanted to protest the delay but bit back his words. He knew it would do no good. It was Sunday, after all. He jangled the change in his pocket his fingers, singling out the 1933 Indian head gold eagle, and nodded. "Anything?" he asked Evie.

"No prints on the bottle. A bruise on the right side of her neck." She pushed the sleeve of Elizabeth's blouse up about three inches. "Bruising on both wrists."

Hugo clenched his jaw and turned from the doorway of the room. Junior followed him from the building. In the parking lot he turned to Junior. "Same plan. You check out Dixie's place. I'll take the Paradise."

He drove away from the motel, his white-knuckled grip on the steering wheel the only outward sign of the rage just below the surface. The coroner's words stung. Elizabeth's death was on him. He'd been blind to the perversion staring him in the face. Well, he was seeing clearly now and he needed to find Stanton before anyone else did.

Twenty-Eight

THE PROBLEM, JUNIOR realized, was that Baldwin County was a large rural area dotted with fields of corn, soybeans, potatoes, and pecan orchards. Stanton could be anywhere in any of the little communities that dotted the shore of Mobile Bay or hidden out on a farm somewhere in one of the small inland communities. Or he could be long gone down the Florida panhandle.

But Junior didn't think he would run. The Chief struck him as a man who would stick it out, use his sense of righteous indignation and control over the community to bluff through the accusations. The question remained, where to find the needle in the haystack. Both he and Hugo were handicapped because they were outsiders. He didn't have a lot of faith in the local police force. At the end of the day, they might have to call on the Sheriff's department.

He passed through the heart of Spanish Fort at the top of the hill and scanned the occasional businesses and side roads that intersected with Hwy 31 as he continued east. He found nothing but the quiet of a scorching late summer day. Nothing stirred until he made a right onto Hwy 181 toward Malbis Plantation. About a mile along, he passed the Standard Oil station on his right. It was open on a Sunday afternoon but quiet, no cars at the pumps.

The dome of the Greek Orthodox Church sat a couple hundred yards further along on the left side of the road. An ancient priest had just gotten out of an equally elderly sedan as Junior drew near and was making his way up the steps toward the main entrance.

On impulse, Junior pulled into the parking lot. The priest turned toward the sound of his car and waited.

"Your Holiness," Junior said as he reached the top of the steps.

The priest gave a slight nod in greeting.

"I'm trying to locate Buzz Stanton." He took his shield out for the priest. "He's the police chief in Spanish Fort. You know him?"

"I know him."

"It's urgent I find him."

"Well, as you can see, there's no one here but me. Which, sadly, is the case more often than not these days. But I did see him earlier this afternoon."

Junior felt a little jump of his heart. "Where was this?"

The priest nodded across the way to the service station at the intersected of Hwy 90. "He was pumping gas."

"Can you be more specific about the time?"

"At least two hours, I would think. Maybe a little more. I was on my way home from a nice leisurely meal with parishioners after the noon mass."

"What was he driving?"

"A truck. Red."

"Did you see him leave?"

"No, I'm afraid not. I didn't stop in at the station, only drove past on my way home." The priest paused a long beat then said, "I expect he was visiting a friend in the area." He pinned Junior with a knowing eye.

"Thank you, Your Holiness."

The priest nodded and watched as Junior hurried down the steps and sped away.

Two miles further south, he turned onto a county road and followed it to the little white house where Dixie lived. Her yellow Volkswagen was parked in the shade. Stanton's truck wasn't anywhere to be seen.

She opened the door as he walked up onto the porch, blocking the opening with her body.

"What's happened?" she asked.

Junior could see the vein at her neck jumping.

"I'm looking for the Chief. Know where I can find him?"

She let out her breath. "Not here. Obviously."

"But he was here earlier."

The quicksilver movement of her eyes betrayed her. She knew she was caught out. For an answer, she turned her head and looked toward her car.

"How long ago?"

"Early. The other detective hadn't been gone but about twenty minutes when he showed up."

"Did he stay long?"

She looked back at Junior and narrowed her eyes. "Not as long as he would have liked."

"Why's that?"

She simply stared at him.

"I need something specific."

"Five minutes."

"Short visit."

"It doesn't take long to decide you're not welcome when you're staring down the barrel of a shotgun. The racking sound can be very persuasive."

Junior's eyebrows shot up and he studied Dixie with a new appreciation. "Then I don't suppose you know where he was headed when he left?"

"Don't know, don't care."

⁂

HUGO FLOORED THE gas pedal as soon as he hit Hwy 98. Traffic was light for a Sunday in the peak summer beach season. He covered the ten miles to the Paradise in record time. A man was getting out of one of three cars parked in front of the bar. Another stood beside the entrance lighting a cigarette.

Hugo roared into the parking lot, slewing pea gravel in his wake. He fishtailed across the lot and swerved to the side to round the building. There, in front of the three rooms that comprised the motel aspect of the establishment sat a red Chevrolet pick-up. He braked hard and came to a stop blocking the truck with his car.

He slammed the Thunderbird into park and was out of the vehicle before it stopped rocking. From the corner of his eye, he marked the man from the bar entrance as he rounded the corner of the building. In three strides Hugo reached the motel room, his right foot raised in mid-stride and smashed it into the door in one continuous forward motion.

The lock splintered and the door flew back against the interior wall as Hugo's momentum carried him into the small space where Buzz Stanton was swinging his bare legs over the side of a bed against the far wall. The right uppercut carried through Hugo's arm with force and without thought into Stanton's left jaw. It caught the Chief as he was rising from the bed and lifted him up and straight back, his arms thrown out wide.

Hugo's rage and his forward motion had him on top of the policeman spread-eagled on the bed, his knee striking Stanton square in the chest, pinning him to the bed as his left fist smashed against the right cheekbone. He delivered a right into Stanton's left temple as the deafening roar of a shotgun barely penetrated Hugo's blood lust. Hands grabbed him on either side and pulled him off the bed and forced him onto his knees on the dingy, dirty carpet.

Hugo shook his head trying to clear his vision, to bring the room into focus through the red curtain of his rage, straining against the men holding him, panting with exertion and the volcanic force of his anger.

"Enough!" a deep voice bellowed.

Hugo stopped struggling and looked up into the double barrels of a shotgun Manon held inches from his chest.

A groan came from the bed. Hugo knew he had to get control of the situation before Stanton came around fully.

"You might want to think about this," he said to Manon.

"Nothin' to think about. White man come bustin' into

my establishment, beatin' up on the local law." Manon shook his head. "Just doin' my civic duty."

"I doubt a local court will see it that way when you've been harboring a murderer."

Manon's eyes flickered with an instant of doubt.

"And there's the matter of ATF. The illegal liquor and cigarettes." Hugo shook his head in a knowing gesture. "Obstructing a policeman in the line of duty." Hugo felt the pressure of the two men who were holding him ease a bit. "Months in a cell as the case is slow walked through the system." One of the men released him and moved cautiously toward the door of the room.

Manon raised the barrel of the gun and rested it on his shoulder just as Stanton sat up on the side of the bed. Hugo pulled free of the other man holding him, sprang to his feet as he pulled his cuffs from his waistband.

The first blow he'd delivered had done the trick. Stanton was awake but still out of it, unable to resist, unable to run. By the time Hugo had read him his rights, all three men from the club had faded into thin air.

⚜

THE ROOM STANK of whiskey. A pint of Jim Beam had been knocked off the night stand at the outset of the altercation. Hugo shoved Stanton onto his side on the bed, his hands cuffed behind his back, and went to the car for the radio. There was one lone chair in the room, a straight back with a cracked red vinyl seat. He positioned it against the side wall between his captive and the open door, ready for danger from either direction. Then he sat and waited as the adrenalin rush began to subside and his heartrate slowed.

Stanton watched him. Blood trickled from his nose and mouth.

Hugo spoke into the radio. "Spanish Fort."

"What's up?" Peggy Sue's voice came back at him.

"I'm low on gas. Need to fill up. Let Detective Knight know. Tell him to meet me at the rendezvous."

"Got it."

Hugo switched to the Mobile Police Department's channel. "I need a black and white. No lights, no siren." He gave the directions then turned the radio off.

Stanton coughed and a small spurt of blood sprayed the chenille bedspread. "I need a doctor." His speech was slurred. Small bubbles of blood formed at the corner of his mouth as he spoke.

"You'll live." Hugo settled back in the chair, relaxed yet alert, a position he knew well and could maintain for hours. Ever watchful, rarely blinking, ready for any movement that would give the enemy away whether in the misty night jungle or the physically fit and slightly coiled prisoner on the bed in this dingy, sad motel room. He knew both jungles and the violent creatures that inhabited them.

And he waited.

The minutes ticked by. Stanton coughed again. More blood. He cleared his throat. "I need to sit up."

Hugo nodded and Stanton maneuvered himself into a sitting position on the edge of the bed, his feet flat on the floor. He stared at Hugo through eyes that smoldered with rage.

"I think my jaw's broken." His speech was clearer now that he was sitting up. A giant knot had popped up near his ear on the left side of his face.

Hugo's shoulders lifted in the barest of shrugs. "Could be."

"What's this about?"

"You're a smart enough guy. I think you can figure it out."

"You think I killed Ruby." He hawked and spat bloody phlegm onto the floor.

"We've moved way beyond that."

"The retard?" Stanton gave a humorless grunt.

Hugo refused to be goaded. He had his man. As much as he wanted to slam Stanton's head through the cinder block wall and finish the job he had started, he knew the sweetest revenge would be the public shaming that would come. Stanton's image was his Achilles heel. It had cost Nelson his life. A quick death wasn't enough. With Elizabeth dead, there was no one else to be hurt by the airing of Stanton's perversion. He would have his pound of flesh then Yellow Mama would have what was left of Stanton.

The look in Stanton's eyes changed to one of cunning. "You've got this all wrong. I loved Ruby more than anything."

Hugo clenched his jaw then released it. "So I've discovered."

Stanton dropped his gaze. Hugo could almost hear the calculating thoughts running through the Chief's mind. Neither man spoke again until the sound of tires on gravel drew Hugo to the doorway of the room as Junior got out of his car.

Junior sized up Hugo's appearance, his disheveled hair and red knuckles. He took in the splintered door frame.

"Christ, Hugo. You've got to do something about your wardrobe."

"It's at the top of my list."

Junior's gaze drifted to Stanton sitting on the edge of the bed. "Anything to be worried about?"

"Nothing serious."

"My car or yours?"

"Neither. A squad car'll be along shortly."

"Spanish Fort?"

"Mobile. Our case, our house."

"Goode'll be all over it."

Hugo nodded.

"He say anything?"

"Not yet. But he will."

The patrol car pulled up trailed by a Spanish Fort cruiser. Boo was behind the wheel of the local car. He came to stand with Hugo and Junior as Stanton was hustled out of the motel room.

Stanton glared at Boo, hawked and spat at his feet, then slid onto the seat of the Mobile Police vehicle with no resistance. Hugo told the driver to swing by Mobile General to have someone take a look at his jaw before taking him to lock-up.

As the car pulled away, Boo asked, "Resisted, did he?"

Hugo grunted.

"Good."

Junior felt the acid burn at the back of his throat. At best they had a circumstantial case. There wasn't a single shred of physical evidence to place Stanton at any of the murders.

"Someone should warn Elizabeth," Boo said as he turned toward his car.

Hugo glanced at Junior. "Elizabeth's dead."

Boo whipped around. "Dead!"

"At the Thunderbird. Room seven."

Boo dropped to his knees. He looked like a rag doll in a policeman's uniform. All the life had drained from his face, his arms limp at his side, his knuckles in the hard packed dirt of the parking lot. "How—"

For a moment, Junior thought he would faint. He squatted next to Boo and placed a steadying hand on his shoulder.

Boo looked at Junior, trying to focus his gaze. "How?"

Junior just shook his head.

"She didn't—"

"No," Hugo said. "She didn't." He got into his car and spoke to Junior through the open window. "See that he gets back to Spanish Fort. Then I want Davis Talbot and Betty at the station. Keep them separate."

⁕

JUNIOR FOLLOWED BEHIND Boo's cruiser even though he had insisted he was fine. Instead of returning to the Spanish Fort police station, he hung a left just past the D'Olive Creek bridge toward the Causeway. Junior sighed. He figured Boo was headed to the Mobile station. Or to see Alma, give her the low-down. Or, possibly, to the latest crime scene.

But Boo drove past the Thunderbird Inn where a Spanish Fort cruiser and a hearse had joined the two vehicles of the forensic team. A quarter mile along the Causeway he made a hard right as soon as he passed over the Apalachee River bridge. The rutted pig trail made a hairpin turn back toward the water and the Dirftwood Bar. The establishment operated as a private club to skirt around the state's Sunday blue laws and was open for business with a handful of cars in the parking lot.

Junior sighed again and picked up his radio. He explained his location to Hugo.

"What do you want me to do?"

Hugo was silent a moment.

"Buy him a beer. Let him talk. See if he has anything useful to say. But don't get drunk."

"I never get drunk.

"True."

"What about Talbot and Betty?"

"I'll send a black and white. Two visits from the police in one day might just do the trick."

"The chief won't like it."

"That's the bonus. In fact, I'll send them to Talbot, Sr.'s house first. That'll bring the heat."

"Tread lightly."

"We're way beyond that."

"The chief might pull the case."

"I don't think so. He's already distancing himself. Not sure why. Maybe he got wind of ATF sniffing around. Whatever it is, he'll want someone between him and any political heat."

"Is ATF sniffing around?"

"Who knows but something's keeping Goode at arm's length."

* * *

JUNIOR CLIMBED THE steep steps to the geodesic dome and found Boo on the east side of the structure mounted on tall stilts at the water's edge. He sat low in a canvas chair on the wrap-around deck. He was halfway through a bottle of beer. The day was fading quickly, the view of the eastern shore in sharp focus from the last rays of a setting sun behind them. He tried to determine where in the sea of foliage Boo's camper was anchored but the distance was too far and he finally settled on a general area.

"Best time of day," Junior said as he sat in a chair beside Boo and nodded to the waitress to bring him the same.

Boo grunted and sipped his beer.

They sat in silence a while, watching the sun travel up the face of the bluff.

"There's no one left," Boo said.

"How's that?"

"Henry, Ruby, and now Elizabeth. All of them dead. No one left to mourn, to remember. Isn't that the saddest thing you ever heard?"

"There's Stanton. And his wife."

Boo made no reply. Junior took a sip of the cold beer the waitress brought. The light was almost gone when Boo spoke again.

"She was only twelve."

Junior remained silent.

"We got out of school early that day. Bad storm brewing so they sent everyone home. We decided not to ride the bus and killed time along the way, acting the fool, the wind blowing her hair every which way. I remember feeling happy. More than happy." He fell silent as they watched the dusk settle in.

"Ruby hadn't been herself all summer. Never wanted to go out and adventure like we used to do. Sometimes she would stare at me so hard it was like a punch. Things seemed better when school started back up. We rode the bus together like we always had. We only had two classes together, but we had the same lunch period.

"He was there when we got to her house. Stanton. In his undershirt and uniform pants. No shoes. I remember being struck by the fact he didn't have on any shoes. Her mama was in her housecoat, a silky flowing blue thing. She was upset; you could tell. I felt embarrassed but didn't really know why.

"He looked at Ruby then at me and I remember being afraid. He took me by the back of the neck and squeezed. Real hard. I thought I'd pass out. Then, he let go. Said, *get on home, boy.*

"The next morning, he gave Ruby a ride to school. She didn't come near me all day. Sat with a bunch of girls she didn't even like at lunchtime."

Boo drained his beer bottle.

"After that we weren't friends anymore."

Junior felt the weight of Boo's words deep in his core. He understood the depth of their meaning. Two beautiful women had been at the mercy of a monster. A monster with the power of position, physical strength, and a willingness to demand compliance by whatever means necessary.

Henry's death was looking less and less like an accident. They had their motive.

Twenty-Nine

STANTON'S FACE WAS swollen, and his left eye turning an ugly blue. He had a cut on his lower lip. The bandage around his head looped down under his jawbone near the back of his throat and again at the tip of his chin. Hugo pulled out a chair across the table from him and assessed the damage.

"Feeling better?" he asked.

Stanton made no reply.

Hugo leaned back in his chair and studied his adversary. A man accustomed to being in charge, someone who dictated what happened and when, someone no one dared question. A man with an ego. That's where he would start.

"How did you get Nelson to go with you? He was afraid of the dark, the storm. Hell, he was afraid to even go into Elizabeth's yard." Hugo tilted his head slightly. "Don't tell me. You're the Pied Piper. Everyone simply falls in line with whatever you want. Is that it?"

Stanton remained silent.

Hugo took out his notebook and flipped through the pages, stopping occasionally to read a note. Then he put it back in his pocket. "Nothing to say? No one's skirts to hide behind?"

"Where's Goode?" Stanton's mouth barely moved as he spoke.

"Ah. *Those* skirts. Well, here's the thing. Goode's a politician of the old school variety. He knows when to fade into the background, to hear no evil, see no evil, speak no evil." Hugo opened the file on the table. "He'll be along. Eventually. I'm sure someone started scrambling to find him in whatever fishing hole he favors the minute they knew you were in custody. But I wouldn't count on him to throw you a lifeline."

"What kind of game are you playing at, August?"

"Didn't anyone tell you? I don't play games. That's why I'm so popular around here." He gave Stanton a knowing smile. "Tell me again why you called Goode rather than the Sheriff or the state police."

No answer.

"I'm guessing it's because you knew he would cover your backside. But he didn't figure on the body count, did he? Now, he's as hard to find as gnat in a snowstorm."

No answer.

Hugo grunted. "Let's try this one. Is Goode in on the smuggling operation? Does he make sure a blind eye is turned when Dubya rolls through Mobile in his Caddy, weighed down to its axels?"

Stanton sat back in his chair. "Once I'm out of these cuffs I'm going to beat you 'til your mama wouldn't know you. Then I'm going to have your job. You'll never work in law enforcement again. I didn't kill Ruby. I didn't have anything to do with Nelson's death. You're spitting in the wind to see if you can hit anything." He leaned forward, the chords in his neck standing out, his nostrils flaring, and fixed Hugo with a look that would quell a lesser man. "There's nothing there. And mark my words August, I'll walk free and you'll be the one caught in the fallout."

⁂

CHIEF GOODE WAS leaning against the wall of the hallway when Hugo left the interview room.

"Chief."

"Tell me you have hard evidence that Buzz was involved."

"He's guilty. Hard evidence is sketchy at the moment, but I'll find it."

"What the hell, August? Not only did you arrest him on a whim, you broke his damn jaw. What about this looks like a sound case to you? All you've done is stir up malicious gossip, put the department in line for wrongful arrest, and now everyone's guard is up. How's any of that supposed to solve the case?"

Hugo looked into steel gray eyes filled with contempt. He gave a little meh movement of his head. "Malicious gossip has its uses. And, under the circumstances, I would think a murderer would already have his guard up."

"Cut him loose.""

"You sure you want to put a serial killer back on the street?"

"Christ. What's wrong with you? You think this is the

movies?" He shook his head and swore. "Someone killed the man's niece—"

"Cousin."

The vein at Goode's temple stood out. "Niece, cousin. No one cares. She was his kin. He didn't kill her. And that boy. Drowned. No one thinks any different but you." His lips thinned and he shook his head. "And now you say there's no physical evidence." He turned to walk away.

"So, what's the excuse for body number three?"

Goode whipped back around. "Three?"

"Elizabeth Stanton. Ruby's mother."

"When?"

"This afternoon."

"How?"

"Undetermined."

"What the hell does that mean? And why didn't I know about this?"

"No visible cause of death. We'll have to wait for the autopsy. I want to hold him until then. As for why you're just hearing about it, you've been hard to find lately."

"So what's supposed to be his motive?"

Hugo knew he had to give the chief something or Stanton would walk free. "She was the last living witness."

"Witness to what? So far you haven't given me anything that would suggest a motive."

"Ruby. She was his victim." Hugo felt like he was betraying her with his words. To give voice to the dark secret she had lived with all those years somehow besmirched the victim rather than the perpetrator, as if she was somehow in the wrong. Once he spoke the words she would be forever tainted by his sin. But he also knew it was the one thing that would sway the chief. "I think he's been molesting her since she was a kid.

"Aww, jeez." The chief stared off into space, then shook his head. "And why do you think that?"

"Her autopsy. Old scarring according to Dr. Allen."

"Is he sure?"

"You can ask him, but he looked pretty grim after the autopsy."

"It could have been someone else."

"It could have but I don't think so. He was obsessed with her. Has been since she was born according to his wife."

"That proves nothing. Hell, her father may have done it."

"We'll have the blood test results. Then we can see if Stanton's a match. As for the father, he could be our fourth victim."

"What the hell are you talking about?"

"Dead. Shot gun blast to the groin. While quail hunting with Stanton."

Goode's shoulders slumped and he exhaled a deep sigh. "When was this?"

"Two years ago."

Goode grunted. "I remember." He remained silent for a long count. "When's the autopsy?"

"Tomorrow morning."

"Type up a detailed, and I do mean *detailed*, report. I want it on my desk. Tonight. I'll expect the autopsy on my desk as soon as it's finished. You better pray Allen finds something." With that he walked away.

Hugo breathed a sigh of relief. A little over twenty-four hours to find something. Anything.

☙

HUGO FOUND JUNIOR at his desk when he returned to the detectives' bullpen. He listened to the details of Boo's revelation with a clenched jaw. More than anything he wanted to go down to the cells and bang Stanton's head against the bars to the point of death. He took a deep breath, forcing his mind to bank the fires of his rage and focus on the end game.

"Everything we have is speculation and innuendo. Let's interview Talbot. We need to eliminate him." Hugo picked up a file folder from his desk. "But first, we'll see what the dutiful Betty has to say."

Junior took his usual stance against the wall of the interview room as Hugo sat across from Betty. She was pale and kept glancing from one to the other as Hugo studied the documents in the file folder.

The harsh light did not favor her, he thought, as he looked up. She would forever be a Betty and never a Ruby.

"Tell me about Thursday," he said.

"What do you want to know?"

"Let's start with Ruby going to lunch."

Betty shrugged slightly. "She left about one-thirty."

"And?"

"And what?"

"When did Davis call you into his office to tell you to type up the divorce petition?"

Betty blushed deeply and she stared down at her hands clasped on the table before her. "About an hour later. He made a few phone calls after she left. I could hear him talking through the closed door. Then he buzzed me to bring my steno pad." She swallowed and looked up. "The standard details, he said. Fifty-fifty. That would be the starting point for the negotiations. Irreconcilable differences, the cause. Then he laughed. *Buckle up, Betty*, he said. *It's going to be a fight to the death.*"

"And the non-existent phone call?"

"I worked on the petition. Kept making typos. I couldn't believe he was going to actually file for divorce." She blinked back the threat of tears. "I tore the paper out of the typewriter and threw it in the trash. So many mistakes!"

Betty fell silent. Neither Hugo nor Junior made a sound. With a deep breath, she began again. "The phone rang. It was a salesman for office supplies. Another boring, ordinary daily task. As if nothing had changed. When I hung up, I just sat there staring at the phone. Then I wrote the message on a notepad and took it to him."

"After that?"

"I knew he was trying to call her. I could see the light on the phone line every time he picked it up." She glanced at Hugo, then away. "It was Thursday. Their night."

"What time did he leave the office?"

"Late. Almost six o'clock. He never works late. He was waiting for her call. Waiting to hear the plan, set the time."

"And the divorce papers?"

"I told him I would have them ready for him to sign first thing on Friday."

"Did you?"

"Yes. I typed them after he left the office."

"Where are they now?"

"In the trash. He signed them when he got to the office Friday and wanted me to walk them over to the courthouse but Ruby wasn't there. I told him it wouldn't be good to leave the phone unmanned. I used that as an excuse to take them later in the day." She looked Hugo in the eye. "And then you came."

"Did he tell you not to mention the divorce papers?"

She shook her head.

"Because he knew you wouldn't say anything."

A tear rolled down her cheek.

⁂

DAVIS TALBOT, SR. sat with his son in the drab gray interview room. His face set in stone, the color in his cheeks high. A right royal rage, Hugo thought. Good. He would start by goading him.

"Mr. Talbot, I'll ask you to step out of the room."

"No."

"This is an official interview."

"I'm his lawyer. He's not saying a word without me present."

"That's probably wise. He hasn't impressed me with his smarts so far."

Hugo sat across from the Talbots and studied the son. He could see the appeal. He had inherited his looks from his mother. High cheekbones, piercing blue eyes, a head of wavy dark hair. But there was weakness as well. Neediness that translated through a less than upright posture, a habitual ducking of the chin and questioning squint of the eyes with the hint of a mea culpa smile. Someone who got away with bad behavior on his looks and innocent little boy appeal. Always forgiven on the false promise to never break the rules again. Until next time.

"Tell me about the divorce," Hugo said.

Talbot, Sr. gave his son a sharp look. "Divorce?"

Davis sat up straighter. He didn't look at his father. "There's no divorce."

"Well, not now. Ruby's dead so the incentive's gone. But we have the papers so let's not waste time with he said, she said. That was your intent as of Thursday. So what happened? She change her mind? Or did you get cold feet?"

Davis was angry. Hugo could see it in the firm line of his lips, the furrowing of his brow. He stared off into the corner of the room but said nothing.

"Lissa would have made life hell. You realized that when you got to The Club, stepped into your privileged world. A reality check because you knew the nature of your wife. You lost your nerve, is that it? But now you're in a corner. Ruby was every bit as dangerous as Lissa. And she wasn't afraid to turn your world upside down. How could you break it off? Especially after the proposal and her swaning off to do what women do in a moment like that."

Davis glanced at his father. "It wasn't like that."

"Then tell me how it was."

"I wanted to marry her. I love her."

"But?"

"No buts. I told her that morning I was going to file the papers. Nothing Lissa could say would have changed that."

"But when it came down to it, you couldn't tell your wife."

"She already knew."

"You said she didn't know."

"They always know, don't they?"

"Did your wife reveal this to you before or after the murder?"

"She never mentioned it." He kept his gaze focused away from Hugo, away from his father. "It was something Betty said."

"And that was?"

"*I shouldn't have told her.*" He looked at Hugo then. "After you left the office. She just blurted it out. I didn't take it in at the time. I couldn't believe Ruby was dead. I wasn't really listening. But later, after I went home. I don't know. Lissa was so calm. So matter of fact, the way she always is when something needs to be dealt with."

"You think Betty warned her about the divorce petition?"

"Yes."

Junior slipped out the door of the interrogation room. Hugo sat back in his chair. He could see how the defense would use this to divert suspicion, deflect guilt. Davis had not said definitively that Betty had informed Lissa of the threat to the marriage. It was all innuendo.

Hugo ran back through Davis' timeline with him, trying to find any holes in his story. The time of death window was tight, midnight to 2:45 a.m. If Dubya and Dixie were telling the truth. The coroner hadn't been able to narrow it any further.

"Where were you yesterday through today?"

Davis stared at him.

"Between noon Saturday and now. And be specific."

"What's this about?" Davis, Sr. asked. "That boy?"

"If you mean Nelson, then yes. That boy."

"I think we've answered all the questions we're going to. This interview is at an end." Davis, Sr. pushed back his chair and stood.

"Suit yourself," Hugo replied. "We have motive, means, and opportunity. That should be good enough for a grand jury."

Davis cleared his throat. "I was home in the morning yesterday. Worked in the yard a bit, then got a shower and holed up in the study. I couldn't stand Lissa's presence, the pretense that nothing was wrong. I had to get out of there. I knew no one would look for me at the office so I left the house about eleven and headed downtown." He cleared his throat again. "But someone did. Stanton. When I came down to my car at around two, he was parked blocking me in."

"Is that when you got the beating?"

"He was drinking but not drunk. I could smell it on his breath. Came in close, inches away, chest out, acting the tough guy. Wanted to know where I got off making Ruby out to be a whore, flaunting our relationship. I tried to explain that it wasn't like that, but he hadn't come for an explanation. He wanted his pound of flesh. I knew it was coming but still wasn't prepared for it. He worked me over pretty good then left me in a heap on the pavement."

"After that?"

"The guy stacking the paper machines found me and helped me into my car. He wanted to call the police but I told him no. I went to Mobile General and they cleaned me up, took some x-rays. Sent me home."

"What was your wife's reaction?"

"I didn't go to Yester Oaks. I went to my parents."

"And he stayed there until we went to lunch at The Club today," his father added. "He hasn't been out of my sight since he arrived home yesterday afternoon."

"What time was this?"

"Close to four o'clock." He shoved his chair under the table. "And now, we're done."

ༀ

HUGO FOUND JUNIOR with Betty in the other interrogation room. They were having an easy conversation about the food at the dog track. Junior was good at that, putting people at ease with the mundane.

Betty watched him enter the room. He could see her tense up. He gave Junior a slight lift of his chin in query and Junior shook his head. He settled across from Betty and sat quietly for a moment.

"Tell me about the conversation with Davis after I left his office on Friday."

"He was upset. Told me to get out." She blushed. "He stayed in his office a long time. Didn't take two calls that came in from clients. After about an hour, I saw the light on the phone. The conversation was brief or else he didn't get an answer. After the light went out, he came out of his office." Tears rose in her eyes. "He looked so different. So beaten down." She swallowed against the tremor in her voice. "He said he was sorry. He didn't mean to snap at me. It was just the shock of it all. And then he left."

"That's it? You didn't ask him where he was going? What to do with the divorce papers? Anything?"

"No. He simply walked out."

"What about before he ordered you out of his office? Did you ask him any questions? Say anything to him?"

"I said I was sorry and asked him what I should do."

"Nothing else?"

Betty frowned and shook her head. "No."

"You didn't say," Hugo made a show of opening the file and pretending to read, "*I shouldn't have told her?*"

Betty's frown deepened. "Shouldn't have told who what?" She shrugged. "I don't understand."

"Davis told me this is what you said to him after I left. That you were upset and blurted it out. Later he decided it meant that you had called his wife about the divorce petition."

The room was deathly silent for the span of a deep breath then Betty burst into tears.

Thirty

JUNIOR SAT ON the corner of Hugo's desk and lit a cigarette. "Poor kid."

"Take her home," Hugo said. "You might want to sit with her a bit. Fix her hot tea or whatever it is you do to make the unbearable bearable."

"You believe her?"

Hugo nodded. "Davis Talbot, Jr. is proving to be a self-serving little weasel, but we already had him pegged for that. He's making sure there's somewhere else for a jury to look."

"So, is he a suspect or not?"

"I don't think he did it. His alibi is pretty tight with his poker buddies and the doorman at The Club. But he's scared so he's throwing out breadcrumbs to lead away from him."

"And Betty? She has no alibi."

Hugo shook his head. "She's an innocent. And that bastard just crushed the life out of her. It'll be interesting to see if she finally sees him for what he really is."

"Why wouldn't she? He practically accused her of murder. Or at least of complicity."

"Love. It makes fools of us all. Makes us blind to what's right in our face."

Junior studied Hugo with a side eye. His expression was drawn, weary. He knew his friend was no longer thinking about Betty. He cleared his throat. "What next?

Hugo sighed, glanced up at his partner and pushed his chair back from the desk. "We have twenty-four hours, give or take. The autopsy might give us something. I don't think she was strangled. That leaves drugs and we both know testing takes weeks. If we don't have anything by this time tomorrow, Stanton wins a Get Out of Jail card. I can't have that."

"Then I guess we'd better find something. But where to start?"

"Check with Evie. If she hasn't gone home, she might be able to give us something more to go on."

"Right."

"Boo's story pretty much confirms what we already know. If we can establish the cover-up as motive I think the Chief will keep him locked up. Someone might leak it to Donahue and that would be bad press. And we both know the Chief hates bad press."

"Works for me."

"An anonymous tip from a concerned citizen. Strictly hands off for the department. No quotes. Refer all requests to the Chief."

"Two can play this game."

Hugo grinned. "Exactly."

Junior stood. "I'll take Betty home. I think I know the very person to leak the story."

"Myrtle Crum," they both said in unison. Then they laughed.

"I'll go see Adele. If anyone knows anything, it's her. She's lived next door since before Ruby was born. And she may say she isn't nosey, but nothing happens at Elizabeth's that she doesn't see." Hugo returned his notebook to his back pocket. "And we're not the only ones who know. If we can't keep him behind bars, she'll be in danger."

"Hollingsworth might be able to weigh in on Ruby and Stanton's relationship. In light of our suspicions, he might rethink what he told us."

"Since I'll be over the bay, I'll see if I can round him up. You take Lissa. We've got to nail down every little detail before Stanton manages to bail out."

"You don't think that'll happen?"

"Not for twenty-four hours. Let's make them count."

"And the smuggling operation? Do you think that's just coincidence?"

Hugo jiggled the change in his pocket. His fingers singled out the 1933 Indian head gold eagle coin and he turned it over and over. "Hard to believe I'm saying this, but I think it is. Someone heard the shot in the night. Maybe more than one someone. Then they all started scrambling to cover their backsides. Dixie called up Chapman to bolster the alibi, maybe help move the evidence, but one of them didn't get the timing right. Probably Chapman because he'd been at the Paradise drinking. Dubya stashed all the contraband into the trunk of his Caddy. Might have been worried that the married couple would remember he was a guest and decided not to skip out ahead of the police so he wouldn't look suspicious."

"O'Sullivan's due to give his statement in the morning."

"You take it. Press for whatever you can get. I don't want to call in the Feds until we have our case solid."

The two detectives headed down the stairs of the police department. They ran into Evie as she was coming up.

Junior glanced at his watch. It was almost eight o'clock. "What are you doing still here?" She had dark circles under her eyes, and she looked exhausted.

"Wanted to leave my report on your desk."

"Anything useful?"

She shook her head. "Not really. We do have a blood type from—" she lowered her gaze and blushed— "from Ruby's autopsy. AB negative. Found in only about one percent of the population. We might be able to narrow down who she was meeting at the Thunderbird."

Hugo took the manila envelope from her. "It could have waited until the morning."

She nodded. "I went to Stanton's shack from the crime scene. The footprints match a pair of rubber boots we found under the overhang of the building, and the other set appears to have been made by sneakers. Small in size so my guess would be a woman's pair of Keds. Nothing else you can really determine from them, but I took photos. And the bag. It had clothes and make-up in it. Elizabeth's clothes would be my guess. A pair of slacks, a skirt, two blouses and undergarments."

"Why do you think it was Elizabeth's things and not Ruby's?" Junior asked.

"The checkbook. It was Elizabeth's. There was some cash folded inside. Quite a bit of cash."

Hugo tapped the envelope against his thigh. "She was leaving."

"With Stanton?" Junior frowned. "Why would she do that?"

"Not with Stanton. She was running. That's why she was so anxious when you went to her house this morning. She wanted to take care of Ruby then make her escape before he came looking for her." He gave Evie a hint of a smile. "Well done." Then he turned to Junior. "Give Evie a ride home. I'll run Betty back to her apartment."

"But—" Junior looked at Hugo.

"Go on," he said. "You're due to be off tomorrow, aren't you, Evie?"

She looked up at him.

"I'll cover the autopsies of Nelson and Elizabeth. Get some rest." With that he hurried down the stairs and out the door.

⁂

HUGO WAS ANXIOUS to be on his way, but he knew Betty was fragile. He escorted her up to her apartment and asked if he could make her a cup of coffee or call a friend. She shook her head and looked up at him, her eyes swimming on the brink of tears. He knew that the moment the door closed behind him she would give in to dismay.

He cleared his throat. "Look. Do yourself a favor and

don't go into the office tomorrow. And maybe never. He doesn't deserve your loyalty."

The pain in her expression changed. She blinked rapidly and stared at the middle of his chest. She frowned and the hurt was suddenly replaced with anxiety. "But who will manage everything?" She stared up at Hugo. "The office? The clients?" She sniffed and wiped her nose on the handkerchief Junior had given her at the station.

The look in her eyes told Hugo that, just like that, she had found a new purpose. Her purpose. She would be there for him. She would resume her old mantel of Girl Friday, comforter-in-chief, defender against the cruel world. And just like with all the other women in Davis Talbot, Jr.'s life, all would be forgotten. And forgiven.

⁂

HUGO ARRIVED AT Adele's house in the purple dark of night that comes at the end of long summer days. It was nearly eight thirty at night. He found her sitting in Nelson's swing, rocking gently back and forth. She seemed at peace.

"Bad news and trouble," she said as he walked up. "What now?"

"I'm afraid you're right." He listened to the call of the whip-poor-will and sighed. "Elizabeth's dead."

Adele took his news without comment. They waited in silence as the spell of the night and call of the crickets filled the void, Hugo leaning against the tree and Adele swinging gently.

"Nelson loved to swing at this time of night. *They sing*

to me, mama, he would say." She fell silent for a while. "They're so loud tonight. I think they know."

She stood up from the swing and headed toward her porch. "Come on into the house. I need a drink."

They went straight through to the kitchen where she retrieved a bottle of single malt whiskey from the pantry. The bottle was dusty.

"I don't often indulge. Always had to be mindful of Nelson. But good whiskey never goes bad." She took two glasses out of the cabinet.

Hugo shook his head. "Not for me, thanks. I'll save it for when we have our killer."

Adele grunted and poured a stiff drink. She took a large swallow and motioned toward the table. They sat across from each other and she studied him. "You're a driven man."

"Some think so."

"Violent?"

"When necessary."

"And now?"

"The end justifies the means."

"What do you want from me?"

"The key."

"To?"

"Buzz Stanton."

"Did he kill Nelson?"

"I think he killed all of them. Including Henry."

Adele grunted and took another big drink. "I sometimes wondered about Henry. He was a good man. Trusting. Nothing complicated or devious about him. Ruby adored him."

"What about Elizabeth? How was she with Ruby?"

Adele thought about her answer. "She was kind but distant. But she was that way with everyone. It's hard to explain. She was always there, on the fringe of life. The fringe of *her* life. Like she was watching a movie. She was there but she wasn't. Do you know what I mean?"

"What about with Stanton?"

"Like I told you, he was always over there for one reason or another. He and Henry got on like a house on fire. More like brothers than cousins. They grew up together and I think Henry always looked up to Buzz.

"They played on the football team in school, always hunting and fishing as boys. The usual things that kids do. I kinda had my eye on Henry when I was a freshman, but he was too swept up in Buzz and that rough and tumble life. Then my future husband came along and that was that. But in small towns like Spanish Fort everyone knows everyone and what they're up to. Mostly.

"I thought Buzz and Elizabeth would marry straight out of high school. He was so jealous and possessive of her. I guess, with him and Henry being so close, Buzz didn't notice him slip the fence and take her from under his nose. Everyone was surprised.

"Obviously there were hard feelings in the beginning. I had married the previous summer and we moved into this house. About three months after Henry and Beth married, they moved next door. She was happy then. Pregnant. Buzz was out of the picture.

"Then Ruby was born and suddenly Buzz was underfoot all the time. He'd married Nora that spring. Everyone seemed to think their marriage was what saved his rela-tionship with Henry."

"And his relationship with Elizabeth, how was that?"

"Always attentive. She couldn't walk across the yard from the kitchen to the picnic table with a tray of drinks that he didn't jump up and take it from her. Always hov-ering around her like she was honey. I don't blame Nora for chucking it. That's when she took up sailing in earnest. She's really a very good sailor. Almost always placed in the regatta. And she had her teaching. I don't know why they couldn't have children but in the end, I think she just didn't want to compete for Buzz's attention anymore."

"Did you ever think there was more to his relationship with Elizabeth?"

Adele watched Hugo a long minute and drank the last of the whiskey. "I'm not one to gossip. But I guess it doesn't matter now. The truth is, he couldn't keep his hands off her. Not all gropey like, but always holding her chair, touching her arm, helping her with her sweater. Except one time.

"They were out in the yard. Nelson and Ruby had been playing in the wading pool. I knew he would be tired out, so I started over to collect him. Buzz and Beth were under the oak tree in the deep shade. He was standing really close, leaning down and talking to her near her ear. His expression was hard. She was white as a sheet.

"He had his hand at the back of her neck, up under her hair but I could see the tips of his fingers and his thumb. I think he was hurting her. She took a sharp breath, and he looked up and saw me. Then his hand slid away, and he went to sit in the lawn chair.

"It stayed with me for quite a while but then I decided it was all my imagination. My husband and I were having problems. Nelson wasn't what he wanted, and I was trying to hold it all together. I put the thought out of my head."

Hugo kept his gaze on the scarred wood surface of the kitchen table. He controlled his breathing, focused on staying calm. The silence grew. He finally looked up to see Adele watching him.

"He was having his way with her even way back then, wasn't he?"

"That would be my guess, but we'll probably never know."

"He was always a son-of-a-bitch." Adele picked up the whiskey bottle but then set it back down without pouring another drink. "He killed Nelson's chicken. I don't doubt it one little bit. That's why he was afraid to go into Beth's yard, is my guess. Buzz resented the fact that Ruby loved Nelson and she refused to abandon him. And he knew Henry had given him the chicken. He wanted to keep him away."

"Henry built the sailboat for Nelson, didn't he?"

She nodded.

"That's why Nelson went out into the storm. Stanton knew he could lure him outside with it."

"Will he get away with it?"

"I'd like to tell you no, but we have no real proof."

She sighed and studied the whiskey bottle. "Well, at least he'll suffer."

"Not if he walks free."

"But his life is over, isn't it? People will talk and he'll have lost the only thing that means anything to him. His whole world has revolved around Beth since we were teenagers. What does he have without her? Without his reputation?"

"It's an act of passion. Killers don't think about the consequences in the heat of the moment."

"Buzz does."

HUGO WAS WEARY. It was well past nine and he was contemplating where to start in the search for Hollingsworth. He had used Adele's phone to call his home, the state police headquarters, and the local VFW with no luck.

Better to conserve the precious little time they had with something more useful than driving all over Baldwin County. But where to start? He turned the key in the ignition of the Thunderbird and glanced at the fuel gauge. He was running on fumes. First stop, gas.

The old man was sitting on his stool behind the counter tallying up the day's take when Hugo walked through the door of the service station. He glanced over Hugo's head at the clock. "Closed."

"Need gas. And I thought you didn't close 'til ten o'clock."

"Been thinking on retirement. Got me actin' foolish and irrational."

Nothing about the old man suggested foolishness or irrationality. "Retirement, huh?"

He motioned with his head in the direction of the new Texaco station. "Everybody wants spit and polish these days. Can't make enough money on orange soda to stay open with the likes of that undercutting me on gas."

"I'll pump it myself."

"Go on then," the owner said as he counted out change into little piles on the counter.

Hugo leaned against the Thunderbird as the numbers on the pump rolled over. He saw that the Texaco was closing up. Across the way a lone street light illuminated the parking lot of the police station. Two patrol cars were parked side by side. He wondered who was making the rounds tonight. Probably not Boo, he decided. It was a given that no one else in Spanish Fort was going to burn the midnight oil to find evidence that their Chief of Police was a stone cold killer.

The traffic light changed from red to green. The pump shut off automatically when the tank filled. But Hugo didn't move. Why had Stanton run the risk of stopping in at the station if he had Elizabeth in the car?

⁂

IN THE END, Hugo hadn't been able to see a way forward with the investigation, so he went home. After a long hot shower, he fell into bed and slept deeply until almost five in the morning. He drank coffee and reviewed his notes as the sun began to come up over Mobile River. A check in the armoire in his bedroom revealed what he already knew. Junior was right. He needed to do something about his wardrobe. It would have to be the Hawaiian shirt for another day. He shook it out, smelled the armpits, then put it on.

He was mindful of the time as he sat at his desk at Mobile Police Station reviewing everything on the case. Nelson's autopsy was scheduled for eight o'clock to be followed by Elizabeth's. As he walked up the steps of Mobile General Hospital, Evie got out of a taxi. He waited for her.

"I thought you were going to sleep in."

"That was your idea." She continued on toward the door of the building. "Come on. We don't want to be late."

The findings in Nelson's death gave them very little information they didn't already know. He had scrapes and scratches all over from the march through the woods down the embankment to the bay. His pajamas were a torn, ragged mess. Bruises circled his left wrist. There was water and sand in his lungs. Dr. Allen found a large bruise in the center of his back, suggesting that force was applied to keep him under. Petechial hemorrhaging indicated suffocation.

Elizabeth's case wasn't much different. The bruising on her wrists suggested she was controlled with some degree of force. The thumb sized bruise at the base of her throat was older. Beyond that she appeared to be a healthy forty-year-old woman. Necessary blood and tissue samples were taken for drug testing. Dr. Allen was about to turn the procedure over to his assistant when Hugo said, "Check for semen."

Dr. Allen and Evie looked at him then at the body.

"Is that necessary? Under the circumstances?" the medical examiner wanted to know.

"Check."

Dr. Allen looked at Elizabeth's body and exhaled a whisper of a sigh. "I'll ask you to step outside."

Hugo and Evie waited in the anti-room of the morgue until Dr. Allen popped through the doors about fifteen minutes later. He nodded at Hugo, started to say something, then changed his mind. As he walked back into the sterile operating arena, Evie glanced at Hugo then followed the doctor.

Hugo was standing on the wide veranda of the hospital staring into space when Evie came out, a brown bag in her hand. She cleared her throat.

He came out of his reverie and looked down at her. "I'll give you a ride back to the lab."

They rode the dozen blocks in silence. Hugo pulled to the curb in front of the police building. As Evie got out, he said, "How long to get a blood type?"

"An hour. Two max."

"I'll swing by in an hour."

⁂

JUNIOR LOOKED UP when Hugo entered the bullpen. He sat back in his chair. "What's new?"

Hugo shook his head. "Nothing but speculation. Adele had her suspicions early in Elizabeth's marriage but nothing you can hang your hat on."

"Went up the hill first thing this morning. Got nothing new out of Lissa. She was annoyed. Didn't want to be late for her tennis game."

Hugo sat on the corner of Junior's desk and stared

across the room to the windows on the far wall. The two men fell silent.

"What doesn't fit?" Hugo finally asked.

Junior took a pack of cigarettes from his coat pocket, saw that there was only one left in the pack, and returned it to his pocket. "The shack."

"Bingo. If Elizabeth was leaving town with Stanton, why go there? If she was trying to escape him, why go there? And why leave her bag in either case?"

"What made her, or them, leave the shack for the motel?" Junior asked.

"Someone wants to draw our attention to the shack. To connect all of this to Henry's death."

"To put a fine point on Stanton."

Hugo frowned. "That makes no sense."

"So what next?"

"Square one." Hugo checked his watch. It was approaching noon. "We go back to the beginning."

"The motel?"

"No. Elizabeth's house." Hugo picked up the phone and called down to the lab. "Evie, let me know when you have a result. Dispatch will find me." He hung up and stood. "Anything on the phone records?"

"Checked this morning. Nothing."

"The bullet fragments?"

"It nicked a rib. Best guess is still a .22."

"Come on," Hugo said. "Let's go pull apart Elizabeth's house and life."

"Should we get a warrant?"

"Everyone's dead. And the dead can't object."

Thirty-One

THE HOUSE WAS unchanged. That is to say, it was clean to a fault. Neat, orderly. And impersonal. No photos, even of Ruby. Hugo wondered who Elizabeth really was. Her home reflected Stanton. Not Henry Stanton, but Buzz. He wondered if Elizabeth's husband, the car tinkerer, hunter, fisherman, ever noticed.

Or had this new controlled, almost sterile environment only emerged in the absence of Henry?

After thirty minutes of combing through the closets, cupboards, and financial papers, they had failed to discover a smoking gun.

"Well?" Junior asked.

Hugo shook his head as they stared out the kitchen window. "We need a snitch. Someone resentful enough to give us something. A direction."

"Peggy Sue," Junior said.

"We'll be in enemy territory. Kith and kin and all that."

"There's nowhere else we can go."

"Agreed." Hugo's fingers found the gold coin in his pocket and turned it over and over. "We should talk to his wife, too. She must have known. Or at least suspected."

"If we don't have something in a few hours, he'll walk. He's hired Compton. The Chief had to set an arraignment for this afternoon. Last on the docket is the best he could do."

Hugo grunted. "Time some luck fell our way. Maybe he'll be brought before the Deacon."

"We could use a little hellfire and brimstone about now."

PEGGY SUE WAS behind the desk when they entered the police station. The older of Stanton's officers was sitting at one of the desks reading the morning paper. The coverage of Stanton's arrest consumed the entire front page of the Mobile Press Register. He gave Hugo and Junior the stink eye, threw the paper down on the desktop, and decided he needed to be somewhere else. He brushed between the two Mobile detectives on his way out the door.

"Don't mind him," Peggy Sue said. "His mama dropped him on his head when he was a baby. Never did know which way was up."

"Which way is up, Peggy Sue?" Hugo asked.

"There's a lot of gossip, as you might imagine. Folks on both sides and those straddling the fence. Either way, I don't see how he can keep his job. Unless he manages to strong arm his way through the city council."

"Is that how he got to be Chief? Strong arming people?"

"Well, I'm not one to say. But Buzz always manages to have his way. Somehow."

"Folks scared of him?"

She looked down at the desk blotter. "I wouldn't say that. Exactly."

"But?"

"Let's just say it's easier to have him on your side than against you."

"I didn't think you were a fan."

She leaned back in her chair. "There aren't a lot of jobs in Spanish Fort. It's mostly farming on this side of the bay. And fishing. I'm on my own so I do what I have to do."

"He's a killer."

"And you have proof?"

"It's mostly circumstantial. That's why we need your help."

"Circumstantial. And you want me to jump off a cliff on that?"

"You've known him a long time. You know who he is. And what he is." Hugo leaned against the high counter. "Be truthful. When Henry died, you thought he did it, didn't you?"

Peggy Sue blushed a deep pink and looked away from Hugo's intense scrutiny.

"Four people are dead. There has to be a reckoning. You know that."

She looked from Hugo to Junior and back. "You think he killed Ruby? Why? He worshipped her."

"Because he was losing control of her. She was going to marry her boss. Move to Mobile, out of his reach. Out of his control."

She shook her head. "But Elizabeth was still here. Henry was out of the way. He had what he wanted."

"Yes. He had what he wanted. He had both of them."

"What!" Peggy Sue's chair scraped backward as she stood suddenly. "That can't—what are you saying?"

"You know it's true."

She shook her head again. "I can't believe it. Henry would have stopped it. He would have known." Her forehead creased in a deep frown. "Wouldn't he?"

"I think maybe he did. When Ruby came home for Easter break, I think he saw something. Or suspected something. And that's why he's dead."

Peggy Sue dropped into her chair staring straight ahead at the switchboard. She ran a hand through her hair. "This can't be true. Nora never suspected—" She looked up at Hugo and Junior. "She knew about Elizabeth. Has for years, I expect. But Ruby. That can't be. She was wild. Slept around. Did whatever she wanted." She took a deep breath. "God Almighty," she whispered.

"Tell us what you know, Peggy Sue. The clock is ticking and Stanton will be out of jail before nightfall if we don't find something."

She was silent a long beat. "You need to talk to Nora."

"Will she talk to us?"

"Yes. I think she will."

"Where can we find her?"

"It's Monday. School's out for summer so probably at home."

Hugo fixed Peggy Sue with a steely look. "Don't warn her."

"No. I won't."

She seemed shell shocked, something Hugo had seen far too many times.

∗∗∗

AS THEY CLIMBED into the Thunderbird, Junior reached into his coat pocket and brought out the pack of Marlboros. He took the lone cigarette from the pack. "Stop at the station for a minute. I need smokes."

"It can wait."

"It won't take a minute. He doesn't have any customers."

"You need to quit," Hugo said as he pulled across the street and into the service station.

"Maybe I will," Junior replied as he got out of the car on the run.

Hugo sat with the motor idling watching the intersection of Hwy 31. A car traveling south on Spanish Main came to a stop at the light and made a right-on-red heading down to the Causeway. Hugo watched it travel down the hill. Suddenly he got out of the Thunderbird and went inside where Junior was collecting his change and cigarettes.

"Yesterday. You saw Stanton leaving Elizabeth's."

The old man squinted his bad eye almost shut. "Saw him come down Spanish Main. Don't know where he'd been."

"And he was alone?"

"I didn't see nobody."

"Elizabeth wasn't in the car with him?"

"Didn't see her. That don't mean she wasn't with him, I reckon."

Hugo stared across the intersection toward the police station. "And he went straight to the station?"

"Yep."

After a long pause, he said under his voice, "How did she leave the house?"

"Could have been with Nora, I reckon."

Hugo whipped around to face the old man. "What?"

"Nora. Come along after. Headed to the Causeway."

"From Elizabeth's house?"

He shrugged. "Don't know. But she come from that direction so that would be my guess."

"And Elizabeth was with her?" Hugo felt his heart racing.

"Couldn't say. Was pumping gas and didn't pay close attention. She turned right and I looked up and saw the back of the car when she was down the road a ways."

⁂

TIRES SQUEALED AS Hugo took the curves of Patrician Drive at speed. The carport was empty when they pulled into the Stanton's driveway. No one answered the doorbell or Hugo's banging. They found the back door unlocked. No one answered his call as they entered the kitchen and quickly made their way room to room.

"Why didn't I see it?" Hugo asked as he stood in the kitchen going through a stack of the Stanton's mail sitting on the table. He dropped the letters where he had found them. "It's the oldest motive in the world and it was staring us in the face the whole time."

"We don't know it was her. Besides, everything points

to him. Why would Nora kill Nelson? Or Henry, for that matter? Assuming his death wasn't an accident." Junior opened the refrigerator then closed it. "And where is she, anyway?"

"Not here, obviously. So where would she go?"

"Peggy Sue might know."

"No. We don't want to spook her." Hugo moved to the sink and stared out the kitchen window at a partial view of Mobile Bay. "The yacht club," he said and headed toward the door. "That's her safe place. That's our best chance of finding her."

✺

VOLANTA DRIVE OFF old Hwy 98 descended steeply down to the protected cove of the yacht club and Mobile Bay. There were a few cars in the parking lot. One of them was Nora Stanton's station wagon.

They entered the long, enclosed porch across the front of the club, the jalousie windows open to catch the slight breeze, ceiling fans turning slowly overhead. A man with a captain's hat pushed onto the back of his head came out of the main building.

He gave Hugo and Junior a quick up and down. "Help ya?"

"We're looking for Nora Stanton. She keeps her sailboat here, doesn't she?"

"Sure." He nodded toward the long row of slips running out into the canal. "That'll be her down near the end."

All three men looked out along the line of boats. They

saw Nora as she was hefting boxes onto the third boat from the end of the dock.

"You're lucky you caught her," the man said. "She's about to head out for a night sail down along the coast."

Their footsteps drew Nora's attention as she cleared the bow line. She studied Hugo's face then looked off toward the wider waters of the bay as Junior took a position at the stern of the boat.

"Mrs. Stanton," Hugo said, "we need to have a little chat."

She gave an almost inaudible grunt and a small shake of her head. Then she threw the line to him, and he tied it to the cleat hitch.

"I don't think you'll be sailing today," he said as he offered her a hand.

She looked up at him. Something she saw in his expression seemed to defeat her. With a small nod, she stepped out of the boat.

They made their way back to the porch of the club house and took a seat around one of the tables. A waitress came through the door with drinks for a couple on the other end of the porch. Nora waved her over and ordered a gin and tonic.

"It seems I've left it too late," she said as she spoke for the first time. "I should have kept sailing yesterday."

"Why didn't you?"

She gave a rueful half smile. "The satisfaction of it all. Nothing really happens around here unless it makes the paper. After all these years I needed to see it in black and white. I needed to know that he had been well and truly exposed, that everything he valued had been destroyed."

"When did you know?" Hugo asked.

"I've known for a lot longer than I allowed myself to know." She toyed with a book of matches on the table. "It's insidious, isn't it? It seeps in around the edges, toys with your mind until you can't not see. But by then you're in too deep. All your life has drained away through a thousand little cuts. You become numb to the pain."

She fell silent and watched the activity on the water as Hugo and Junior watched her. Finally, she turned her attention to them. "What gave it away?"

"The shack. Elizabeth's bag. It didn't fit the story."

She studied Hugo. "You're too clever by half." She sighed. "Poor Henry. I couldn't let him get away with it."

"Tell me about Henry."

"He saw something. When Ruby came home for Easter. He and Buzz had a big falling out. They fought. Henry wouldn't have him around his house. Around Elizabeth. That ate at Buzz." She gave a slight shrug. "Then Henry died. Ruby came home. All his problems were solved."

"Why Ruby and Elizabeth? Why not kill him?"

She was silent a long moment. "It's all her fault."

"Whose fault?" Hugo watched the color rise up her throat to her face. The first hint of emotion to mar her cool self-control.

"Elizabeth." She looked Hugo in the eye. "She thought she could escape by marrying Henry. Instead, we all paid the price."

"But Ruby? She was his victim, too."

"The pair of them, the bookends of his obsession. He had to have both of them to feel complete."

"His death would have ended all that."

Her brows rose. "Where's the suffering in that?"

"And Nelson?"

"Let's call it incentive. No one was going to see beyond his facade without the death of an innocent. You lot couldn't find your backsides with both hands. So I gave you a roadmap." She almost smiled. "I knew his death would fire you up. You're the Archangel, after all. I knew it the first time I saw you."

The waitress brought Nora her cocktail. She squeezed the lime into it and took a drink with a sigh of satisfaction.

⁂

AT HIS LATE afternoon arraignment, Buzz Stanton was released from Mobile police custody. Against Junior and Hugo's protests, the presiding magistrate wouldn't allow charges to be brought in Mobile for the death of Henry Stanton. The file and Nora's confession was handed over to the sheriff of Baldwin County. With no substantiating evidence, they had no grounds on which to charge him with Henry's murder. They would need more than her suspicions. She would be transferred to their custody the following day for the murders of Ruby and Elizabeth Stanton as well as the death of Nelson.

Junior was finishing up the last of the paperwork to expedite the transfer when Evie walked into the bullpen at nearly eight o'clock.

"Hey," he said. "What are you doing here so late?"

"The last of the lab work. Thought you'd want to know.

"The blood type from Ruby's encounter on Thursday night doesn't match that from Elizabeth. It does match the cook. That'll carry more weight because it isn't a common type but since Dubya's statement implies it was consensual—" she shrugged.

"And Elizabeth?"

"Nothing to compare it to."

"My guess would be Stanton."

"We won't know without a sample from him and it's type O. Pretty common."

"Well, it's Baldwin County's headache now."

She nodded.

Junior noted the dark circles under her eyes and the overall signs of fatigue and disappointment. "Why don't you go collect your things and I'll give you a ride home?"

She started to speak, then simply nodded. "Thanks. I'll meet you out front?"

"Ten minutes?"

Evie nodded again and started toward the stairs.

When Junior got to the street, he didn't find Evie waiting by his car but Donahue. He paused briefly on the bottom step of the courthouse then carried on to his vehicle. "Donahue," he said.

"Detective Knight. I was in the area and saw your car. Thought I'd get your opinion on the recent turn of events in the Stanton murders."

"How'd you know it was my car?"

"Maybe a little birdie told me."

"Uh huh." He unlocked the car door. "You know I can't comment on an ongoing case."

"Is it ongoing? I heard it had been punted to the Baldwin County Sheriff's jurisdiction."

"If that's the case, why question me?"

"It's the Gorton boy. I'm not sure how his death fits into the scenario."

Junior took a pack of cigarettes from his pocket. "I read the paper. Seems you've got a theory about all of it. Don't know that I have anything I could add. Besides—"

"You can't comment on an ongoing case."

Junior grinned and watched Evie coming down the steps of the courthouse.

"Maybe I should ask Myrtle Crum," Donahue said.

"Mrs. Crum's a nice lady. Always happy to be helpful. Can't say that she'd know anything about any of this."

"Still—"

Junior shrugged, "Still." He moved to the passenger side of his car and opened the door for Evie. Once she was settled, he pulled away from the curb with Donahue standing there watching them go.

Evie was quiet. "Thanks. It's been a long day."

"A long few days."

She nodded and yawned.

By the time they reached the YWCA she was asleep in the passenger seat. Junior slowed then picked up speed as he turned the car toward midtown. The porch light was on when he pulled up in front of his house. By the time he had parked and circled the car to open Evie's door his grandmother was standing on the porch.

Evie roused and looked around. "This isn't the Y."

"No. It's much better. Grammy has supper warming in the oven."

Evie made no move to get out of the car.

"You'll rest better after a good meal."

She frowned. "I can't put your grandmother out like this." She glanced at the clock on the dash of the car. "It's eight-thirty."

"Grammy will be offended if we don't eat. Besides, there's peach cobbler for dessert."

Evie looked toward the porch and Junior's grandmother waiting there. "I don't know, Junior—"

"Well, I do." He held out his hand and she took it.

Before they reached the steps of the porch his grandmother was tut-tutting. "Look at the two of you. Worn to the bone. And empty to your toes if I'm any judge of things." She opened the screen door and gestured toward them. "Well, come along, then. I'll have supper on the table in a whipstitch." She tut-tutted again and mumbled under her breath about late hours and ruining their health as she lead them across the living room toward the kitchen.

Junior glanced down at Evie and saw the hint of a smile on her lips and knew the magic that was his grandmother had been the right call.

⁂

HUGO FELT HOLLOWED out, empty to his core. Nothing about the case had been resolved to his satisfaction. Stanton was once again a free man. He might even succeed in sweeping everything under the rug as the malicious lies of an unhappy wife.

He would have to tell Adele before she heard it from someone else. At least they now knew Nora's reasoning for luring him to his death. An innocent caught in the fury of her rage over the long festering infidelity of her husband. The fact that Nelson had looked to her for guidance and caring only accentuated the perfidy of her actions.

He sat in the Thunderbird inert with the weight of it all. Life, he decided, didn't always favor the just. He would do what he could to balance the scales. With that, he turned the key in the ignition and headed toward the Bankhead tunnel and the Eastern shore beyond.

Once again, he found Adele in the swing in the side yard. She listened to his tale of discovery and disappointment. Finally, she nodded.

"Don't let it fester," she told Hugo. "If there's a God, sooner or later Buzz will get what he deserves. Besides, punishing him or Nora doesn't change anything. Nelson is still gone. I'm still left with the imaginings of what he suffered that night."

"You can't dwell on it, Adele."

"No. I suppose not. The preacher came by today and said much the same thing. Still."

Yes, Hugo thought. Still.

"Will you be okay?"

She nodded.

HUGO STOPPED AT the intersection of Spanish Main and Hwy 31. The old man could be seen through the plate glass of the service station sitting at the counter whiling the time away. Neither he nor the Texaco had any customers. When the light changed Hugo drove south across the intersection until he found himself pulling into the parking lot of the Paradise.

There were few cars parked in front of the juke joint. Hugo saw Manon behind the bar when he stepped through the door. The few patrons turned and gave him a glance before returning to their conversations or watching the musician playing a brass guitar on the tiny corner stage.

Hugo stood with his elbow on the bar top near the door of the establishment. Manon made his way toward him, polishing the wood surface with a damp rag as he came. He stopped and waited when he reached Hugo.

"Quiet night."

"Mondays usually are."

"Who's the singer?"

"Some kid working his way to New Orleans."

"I like the sound. Never saw a guitar like that."

Manon waited in silence.

"You read the papers?"

"Most days."

"You read today's paper?"

He nodded.

"Things are about to get messy." Hugo took out his wallet and put two dollars on the bar. "Buy the guitar player a beer. And, if I were you, I'd give the place a good cleaning. You never know when company might drop in."

The two dollars disappeared into Manon's pocket and Hugo left the bar. Outside he went to the public phone mounted against the wall of the building. After thumbing through his notebook, he dropped a dime and dialed a number. "I'd like to leave a message for Agent Roberson," he said to the voice manning the phone of the ATF office in the after hours. When he was done, he got in his car and drove away.

As he crossed the bridge over D'Olive Creek he slowed to make a left. There was no traffic, yet he came to a stop and sat in the middle of the intersection with the motor idling. He took the photograph from his shirt pocket and studied the faces. The Dirty Dozen, they had called themselves. Cocky, full of life, the bravado hiding the underlying fear and uncertainty. By the time he'd flown the Freedom Bird, their numbered had been decimated by half. He stared through the windshield of the car. Where were the rest of them now, he wondered. After a moment, he continued straight ahead until he reached Hwy 31 and took a right.

The porch light was on at Dixie's house. He could see the ghost of her little yellow Beetle off to the right. She was home.

He parked and by the time he reached her front steps, she was standing in the open doorway.

She leaned her shoulder against the door casing and looked up at him. "This is a surprise."

"Yeah. To me too."

"Everything all right?"

"Is everything ever all right?"

"Uh." She studied his face for a long beat. "So, what brings you here?"

Hugo looked away with a slow grin and said, "I decided I'm the lonely type after all."

"Not afraid of being compromised?" she asked as her long lashes swept low on her cheeks.

"I kinda like the idea, actually," he said as he leaned in.

"Well," she looked up into his whiskey brown eyes, caught the front of his Hawaiian shirt, and gave it a gentle tug, "I guess you'd better come in then."

Acknowledgements

SO MANY PEOPLE with their unique stories and voices have created the rue from which the characters in this series have developed. I'm thankful to each of them for what they have added to these works of fiction.

Lolita Dickinson, artist extraordinaire, graciously gave of her time and expertise to help me visualize the character of Ruby in *She Had to Die*.

I want to especially thank the Vietnam veterans, specifically Reid Lyon, US paratrooper, who have personally shared their stories with me and those who have written about their experiences. From them I have drawn the essence of Hugo. It goes without saying that Ginger Davis McSween has continued to be a font of knowledge about the Vietnam era. I thank her for all those little nuggets that bring the staid facts to life.

This book is, of course, a work of fiction. There are instances where poetic license was necessary for the purpose of story. That said, without the fundamental facts of how the Mobile Police Department operated in the sixties and seventies, this story would have no legs. For that I'm grateful for Joseph (Joe) V. Connick, III, a former sergeant for many years with the Mobile Police force. His engaging stories have added so much flavor and legitimacy to this novel.

We all know that one person who is a bookworm and critique extraordinaire. That's Tricia Campbell who gave such wonderful feedback on this story.

Becky Bayne of Becky's Graphic Design, LLC, is many things. I simply call her a life saver. Her talent, patience, and kindness have made this project a physical reality.

I feel blessed to have such generous, talented, and kind people in my life.

About the Author

REBECCA BARRETT WRITES historical fiction, short stories of life in the South, and children's stories. She fell in love with cozy mysteries after discovering Lillian Jackson Braun's series. In 2024 she began writing the *Cat Callahan Mystery Series.*

The Rat Catcher was her first novel in a gritty detective series set in the deep South of the sixties featuring Hugo August, a Vietnam veteran, as her protagonist. The second book of the series, *She Had To Die*, is available as of August, 2025. The third book is still rummaging around in the attic of her mind.

The product of front porch socializing and an avid reader since the book mobile began coming to their farm when she was a child, Rebecca now happily lives in the lovely village of Fairhope, Alabama, situated on Mobile Bay, where she finds inspiration all around her.

To enjoy samples of Rebecca's short fiction, visit:
www.rebeccabarrett.com

Rebecca can be reached by email at:
barrett.author@gmail.com
She'd love to hear from you!

See also, Book One of the Hugo August Detective Series:
The Rat Catcher

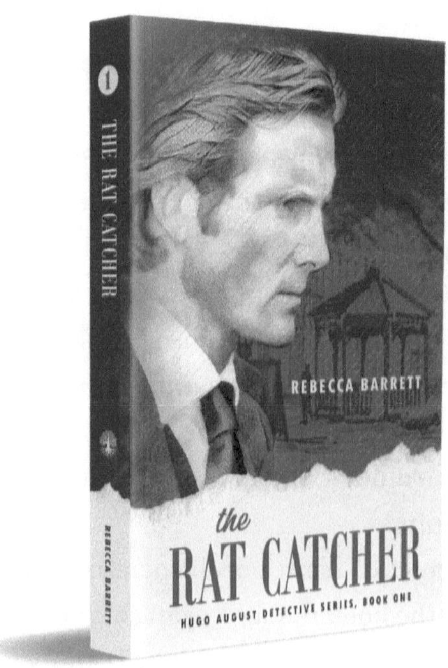

Leave a Review!

FOR A SELF-PUBLISHED author like myself, reviews mean the world! Please leave an honest review on Amazon, BookBub, Goodreads, or the platform from which you purchased this book. Don't worry, you won't hurt my feelings. Tell me what you truly thought. I read each and every one!